Lincoln's Assassin

Maj. Rathbone.   Miss Harris   Mrs Lincoln   President.   Assassin.

THE ASSASSINATION OF PRESIDENT LINCOLN,
AT FORD'S THEATRE WASHINGTON, D.C. APRIL 14TH 1865.

Lincoln's Assassin

A Novel

The Unsolicited Confessions of *J Wilkes Booth*

J. F. Pennington

Skyhorse Publishing

Library of Congress Cataloging-in-Publication Data is available on file.

Jacket design by Dominic Allen

Print ISBN: 978-1-63220-660-2
Ebook ISBN: 978-1-63220-878-1

Printed in the United States of America

Recollections
from the Kentucky wilderness
in the 52nd year of my life
October 1890

For Viola and Sebastian—
Remember me, babies, in your prayers.

***

Why would he risk his own life to claim that of the president? Who were his urgers, and what had they promised?

***

Where did he learn the password that allowed him to cross the Navy Yard Bridge after the shooting at Ford's Theatre? How had he planned to complete his escape, where did his route lead, and when was it clear everyone had betrayed him? Could he have eluded the men sent to intercept him at Garrett's Farm, and did his deed earn him the reported $25,000, enough to keep him quiet—and anonymous—for the rest of his natural life?

***

He was a member of America's most prestigious theater family—generally held in higher regard than his now-more-famous brother Edwin, and receiving a greater annual salary than the U.S. President, but by the end of the Civil War he had all but abandoned his theatrical career and become strangely obsessed.

***

Introduction

At approximately 10:15 P.M. on Good Friday, April 14, 1865, 26-year-old actor John Wilkes Booth shot and killed President Abraham Lincoln in Ford's Theatre, Washington, D.C. Newly celebrating the close of the American Civil War and the Union victory over the armies of the Confederacy, Lincoln and his wife Mary Todd, with guests Major Henry Rathbone and his fiancée Ms. Clara Harris, had been attending a performance of Tom Taylor's *Our American Cousin*, starring the first diva of the American theater, Laura Keene.

Members of the audience reported the assassin crying, *Sic semper tyrannis!* ("Thus ever to tyrants," Virginia state motto), before ironically tripping over American flag bunting as he leaped from the presidential box onto the stage.

Booth escaped swiftly through the rear of the theater and into the night, but government reports claimed he was killed twelve days later in a pre-dawn incident at Garrett's Farm, Virginia. Yet the body of the man who was shot in the head and burned in a tobacco-shed fire before being covertly transported to Washington was never wholly identified. Family members and friends were barred from viewing the remains, the only photograph taken of the corpse was never printed then subsequently misplaced or lost, and a strangely ceremonious martial court presided over a secret burial. Rumors immediately began to circulate that the real John Wilkes Booth was still alive.

A crudely fashioned barricade inside the presidential box and a back-stage exit pre-arranged with members of that night's acting company, along with knowledge of that day's password to access the Navy Yard bridge confirmed many of Booth's preparations had been secured in advance, and the soldier who was to have stood by and guarded President Lincoln was curiously away from his post.

Lincoln's assassination was but one part of a daring and intricate plot to completely debilitate the otherwise jubilant North. The same night this plan nearly claimed the lives of the bed-ridden secretary of state, William Seward, and one of his sons, and was allegedly to have also included the subsequently implicated Vice President Andrew Johnson and a conspicuously out-of-town General Ulysses S. Grant, each of whom were initially to have joined the president at the theater.

While his fellow conspirators were neither as successful nor as stout as he, the charismatic Booth's escape was so artfully designed that his near interception could almost only have been accomplished by those who knew its particulars, who also understood Booth's southern sympathies, how far he would go to serve them, and have been able to use his infamous dramatic passions to their own ends—before calling out the hounds to ensure the trail could not be traced back to them.

Pursued by Federal troops while another assumed his place—unaware the orders to bring the assassin back to Washington alive were never meant to be obeyed—a tired and crippled Booth managed his way to relative freedom, leaving behind all of his personal belongings except sixteen pages of the diary in which he had begun a romantic stage play.

Twenty-five years later, Booth lives in the primitive Kentucky wilderness cabin where Lincoln himself may have been born. Forced into a life of nameless exile and haunted by the past, Booth is as unable to claim the glory he thought would be his as he is to forget the fatal incident that put the country into mourning and rang the final curtain on the questionable career of the youngest member of the nation's most prominent theater family.

Contents

ENTR'ACTE: *The Diary*

ACT IV *Contrition*

EPILOGUE: *The Dawn*

CURTAIN

Prologue
The Dream

The bearded tyrant sat grim and still. The makeshift door-brace eased precisely into the knife-cut mortise as a fragile darkness assumed its place with eternal acceptance. No guard had there been at the top of my quick, rose-carpeted steps. No guard except the conscience I had long persuaded to watch me past the carved colonnades of the outer balcony. And from my temporary cloister, these twice theatrical wings of daring which could wax or melt in an instant—my heart speeding as if the deed were done, the labyrinth sprung—I once more studied my final entrance.

The moment held its breath as next my fingers moved to part, if slightly, the damask curtain that now alone separated our cause from his unbearable will, true victory from an untenable surrender, my haunted night from the all-harkening day.

The tyrant's gnarled knuckles clawed into the lupine-scrolled arms of his rocking chair perch, and his eyes fixed upon the evening's play, while he was yet aware that half the house rather watched him—for a movement, a sign, some memento to take home from the theater; the monograph, perhaps, of a once favorite player. This would my hand supply as never before.

Fine powdered ladies in their veils and bonnets, tall grinless gentlemen with their canes and capes, although forgetful of the solemn night's duty, forced appreciation of fatuous comedy while surely urged beyond noting the execution of a well-framed speech. Their ancient spirits cried for them to witness the justice done to creation's two-thousand-year-old ritual, turned westward· toward the fractured summit. The fabled robe of old stretched as velvet upon the seats throughout the house, its purple plush full-soaked with scents of perfume or cigars. Again, the dice profaned the cause with play.

Their usurping standard presumed its place in folded drapes out front the box wherein their blasphemous master dreamed. The rifting stripes and impenitent stars signifying only a shroud to cinch his steps from imagined resurrection. And his plump Calpurnia, decked in more finery than her frame or character could support, drunken with her pride and porto, clutched at his side, somehow knowing that next, this dusk of Ides, this modern feast of sacrifice and expurgation, this Good Friday—the Gods of nature would laugh and revel and be appeased, this Gessler would be mine.

Mrs. Mountchessington exited in a flurry and, there, too, a single player stood upon the stage. His cue well met, his lines well-spoken, I crossed and played my business out. Half a stride, then face to face, I cheered the motto of my faith and countrymen. The powder flashed, the bullet rang, those steel-gray eyes last looked on me.

Act I

An End to Exile

War Department, Washington, April 20, 1865,

☞ $100,000 REWARD!

THE MURDERER

Of our late beloved President, Abraham Lincoln,

IS STILL AT LARGE

$50,000 REWARD!

Will be paid by this Department for his apprehension,

in addition to any reward offered

by Municipal Authorities or State Executives.

$25,000 REWARD!

Will be paid for the apprehension of **JOHN H SURRATT**,

one of Booth's accomplices.

$25,000 REWARD!

Will be paid for the apprehension of **DAVID C HAROLD**,

another of Booth's accomplices.

LIBERAL REWARDS will be paid for any information that shall

conduce to the arrest of either of the above-named criminals,

or their accomplices.

EDWIN M STANTON, *Secretary of War*

April 14, Friday the Ides—Until today nothing was ever thought of sacrificing to our country's wrongs. For six months we had worked to capture. But, our cause being almost lost, something decisive and great must be done. But its failure was owing to others who did not strike for their country with a heart. I struck boldly, and not as the papers say. I walked with a firm step through a thousand of his friends, was stopped, but pushed on. A colonel was at his side. I shouted sic semper before I fired. In jumping broke my leg. I passed all his pickets, rode sixty miles that night with the bone of my leg tearing the flesh at every jump. I can never repent it. Though we hated to kill, our country owed all her troubles to him, and God simply made me the instrument of his punishment. The country is not what it was. This forced union is not what I have loved. I care not what becomes of me. I have no desire to outlive my country. This night (before the deed) I wrote a long article and left it for one of the editors of the "National Intelligencer," in which I fully set forth our reasons for our proceedings. He or the South.

Friday, April 21—After being hunted like a dog through swamps, woods, and last night being chased by gunboats till I was forced to return wet, cold and starving, with every man's hand against me, I am here in despair. And why? For doing what Brutus was honored for what made Tell a hero. And yet I, for striking down a greater tyrant than they ever knew, am looked upon as a common cutthroat. My action was purer than either of theirs. One hoped to be great himself. The other had not only his country ground beneath this tyranny, and prayed for this end; and yet behold now the cold hand they extend to me. God cannot pardon me if I have done wrong. Yet I can not see any wrong except in serving a degenerate people. The little—the very little I left behind to clear my name, the Government will not allow to be printed. So ends all. For my country I have given up all that makes life sweet and holy, brought misery upon my family, and am sure there is no pardon in heaven for me since man condemns me so. I have only heard of what has been done (except what I did myself), and it fills me with horror. God! try and forgive me and bless my mother.

Tonight I will once more try the river with the intent to cross, although I have a greater desire and almost a mind to return to Washington, and in a measure clear my name, which I feel I can do. I do not repent the blow I struck. I may before my God, but not to men. I think I have done well, though I am abandoned with the curse of Cain upon me, when, if the world knew my heart, that one blow would have made me great, though I did desire no greatness. Tonight I try to escape these blood hounds once more. Who, who can read his fate? God's will be done. I have too great a soul to die like a criminal. Oh may He, may He spare me that, and let me die bravely! I bless the entire world. Have never hated or wronged anyone. This last was not a wrong unless God deems it so. And it's with Him to damn or bless me. And for this brave boy with me, who often prays (yes, before and since) with a true and sincere heart, was it crime in him? If so, why can he pray the same? I do not wish to shed a drop of blood, but "I must fight the course." 'Tis all that's left me.

Scene I

Oh! The snow, the beautiful snow,
Filling the sky and the earth below;
Over the house tops, over the street,
Over the heads of the people you meet;
      Dancing,
          Flirting,
              Skimming along,
Beautiful snow! it can do nothing wrong.

– J. W. Watson's Beautiful Snow, *or*
Remorse of the Fallen One

Strophe

I

There is no beauty in these woods. No hope, no thought of reconciliation or forgiveness. These ancient oaks and bearded hickory house their nests from year to year, shelter numerous cardinals, tufted titmice and warblers of senseless songs and ceaseless flights to be, awaken my sleepless nights each day before dawn, block the sun. The four-coursed brook that winds and sinks and echoes cyan past my cabin's only window, soothing the silent deer and slinking yellow cat, mutters only jumbled syllables of forgotten claims and oaths. And every boot or broken twig sends me running that I might not face the intrepid hunter or happy traveler from Hickman or Union City who would exploit or explore the half-cleared knoll where I broodless roost. Or was it but some white-faced Hereford strayed too far from Ainsley's farm?

I would not have expected to see swamp sparrows here amid the thickets of willow and alder. It is as if they followed me up from those days of my pursuit, their streaked-gray breasts constantly beating with the sound of my own shadow-fearing heart, their striped crowns masking intent. The sweet and gurgling song of this harlequin, poised and practiced to play the executioner with a skulking smile, his throat somehow mimicking mine, as I am cast headlong, head lost, into the depths. And still the black-capped chickadee calls for light, "Phoebe, phoebe!"

I know my neighbors, all of them. Have watched them drink or dance or sup from where I sneaked beneath their sills; laugh in the hours after dusk, the lamplights tinting the magenta roses of their cheeks and wants. And seen them, too—long after, from my place of hiding, when my own head ached for want of company, my heart for her—turn those lanterns down and guide their shadows beneath the legacy quilts where solemnly they shared their trusts. I know them well, but they know not me.

And how many years later do I still think of her love? Surely I felt something. What, if not that one thing? But if by day I confidently mount the hill where dreams have seen my death, felt fully the truth that otherwise seeks shelter and disguise in night, which valley do I look upon? What age is this that finds me fettered here, the pinioned deliverer, silhouetted by the flame I thought to bestow? On what parade of political peccadilloes do I spy, that I may say, or must admit to having written the prologue and introduced the stumbling understudies from the corps of stock characters? Or, if I recognize my place, allow the current to upsweep me as it wills, perhaps it is not the motion of myth or past experience, but a haunting wind of future events that lifts my fears.

These woods have called me here to die or dream that I am better dead, that I should have taken one of theirs. And in the shadows of these trees, the broodings of this restless night and howling forest, the passages of time and doorless fate; in the candlelight of these confessions, while a schoolboy named electricity illumines half a stormless hemisphere, I stumbling stalk the shadow that has followed me forever, and watch and

hear and fear the purposed sands that drain and spill to fill
my tomb and catacombs.

II

There is no beauty in these woods. No scent of myrtle, myrrh
or hyacinth, violet or jasmine—nor amity in the squawking
jay, who every morning seeks not my company, but some
seed or kernel only by my path. The several songs of
woodthrush, veery, field sparrow, scarlet tanager and whip-
poor-will are threnody to the thoughts that steal my hours.

I sit alone by the fire in my silent, shuttered hutch,
underneath a still and starry sky in a still more silent,
hibernating wood, while moths strike at the window of my
will. One, two, three—and after a time, another, another, a
pause, and then a third; vainly try to rap the beat of the knock,
gain admission to the secrets that are only theirs already. And
just as this last series rings familiar, there comes a fourth.

My thoughts are rusty moths seeking entrance to the
harbor of some more sensible, truer light. I feel its warmth,
sense its flames that might teach or melt or burn, hope beyond
desperation that there will be relief of either outcome.

Last night my grating recollections finally sang my mind to
peace, pitched their whirring, swirling colors faster and more
loudly than my conscious eyes though closed could trace. But
when I woke in the hours before dawn, unsteadied by that
haunting dream wherein my soul may not be mine, my body
fairly chilled and soaked in fevered sweat, I could not trust to
sleep again, that he would yet be there. Then, at the moment I
fell back again, gave the hands of chance their grip, I heard a
plaintive cry and wondered, wondered into the light. That
scream was mine.

I live like the animal I have always been. Alone in the hole
of my wintry birth and constant hibernation, I am savage of
spirit, bereft of soul. No human grace or beauty blesses this,
my heart. How many mistakes have I made only to feel I have
made them each singly, or not at all? Is there not some friend,

some one, some God who might take some share? Yet who would hear me even if I should cry?

The horrible crime I have committed—upon man, upon myself—I needfully re-examine with imperfect and preserving eyes that through a self-forgiveness I may live with the savagery of my own being.

Antistrophe

How does one reconcile and repent? How do they? If only through cursing me, they have sinned again. Either I am too protected, too shallow, unreflective, or, they will not see.

The God whom I had cursed and spit upon has not forgotten me. He howls at me and taunts me with his justice. The crippling of my spine, which twists my back and humps my shoulder, recalls the hunched Plantagenet for whose portrayal I was acclaimed. That usurping Richard of England whose stampeding fury found its final judgment afoot. Every twist, from my scar-knotted neck on down, presents a choice between that reining truth and my own.

What madness is this that courses through my veins, ices summer's lazy whims and fires winter's snug content beyond hearthside warmth, melts satisfaction into senseless pools and spoonfuls of despair? If I were free to roam about, pronounce my craft or answer to my name, would I be as miserable?

I have been cursed, not unlike he who committed the "first murder." I could no sooner blame him than I would wholly myself. But perhaps the Universal Church's principle has penetrated your imagination as well. Or can you too understand the frustration that led the honest Cain to envy and kill his favored brother?

One night two winters ago, while the Great Blizzard of the East was laying untimely claim to four hundred frozen souls, I walked down to the river. Only its half-iced lullaby, deeply submerged and secreted, could be heard alongside the worried exhalation of the north wind. I swallowed a large mouthful of brandy from my hip flask and soon found myself sitting comfortably in the snow.

Oh, Father! I thought as I lifted my eyes to the pinpricked canopy of ebon. *Who is your son? And why is he here, so far from love and dreams? What doubts are mine that I would not share them with you?*

The night was over clear, the moon three or four days past full but bright. I fixed the great and lesser bears, Orion and two or three of the planets. All these I could discern, still not a glimpse of my own bearings.

I let my eyes wander those always strange yet familiar heavens until they led me to a quadrant with which I seemed to find some natural affinity. The seven sisters, they are called. There, I thought, there. And just then a meteor streaked its sputtering tail across the sky from pole to pole. Could I be sure? But no sooner had I questioned this, this sign, this symbol or measure of divine will, when another streaked in almost the same path, but on an opposite course, now south to north.

"Thank you," I said aloud to no one, while a comic gust of wind shook the laden branches of the surrounding pines, whistling once or twice about my head before moving on. *Thank you*, I thought to myself, what only I could answer.

But tonight, those signs are absent, tragic, nowhere. Tonight, I let them laugh that I should fill my veins again to end the score and four winters during which I have nailed my hopes and very life to this hutch, these woods, these trees that only cross the heavens out.

***

Thursday December 31, 1863. Washington City.
New Year's Eve. A light snowfall. Hackney cabriolets and coaches, gigs, phaetons, large-wheeled tilburies and private carriages of all kinds deposit their contents of costumed gentry at the entrance of the stately NASH home. FOOTMEN wearing glazed chapeaux greet the procession, open carriage doors and assist GUESTS up the wide, polished stone steps, while DRIVERS steady steam-snorting

HORSES.

Inside, disguised MANSERVANTS take hats and capes and canes, and lead the way to the reception room. TWO ACTORS, dressed as Romulus and Remus, exchange quick greetings with a group of similarly masked and anonymous HOSTS and certain sober MEN by the names of Crowe, Jones, Kennedy, Lester, McCord, Reed, and others. Dutch-capped MAIDS bustle about attentively, as the Two Actors separate.

In a corner of the room stands MR. PIKE, friend of General Lee, his large and powerful stature towering over the others. Pike's granite-featured face, as those of the men he addresses with quick successions of filial embrace, is uncommonly grim, but perfectly suits the long, feathered Indian Chieftain Headdress he sports.

In another section of the room, a man named LUTZ in the attire of a riverboat gentleman and on whose arm is the actress LAURA KEENE dressed as a Southern Mammy, her ringlet tresses wrapped under a gingham kerchief, are gathered with a group of seriously demeanored men.

A small ORCHESTRA plays under an indoor arbor as the entire room heaves and glows with the sounds and colors of festive songs and draperies and candles, whirs with the rustlings of feathered masks and costumes.

Among the flurried pageant of curvets, caracoles and capers, the occasional waltz or minuet or jig, appears a beautiful YOUNG WOMAN. Auburn hair, emerald eyes behind a silvery mask, a carnelian and pearl dress that accents her complexion, and a smile that glints as she dances. She is the picture of the season.

She retrieves an hors d'oeuvre *from the catering table and is soon alone in a corner of the gallery, though she continually nods apologetic pardons to disappointed dance-suitors. There she stands, somewhere between a fidgeting girl and swaying enchantress, lost among lacy billows of ruffled silk over hoopskirts delicately hung with rosebud garlands. An unexpected, open-mouthed yawn brings the YOUNG WOMAN to THE ACTOR's side with a smiling, arched-eyebrow rebuke.*

Here is a romance. No crash of symbols, rolling flats, descending backdrops, flickering lights. No exotic locale, time-pressed moment, glorious protestations or oaths; simple, careless, conversational romance. They stand together, hardly aware of their surroundings, lulled by each other's breathless harmony.

***

As the scene of the tyrant haunted my nights, so did this one burden my days. I knew that evening was the key to all—my murderer was there.

Scene II

Flying to kiss a fair lady's cheek,
Clinging to lips in a frolicsome freak;
Beautiful snow, from the heavens above,
Pure as an angel and fickle as love!

The night I tied off my arm for what was to be the last time (was, for a very different reason than I had at first intended) Hand returned after nearly four months. I never really expected to see him again, thought some stranger might find my corpse in years to come and, somehow recognizing it, have it placed on display at a carnival road-show.

Hand seemed so natural, so familiar, as he hobbled his funny form up the path, balancing his traveling bag and a number of paper-wrapped packages. He had gone before the winter snows to see, he had said, if there was any chance I might finally leave this place. Now was he returned.

Quite a sight was he, his body bobbing back and forth upon legs too short yet sturdily perfect. Fingers and palms, huge by comparison to the stubs out of which they protruded, ever-willing to grasp and clutch and, even as they released, defiantly leaving their trace on all. Underneath a wide-brimmed hat his deep black eyes recalled a life of unshed tears. He alone cared for me in moments when no amount of morphine could soothe my fever.

"I 'ave news, my broz'er," came his even, if thick-accented words as he emerged from the wide-open, leather-hinged door. Laying down his parcels he ignored the syringe and spoon outlaid upon the table with certain courtesy and discretion, aware of the beast that had dug its spurs into my sides long before he had come to know me.

Without another word, he reached into his brocade tote and produced for me a copy of the January 1890 edition of *The Century Illustrated Monthly Magazine*, earmarked and folded open to an article about myself, *Pursuit and Death of John*

Wilkes Booth.

"Another mob of lies, I presume," trying to discount the tourniquet I was unraveling.

"Per'aps," he said, pushing it toward me, and glancing at the violin collecting dust in the far left corner of the room. "You 'ave not been playing, I see?"

"At what," I laughed. "A wedding march? Or something new, Onegin's Polonaise?"

"Z'en must you rh'ead," he said, and at his insistent urging I sat down on the stone hearth. By the blinking firelight I read with a somewhat renewed interest in the ancient tale, wondering what Hand had seen to so capture his cynic's attention.

I finished the article in time to see the dwarf falling asleep in the broken armchair across the room, and stared for what seemed a long time into the fire and at the smoke ascending the clay chimney, before I found myself following his example. It had meant nothing to me.

***

I awoke the next morning as Hand lifted a smoldering pot out of the fire and placed it upon the table next to two cups he had set out for us. Both were color-worn and chipped, and only the one somewhat dutifully set before my place, of all my collection of six or seven, remained upon its own patterned saucer. Yet he had set out no spoons.

"You do not see, do you, *mon vieux*?" he queried, less disappointedly than I would have been, and perfectly pouring off the steaming tea. He always understood.

"I am afraid I do not."

"No," he nodded. "Per'aps you will understand z'is."

He produced two letters bundled together with coarse twine. One was written on a rough and colorless parchment, the other upon a delicate stationery, and surely in a young woman's hand. They were both addressed "Father." I looked up at Hand with some surprise, but he had already removed

25

himself back toward the hearth.

He waited patiently for my reaction as I quickly read the two short notes.

"But how; what?!" I exclaimed.

"I 'ave been to New York. Man'attan Island. I saw my cou'zahn *Henri*. Your broz'er would not see me. 'E 'ad *Henri* deliver z'ese z'ings to me."

"My brother? Edwin?"

"You are surprised? You must not be so. You z'ought 'e waz dead, per'aps? 'E ees not so very much h'older z'an you. And, of course, 'e knows you leeve. 'E ees your broz'er."

Hand knew the cursory import of his statement. Edwin and I had ever been rivals more than kinsmen, though at times we seemed to struggle that it was not so. He, in his silent refusal that it should be true, and I awkwardly trying to balance the pathetic unproductiveness of his method with occasional pleas for recognition and reconciliation.

It had been never worse than the August Friday he enjoined me to play opposite him, as Richmond to his Richard III at the Holliday Street Theater in Baltimore. It was the part in which I had debuted two years before, but I was yet 19 years of age and scarcely known outside my township. He was 24 and already marked to succeed our father as the country's finest tragedian. For the occasion of our first performance together, he booked for me an excellent room at Barnum's Hotel with a curtained bed and a well-filled basin.

It was, at the heart, as true an act of filial devotion as I could ever hope, and yet he took every opportunity to turn the screws against me. Somewhat, though every line and cue and crossing was memorized, for having arrived at the performance without my script in hand, in event that I "should need for any reason to fill another's part." But mostly for not adhering to the traditional interpretation in all ways, particularly in the fight scene, within which I again exercised my skill by making Richard fence instead of merely foil.

Did I not understand the "horrid dangers" of such

"unrehearsed, unblocked antics"? Or, was I, but "a dilettante, unhappily born" into an otherwise brilliant family? These rebukes I bore to the witness of the entire company, and tried my best to see their merit, though he would never yield an instant to any of mine.

And so I billed myself as only "Wilkes" for three more years, until I could feel I had earned the name of my father. But more of him anon. It was as Richard, at the Petersburg Theater in Virginia, I finally assumed my family name while yielding not my own technique nor interpretation. Which interpretation I may say, was, if startlingly, well-met more times than not. But those were years and days long-vanished even at the time of my transition.

"My brother! And the uncle of my children," I thought aloud. "My children!" I repeated. "I have children?"

I was truly astonished. Among all my suspicions of twenty-five years it was the one thing at which I had never guessed. Not for a moment. Not for I, a father!

"*Mais*, z'ey do not know 'o you h'are."

"Then I must tell them. I must go to her! Now!"

"I do not z'ink so," lifting his eyes to mine. "You really do not understand why I show you z'e article?"

"It does not matter. I have children. I have a—"

I stopped myself. Remembered Ella. I had never forgotten her, but now her image, her scent, her voice, every memory of her rushed on me at once. She was the mother of my children! But she had never been my wife. I had no wife. And I had no name.

Hand was still looking at me. He knew this too. And he knew more.

"She died z'e day after z'ese letters were written."

"But—" I started.

"Forget z'at my friend. Forget everyz'ing. Can you not see what 'as 'appened? Z'ey knew eet was you. Z'ey came for you. Z'ere ee'z somez'ing you can do for your children, but eet 'as noz'ing to do wiz' seeing z'em."

27

I do not know how much time passed before I spoke again.

"Do what? What are you talking about? What happened? Who came?" I shook my head, still dazed from recollections of the past.

He grabbed the volume from the hearthside and hopped back over to the table with it under the light of the kerosene lamp.

"Z'ere!" he pointed with a shout, his former accent returning as strong as ever. "Page four-four-seven," a gnarled finger drummed. "R'head!" he commanded with a guttural trill and his habit of placing "h's" where they did not belong. "H'aloud!"

His force took me aback as his finger continued to pound at the specified passage. With some temerity, I began to recite *Captain Doherty's Narrative*.

"I proceeded to the barracks, had *boots and saddles* sounded, and in less than half an hour had reported to Colonel Baker. I took the first twenty-five men in the saddle, Sergeant Boston Corbett being the only member of my own company—"

"Ah!" he screamed with satisfaction. "You see?!"

I began to re-read the segment to myself. Hand was clearly frustrated and half-furiously spun around.

"*Regarde, mon vieux*! L'hook!" He pointed again at the passage. "'. . . be'hing z'e h'only member of my h'own company!' Coh'rbett! Z'e man 'o shoot 'you!' You 'ave never understood 'ow z'e troops knew to go to Garrett Farm. Now you must know," his eyes squinted with increased excitement. "Z'eir 'h'intelligence' came from your 'fr'hiends.'"

"Forgive me," I said. "I still—"

"No," he sighed as he took a chair again. "I do not guess you would. I do not z'ink I would. It eez a 'ard tru'z.

"Garrett Farm was known only by you and z'e people 'o 'elped you plan your h'escape," he continued. "'O h'arranged z'e missing guard, and gave you the navy password. You 'ave h'always wondered 'ow Mr. Pinkerton's detectives could 'ave discovered h'any'zing. Z'e article explains z'at z'e idea to go to Garrett's was Captain Zhett's."

"The same old lie," I reminded. "That is the account of a certain Lieutenant A. R. Bainbridge, who swears he and I were old acquaintances. I know. I never knew Bainbridge. But I knew Captain Jett, and Jett knew where we were headed."

"Yes, you were somewhat—'ow does eet say in z'e arhticle?—'braggadocio.'"

"It says I used 'no braggadocio,'" I corrected with a half-smile and an able reference to the text of the article.

"Does h'eet? Well, we bo'z know better," he smiled broader and without a look at the indicated sentence. "*Mais*, z'is h'ees not z'e point. 'Ow did z'ey find z'eir way into z'at place at h'all? To find poor Zhett and z'reaten 'im? Z'e Virginie countryside ees beeg."

"Yes, you are right. How? That was always my question. Luck, I suppose."

"And why should z'ey h'always 'ave h'eet? 'Luck' to find you; 'luck' to shoot you dead—z'e o'zer you. No. Z'is article tells h'us more. Does h'eet not seem strange to you z'at z'e entire company h'ees under orders to 'take Booz' alive,' and z'e one man 'o disobeys z'ese orders ees z'e only man 'o was 'andpicked for z'e zhob? Do'erty was peeked by z'e War Department and 'e personally peeked Coh'rbett! And Coh'rbett shoots Booz'. Against h'orders! Z'e one man Do'erty might z'ink to trhust."

I looked at him blankly, awaiting the foregone conclusion I could not see.

"I z'ink Do'erty knew 'e *could* trust Coh'rbett. Just like z'e War Department knew h'eet could trust Do'erty. To pick a man 'e knew was sure wiz' 'is gun. To keel you!" he shrieked.

He was right. My heart seemed to stop and I winced with the pain of awful truth.

"Why?"

"Ah!" he shrieked again. "Z'at I do not know. Only z'at you may never leave 'ere." He shook his head with miserable sympathy. "You know 'o z'ey h'are. You know why z'ey

29

wanted Lincoln dead. And z'ey could allow you to tell? Not z'en, not h'ever."

"But I— I'm afraid I don't. I— I might. I mean, I thought I did, but—"

"And z'at ees more z'an z'ey can allow. Z'at ees somez'ing z'at 'as not changed in twenty-five years, you can be sure. Z'ere ees noz'ing else for you to do."

Nothing, but to reflect on what I had just read. Hand knew the source of my preoccupation. Not the article. The letters from my children. Ella. The questions they had raised in a mind long unfamiliar with possibilities of almost any sort and, to be sure, completely unprepared for this particular set of them.

Strophe

I wanted—I don't know what I wanted. To be loved. To be someone, somewhere else. But there was nowhere else. And only myself to be. And, Hand was right, nothing to do. I took my silent leave from him.

I walked down to the brook and slipped off my boots. How long had it been since I had rolled up the cuffs of my trousers and allowed my boyish toes to reminisce in the cooling, sun-spilled ripples. How I had longed for nothing more. Why could I then not be happy?

What still remains unsatisfied? The dreams of youth are ever anxious. Once fulfilled, they show that anxious, stirring sun, require further fantasy. I have shut my eyes too often to drink of their waters, imagining ease where I have found only Lethe. This is time to wake, Wilkes. Splash your face only.

***

The official report of my death runs as follows:

Two weeks after my deliverance of the tyrant's worthless soul, having been informed of my general whereabouts by Pinkerton agents in the employ of the grizzly Secretary of War Edwin Stanton, a squadron of two dozen Union troops assigned to Lieutenant Edward P Doherty was dispatched from Washington by Colonel Lafayette C. Baker, chief of the federal secret service. Doherty, along with his men and former army Lieutenant Colonel E. J. Conger, was placed under the command of the service director's cousin, Lieutenant Luther B. Baker. Arriving in the middle of the night at the Garrett family farmhouse on a fork of the Rappahannock River in northern Virginia, they straightaway confirmed information that David Herold and I were asleep in the small farm's tobacco shed.

With orders to take us both alive, the squadron commander led the troops into a circle about the shed and demanded we give ourselves up lest he should have his men set fire to the barn. This, in the quickening flames of the threat's fulfillment, the scared young Herold did, but before I could be likewise persuaded, a shot rang clear and I fell. A religious fanatic and self-inflicted eunuch named Boston Corbett, a corporal in the army previously in Conger's own command and with his former commander temporarily assigned to duty with Baker, claimed credit for disobeying orders to hold his fire on the excuse that he was carrying out God's will.

A not just slightly dissipated, scarcely recognizable man, weak from days as a hunted fugitive and now mortally wounded, was dragged from the burning shed by his heels, face down, that only his hands were burned. That was enough. The only truly identifiable marks, initials tattooed in younger days upon the inside of my left wrist, were thereby obscured. And the face so mangled that none could guess it was not Booth. The politic addition of last words about mother, who might swear it was not I? And then, this dying man half-paralytically held up both hands, as in one last gesture of defiance, gasped, "Useless, useless—useless!" and fell silent. John Wilkes Booth was dead.

The body, variously described as having been wholly or partly seared or charred from the fire, was returned to Washington where a government-supervised autopsy and nominal identification took place. No family members or close friends were allowed anywhere near it. Two doctors, one alleging to have filled a tooth of mine the previous winter, the other to have performed a minor surgery some years before, testified positively as to my identity. The most distinguishable characteristic being those tattooed if obfuscated initials never found mention in any official reports. The photographer Alexander Gardner, who would soon be asked to preserve the scene of my hanged compatriots, was invited to produce a posthumous portrait of the principle conspirator for the generations to come—though he was not among those who might have recognized me. But the one authorized negative and subsequent print handed over to the presiding military official never found their way to publication—nor even a simple mention in any sanctioned accounting. As far as the government was concerned, this death-mask photo had never been taken.

To all of this, add the quick and secret interment of the body, further confounding already circulating reports of a possibility of which Conger, the Bakers and Stanton—and I imagine even you—were too well aware:

It was not my body. I lived.

Strophe

If Jack Wilkes is alive, why does he not give himself up?

People say the most ridiculous things.

If there was really a conspiracy and he knows who is behind it, why does he not tell the world, and let justice be done?

All right, I killed Lincoln, but I was not alone in my planning. Still, how might I prove that? Who would believe a presidential assassin, and how could I think to be safe after any such disclosure? If those others were capable of implementing such a plan, certainly they would be capable of dispatching only a man such as I.

"I am only confused about one thing," I stated firmly as I entered the cabin to see Hand now busying himself with our supper. He did not look toward me but gave me his attention with a pause.

"If you did not wish me to go, to make some sense of this—to say nothing of my life—why did you bring me that article? Or, more particularly, the letters from my children."

Those last words stuck halfway in my throat. They were still so unfamiliar. There had been no time to get used to them, and now they had only to be accepted.

"What should I 'ave done?" he returned simply. "Lied to you, as all z'e rest?"

"You know me. You knew how I would react!"

"Per'aps. *Mais*, z'at h'ees not my decision."

"And if I decide to go? Will you try to stop me."

"No. I 'ave told you h'only what was yours to know. Z'e rest h'is up to you."

"What would you do? Stay here?"

"If I were you? I do not know. One may never really know z'e oz'er side."

His eyes shone clear, even at their most troubled and deep.

"No. I mean, if I am to leave, what would you do?"

"Z'e traveler z'at journeys west, z'ey say, never sees z'e sun set, never recognizes or admits z'e passage of time. *Mais*, z'e wise man z'at journeys east, finds 'is shadow lengz'ening wiz' z'e day. Z'e night is simply z'e consequence of 'is quest. 'Is nights are shorter and 'e is h'able to keep 'is back turned to z'e seasons. 'E watches h'only z'e rising sun."

The dwarf was absorbed in his own philosophy.

"It is always glorious, golden dawn?" I mused.

But those were not my words.

"What would h'I do?" Hand ignored my last comment, and as an afterthought returned to my original question. "I would myself 'ave h'only one choice. To go wiz' you."

I smiled. He did not return it, but maintained that same

33

familiar attitude.

"And if I forbade it?"

"Why would you? Am I not pleasant company, *mon vieux*?"

"Because these men of whom you speak may already be following you. Waiting for you to lead them to me."

"Z'ey could not follow where I 'ave been."

"No," I smiled. "I am sure of that. Still, they may now be looking for us both. To travel together is to deliver ourselves to them. We do not, my friend, make a just slightly conspicuous pair."

"I suppose," he said with a resolute sigh, "you may be right about some z'ings, h'after all. *Mais*, I shall not leave z'is place, and when you come back wiz' z'e news from Coh'rbett—"

"Corbett? I do not seek him. It is my brother, my children's uncle, who I wish to see. I am once again in his shadow."

"Z'en, go. Go where you must. I will be 'ere when you return."

"What about a disguise?" I wondered aloud.

"Disguise?" he laughed. "'Ave you not considered yourself lately? Z'at beard? Z'at 'orrible h'overcoat?"

He pointed to the shapeless rag hanging on the peg next to the cabin door.

"Of course, you are right," I chuckled along. Then resignedly, "I suppose we must get some sleep."

"Yes," Hand agreed. "*Mais*, I will make for you a fine breakfast in z'e morning," he nodded toward the still unwrapped packages. "Crèpes and zham—wiz' real café. It will be h'Easter Sunday, you know." I watched as he went about preparing for sleep and heard him whisper laughingly to himself, "A disguise?!"

The fire had dwindled to a few crimson embers only, and now Hand turned down the lamp after unrolling his beddings on the packed dirt floor. I sat on the edge of the cot that built out from the cabin wall to form my bed of cornhusks and bearskins.

"Hand?" I spoke his name with a question. He looked up at

me, and through the dark I could still see that strange kindness I had come to understand. "I'm glad you came back."

***

I shall not essay to have you believe there are a host of reasons—or pure altruism of any kind—that cemented the major's loyalty and affection to me. I myself attribute its basis to a single, if unremarkable incident.

It had been some two or three days after we had left the monastery. The recommendation from his cousin came with an implicit trust that we would care equally, the one for the other. Henry's devotion to my family was unquestionable, and I had every reason to expect the same of his own. I was right.

"I, too, h'am a criminal, *Monsieur* Booz'," Hand said to me the afternoon of our second day together. "*Mais*, z'ey are not now 'unting me z'e way z'ey used to do. It seems z'at noz'ing in z'is world matters h'anymore since—excuse me—since you h'are dead."

Hand seemed to understand and quietly respect the simple fear behind all my courage.

"Still, if z'ey should find me, z'ey would not z'ink to drag me all z'e way to Washington City to see me 'anged. Z'ey would shoot me h'on z'e spot." His hands came together with a loud clap. "Z'en, for h'all z'eir talk, z'at is what z'ey would do wi'z you, too, no?"

He looked at me somewhat puzzled, but there was no confusion to be shared.

"I z'ink maybe we can not be sure what z'ey never do, yes?"

Hand was never specific about his crime, the reason he too was hunted, but there seemed an assurance that he was also a misunderstood casualty of war, that he was not merely some treacherous thief or murderer. And although the understanding was ever that I had no reason to doubt or fear,

35

I must say those were perilously uncertain times for me to trust anyone, and I fully prepared myself to sleep with only one eye at a time and kill him if I must.

Perhaps the country was satisfied that John Wilkes Booth was dead, but I knew he was not. And I meant to keep it that way. The only thing I learned about Hand at that time is that he was for many years a free man. At age fourteen he had been sold to Napoleon Turner's circus, with which he traveled successfully for three years. At that time, he bought his freedom on the pretense of being nineteen. His color, remarkable size and condition, as well as an undeniable ability to lie boldface, made it difficult to argue with him about anything and impossible not to believe. It was, as well, only two years' difference.

All this I heard in great detail as we hiked unsteadily through leagues of uncut brush and brambles until the major and, later that same afternoon, I came to one of those myriad and boundless rivers that are part of the great Ohio system. Spring was full-on and the snows of the mighty and ancient Appalachians were by their movements mirroring our own, disguising their wintry hearts in shimmering tracks of westward meanderings.

The woodlands of the West Virginia territory are almost as venerable as their mountain fathers. Their thick interiors still host occasional fragments of a primeval sun, for thousands of years of diurnal coursings have gone unnoticed by their twisting undergrowth. Here, the bubbles of splashing waters and the crackling snaps of a lizard's tread among the leaf-strewn rocks echo the tones of the first language, one that antedates the comparative sophistication heard in the whistlings of the minor birds.

"The water is deep here," I said, overlooking Knob Creek from the bluff on which we stood. "I think we would be better to find a suitable place for fording downstream."

"Z'ere ees no time for z'at, *mon ami*. Are you h'afraid of getting a leetle wet?"

"Afraid, no, but why must we—"

"Because, you forget, eef we h'are not on some *pique-unique*. Z'e time, h'it ees precious."

With this, he began to take off his boots and shirt, tie them into a kind of knot with his bedroll and heave them across to the other bank with surprising ease. I followed his lead and did the same.

The waters were deep, but they were not the least rapid. There could be little problem crossing, after all. With a great splash, the major plunged into the water. Before I could do the same I paused for just a moment with a kind of eerie presentiment. The major did not come back up. I waited. Still nothing. I had no choice but to follow him.

Down into the water I swam until I saw him, eyes closed, silent, still. He lay motionless upon the shingles of the river's bed as if he meant to yield entirely to Echo's unintentional suit. Suddenly, his dark eyes opened huge and looked at me with an animal panic while he began to beat furiously at the water with his arms. As I reached around him, he hit me several times—nearly breaking my nose—before I could guide him to the surface and finally to the other shore.

He never let me forget that date, July 7. Nor could I. It was also the day they hanged Herold, Payne, Atzerodt, and dear Mary Surratt in Washington.

They had not been tried. They had been brutally held before a martial court with paltry defenses and no real chance at liberty. Their hands and feet had remained bound throughout, their faces masked. They had been able to utter not a single word on their own behalf.

This was my first real indication that I had killed the wrong man. Been wrong to think a single death could solve what had begun to tangle. It was a contagion that had long passed into the hearts and minds of the entire North.

I imagine I feel it is my duty to talk of more than vengeance here. For does it not have its more estimable side?

Four people—American citizens—were hanged for the firing of a single bullet. The courage was theirs, the pistol mine. Is it not just that I should speak? What God wills he wills apart from human triflings and desires. He holds us in his hands but does not think or care to close his fingers, cup his palms. Three men and a noble woman committed themselves to his care the morning of their deaths. Four others found mercy in a sentence to live their lives' remainders in a desolate prison.

Once a jury has decided—

There is no such thing as impartiality. What we believe, we will believe.

***

"I h'am sorry," he coughed, as I dragged him up onto the bank. "You h'are very brave."

"What happened?" I asked as he continued to spit out water.

"I cannot swim," he said as bluntly as his accent and condition allowed. "Mais, I was not h'afraid." He coughed again. "I was not h'afraid. Not to die, not to drown. Only for you. Henri would 'ave been h'angry if I left you h'alone."

"I would have been angry, as well. In fact, I may never have spoken to you again."

"You would not like me?" he began before understanding my attempt at comedy. "Oh! I see," he chortled, pleased to have discovered I too could have a sense of humor.

That night we sat about our small fire, the major wrapped warmly in both our blankets, finally allowing me some reign. I had insisted he must care for the mouthfuls of river surely remaining in his belly to manifest themselves as fever during the night. His hair glistening with a thousand stubborn droplets clinging to infinite curls, his skin showing purple in the glow of the camp, his face and mine giving sole expression to the moonless night.

"'Ow might one suppose z'at because a man h'ees possessed of some good 'e might not be equally stricken wi'z an amount of blinding h'evil?" he began to speak while following sparks from our fire as they rose to meet their brother stars.

"So, 'e desired to free my race? What right 'ad 'e to cause z'e blood of countless z'ousands to run as freely? Could h'any end be justified by such means? And 'ow might h'any man, given z'e h'obvious outcome of z'is present 'emancipation' z'ink any negro better for z'e generations of h'enmity to come?

"Was I not educated along wi'z z'e whip—first of z'e plantation, z'en of z'e circus—even as z'ey laughed at z'e 'opof-my-z'umb'?"

"Hop-of-my-thumb" was an expression I recognized immediately, but did not know why. Perhaps I had once heard my father speak of dwarves this way.

"Did I not prove my h'own wor'z by z'e h'industry wi'z which I pursued and purchased my freedom? Why must I share z'at precious commodity wi'z h'innumerable o'zers whose h'outstanding achievement was z'e performance of some command when z'eir h'indolence afforded z'em not a single 'aystack behind which z'ey might 'ide to sleep away z'e afternoon in lazing dreams of h'idle Africa?

"Where h'are z'e proud cities of z'eir black 'omeland? What h'inventions can z'ey claim wi'z which z'ey eased z'e season's natural h'afflictions? Are z'ey free men because z'ey walk upright, or must z'ey not prove z'emselves by more z'an a desire to be equal? Equal! 'Ow should z'ey not be held h'accountable to h'action as was I?

"And I h'am z'e h'aberration!" he drew a deep breath and cleared his throat. "You know, I have a broz'er. A twin, yes. Our moz'er died moments before I was delivered h'and my broz'er, h'Atlas—my own flesh, first born and

39

fully formed—refused to ever h'acknowledge our fraternity. As h'if it would make 'im less z'e man to be related to a 'Mr. Paap.' Poor man carried z'e weight of h'our kinship h'on 'is shoulders," he laughed.

"Z'e 'appiest moment of 'is life was z'e day h'I was sold to z'e carnival. Carted off like some wild z'ing to remind 'im no more of z'e dwarfed and crippled part of 'is h'own character.

"H'our master did not sell me. H'it was my broz'er! I suppose 'e told z'e plantation h'owner I ran away, while 'e 'orded z'e miserable coins 'e received for me, knowing it would buy 'imself not freedom, a lifetime of whisky! Oh! h'it was h'only 'alf enough to purchase 'is papers, and 'e could never 'ave z'ought to save h'it until 'e found z'e oz'er part. Better to drink h'it slowly. Z'at h'is my broz'er!

"Now z'ey will make 'im free, and h'I must once again compete wi'z 'is z'oughts of superiority. All z'is when 'e 'as never distinguished 'imself. 'Ow do I know? Oh! I kept contact with 'im. 'E was still my broz'er. Alz'ough 'e never knew I was watching 'im. Just enough to satisfy myself z'at 'e was wrong to z'ink 'is z'oughts of me. And I was right. 'is only claim is to be normal—man-size.

"I h'am 'is equal in every part z'at matters to a woman, and 'is better h'in every part z'at must make a real man!" He stretched his neck straight above the wraps about his shoulders, as if accommodating his enlarged spirit, then sighed. "If h'eet 'ad been my cane, *Monsieur* Sumner would never 'ave risen!" he mumbled, poking at our fire with a willow branch.

"Abolition! I will 'ave no part of z'at system. What h'ees wrong wi'z slavery? Save z'at eet should be h'inflicted on one race h'alone. Z'ere h'are many whites 'o are equally lame to contribute more z'an z'e force a master's rod can supervise. *Mais*, any man 'o will content 'imself to z'e miseries of z'e yoke, 'o will not toil for 'is own freedom, and 'o would let z'e blood of innocent h'oz'ers pay z'e price 'e 'imself ees h'unwilling to pay, what h'ees 'e, but a leach upon z'e body of society? A 'erded vassal. A mindless drone. What should 'e be, but a bonded slave?

"I love my cou'zahn *Henri*—h'as a friend may love a friend—still, e' h'ees but some puppy dog of a man, willing to cast 'is loyalty toward 'omever 'olds z'e deesh!

"If 'Faz'er Abra'am' was so just, where was 'is son when z'e field was taken? Why did 'e so ve'emently deny z'e rumors of 'is mixed blood, whez'er z'at blood was Afrhican or 'ebrew? 'Ow might z'e pay of 'is beloved 'coloreds' 'ave been so h'unequal, only one-'alf of z'e white men alongside 'om z'ey marched to equal dea'z? If 'e was so great and so wise and good, where was 'is soul and 'eart of 'earts z'at 'e could not see or feel or 'ear z'e sufferings of truly righteous men, 'ose labors were not to h'enslave z'e masses, but to make use of nature's h'own bondsmen? Z'ose beasts, 'o, h'unprodded, would contribute only z'at which z'ey could not depend would be given to z'em? Z'e 'rail-splitter' was ever a 'tongue-splitter,' no'zing more!"

***

What I am about to tell you is surely the most difficult part of my story to explain. You will take it for an excuse, for a flimsy explanation, for a fantasy of self-deception. And you will be justified to the extent that I could never truly hope for you to understand the mechanism of something so inherently unmechanical: Theater.

When it is asked how I could have killed Poor Old Abe, I must respectfully submit by way of reply, how could I not? It was not a drama, you see, of my own design, but a role that I seemed to have been assigned in the space between the ages long past and those yet to unfold. I could as readily view my part as that of some fate-thwarted lover of life's own comedy, some comic fool caught up in the tragedy you would deem the episode to have been.

And, though I understand very well the means by which I

came to play my greatest scene, I can not for an instant expect you to grasp the purity of my motive. You have no sense of the pageant beyond the diversion of an occasional evening. Your very association of the thing with frivolous play prohibits you from approaching it otherwise. This is not your fault. There has never been an attempt to convince you to the contrary. How should I imagine I might? Yet must I endeavor.

The mysteries of the theater are ancient, venerable and, to the detriment of both spectator and this performer, unspeakable by custom. What appears to be mere posturing and apish prattle to some—my own brother among them—is at its depth an investment of the heart and spirit into a different circumstance, a different mind.

When an actor is assigned a role, it may be commonly understood that he must choose a character, a mode of speech unlike his own, an altered gait, a distinctive manner or tic. This may be so for many. But when a man of the theater plays well his part, his choices are removed. The character lives and operates and breathes of its own, approaches its destiny with complete abandon. There is no motivation, as it were. There is necessity alone.

In the jungles of the east, I have heard it told, there are annual festivals wherein whole villages partake of a timeless and primitive ceremony, to which no outsider has ever been allowed. Each year a member of the tribe is chosen to represent a beast of the wild. From year to year the representation changes from boar to bear to jungle cat and on, in a cycle of twelve.

As the rest of the villagers celebrate the season with the gathering and dancing about of a huge bonfire, the elect slips cautiously away from the group and begins a ritual prowling at the village perimeter, granting glimpses only of his newly assumed form. What was a man is man no more. Under the influence of trance-inducing herbs and medicaments, the candidate begins grunting or howling a sort of occasional chorus to the songs of what had been his kinsmen, as their ceremony transforms to frenzy.

When the chanting subsides, the young men of age select each a weapon of the hunt—some lassos, some nets, some clubs or spears—and rally off in search of their prey, while the elders and women and children commence to pray and prepare the banquet table.

To say the chase is only another part of the initiation rite is to neglect the fervor with which both hunters and hunted proceed. Two or three days of intrepid tracking, and reports of knife wounds and teeth marks are not uncommon, it is said, before the beast is overpowered and transported back to the village, bound to the stake that is to become its turnspit.

These are not cannibals to our understanding, though I have heard the fate of the elect spoken of uncertainly—and imagine the possible devotion and solemnity of the feasting itself as each member of the tribe shares in a portion of the sacred meal. But this is not as fantastic as it may appear. There are reasons to believe the Christian religion too with its Eucharistic traditions may stem from as unholy a source.

Why would anyone, you may ask, allow themselves to be thus elected? It is a great honor, for the family as well as the individual, and the days of gluttony and excess preceding the event are in many societies reason enough. Surely you have heard of the triumphant warrior whose heart was plucked from his living chest atop some Aztec pyramid, or the beautiful virgin rewarded for her chastity by being thrown screaming into the depths of the fiery island volcano—of their glory and immortality?

And have you not wondered why it was never the vanquished prince who foolishly chose to lead his people against the empire, or the harlot whose crimes were so grievous and innumerable as to defy the suitability of a simple stoning or branding? It is the hero, the martyr, the saint alone who can be imagined to quiet the spirits of flesh and fire when they call for appeasement.

Actors are born. The first actors were not trained to

populate the theaters, rather theaters built to house the actors—as assassins must be framed to dispatch tyrants.

What makes a good actor? A certain disposition or predisposition, I imagine. What, in the theater, is commonly termed role-playing is actually an ability to channel emotions and even physical characteristics. During a brilliant performance an actor somehow seems to take on the corporal qualities of the character beyond the padding, shadings and vocal schemings. The actor assumes the context of the situation. It is simple really. He allows himself to become a sort of host, a receptacle, the object of universal forces. The willingness to take risks, be vulnerable and submit to the miracle allow him to succeed.

With me it wasn't so much willingness as need, and less a matter of being vulnerable than merely being exactly who and what I am, completely vulnerable, sensitive and—if I have learned anything about myself in this life—even craving of affection.

To assume a role is to embrace fate. One's own and that of every member of life's cast. To submit oneself to what Coleridge at the beginning of the century called the "willing suspension of disbelief." For what may man believe but that all of life is fraught with doubt, and the only certainty is that which he freely and completely invests in it. A poetic faith that whatever shall be must be. And the knowledge of the difference between what is not dared and what is done.

Once committed to the removal of the northern president, whether as hostage for the release of the thousands upon thousands of Confederate prisoners or no, I was committed to his removal. Once I accepted the role, I accepted its liabilities, even if I had to claw and scratch and bite my way through its performance. And you will not understand, you who have never been upon a stage, who think of performance only in terms of the possible attributes of a hired lover. Your broken heart is the only thing in life you have ever taken seriously.

You will say Wilkes Booth is mad. It has been said before.

Sunday, June 3, 1860. Petersburg Theater, Petersburg, Virginia. Dress rehearsal for Richard III. *The DIRECTOR and the STAGE MANAGER have called for a break from the rehearsal process and are talking at the back of the theater. The stage is set as the interior of a royal palace. The CAST, as LORDS and LADIES, laze or mill about listlessly, speaking in Southern accents of the glorious cause of the Confederacy. THE ACTOR taunts and goads an older member of the Cast with a sword from which he has dangerously removed the fencing tip.*

THE ACTOR *(waving his sword wildly)*: Fight, damn you! Fight, fight!

OLD ACTOR *(mimicking reproachfully)*: You are mad, mad!

THE ACTOR *(striking a pose and wielding his sword with great expertise until his opponent must fence or be inflicted)*: I am Richard! And you are my mortal enemy. *(improvising iambic pentameter and taking swipes with every phrase)* This day—I shall see you—gone to hell—an' you will not—defend your honor!

From among the Cast, a YOUNG ACTRESS, who has been watching the two with varied interest, gives an audible gasp and directs the attention of the others to the scene with concern. The Actor pauses and takes half a step back, realizing he has slashed a piece out of the Old Actor's costume. The Director begins to come forward, but stays back to watch what may unfold.

OLD ACTOR *(rising and taking up his sword in self defense; he too removes its tip, begins fencing expertly and with force, while improvising Shakespearean verse between attacks and parries)*: If—you—will not—desist—*(switching his sword into his left hand)* then I —must show—you—I—am—the—better man. Not only—if only—with a sword—in hand.

THE ACTOR *(pleased by the provoked enthusiasm, also switches sword hands):* Well spoken, then. And with—the silvery tongue—that marks each member—of your house—a liar!

As they continue, the Old Actor mounts his assault, backing The Actor upon a riser representing a castle stair.

OLD ACTOR: Is this—but some game—to you? *(switching back to his right hand)* They said—you were—your father's son—and now—I see it—for—a fact!

THE ACTOR *(continues with his left hand, turning the insult into motivation):* And yet—it can—be said—I know—my father's name!

The Cas, now follow the action with some, if mixed, delight as the two actors work their way across the stage.

OLD ACTOR: You are—a fool.

THE ACTOR *(switching back to his right hand):* But not—an old one, like—yourself.

OLD ACTOR: Yet—one—marked—for certain—death.

The Old Actor lunges, the tip of his blade disappears into The Actor's side. The Young Actress lets out a shrill scream and there is a great commotion. The Old Actor tosses his blade aside and rushes to the side of The Actor who has collapsed in a heap. The Stage Manager and Director rush onto the stage.

OLD ACTOR *(frantic as he lifts The Actor into a sitting position, examines the wound):* My God! *(turning to the others)* Fetch a surgeon!

The Director pushes at the Stage Manager who rushes out of the theater.

THE ACTOR *(smiling):* I'm—*(taking a deep breath)* all right. You—*(another gasp as he grabs the Old Actor by the shoulder)* can play a part—when you must. But—*(clutching his side)* Richard is supposed—to win the duel!

The Actor grimaces as the Old Actor joins his strange humor with a crooked smile, wondering at the possible outcome of the performance later that day. The Stage Manager returns with a SURGEON, who quickly allays any fears for The Actor's immediate recovery.

Scene III

Oh! the snow, the beautiful snow!

It was to be our last night together, and I allowed Hand to take me to that place he knew so well. In every town, whether he had ever been before or not, he knew this place instinctively. Where else could a man such as he find the body's simple comforts? He, who truly held the deformities of Richard Plantagenet, with neither throne nor crown nor sceptered treasure to lure his would-be loves. No, nor even the simple poetry of primal lust to express his desires.

In years before I had been invited to go with him many times to these houses of seamy comfort, had ever envied him exercising his matured, if stunted, manhood and wanted the same for myself but could not. Thought little, but that it might be some time, perhaps never, before I should forget Ella long enough to remember only the animal in me.

She had brought the beast in me to bay, and tamed him too. Now I was wild again, but clawless, without instinct. Hiding like some caved or cornered creature with eyes yet mindful and gloweringly green. I had no life, no desire, no animal at all, bleached bones only inside my pelted frame.

When he had done, Hand returned to where I sat in the foyer glancing at a weekly and lost in my own thoughts. Behind him stood a young and pretty girl, scarcely eighteen I should think. With candid simplicity she wrapped a lightly tatted shawl about her shoulders and her half-buttoned blouse.

"Z'ere is a circus on z'e oz'er side of town," Hand addressed me with the tone of the returned warrior. "Our lovely Marie says it will only be 'ere for a few days, and I 'ave promised to take 'er. She 'as never been to one, but knows of my familiarity with z'em."

"Well, then; I can make my way home by myself."

"*Mais, non!* We want you to come. Eet will be good for z'e

z'ree of us."

"But—"

"He is even more handsome than you described," said the girl, with a glint of out-of-place evil in her eyes.

"Z'ere," cried Hand. "You see! H'eet will be good for h'all of us!"

He laughed again as he took his Marie by one arm and seemingly swooped me off the divan with his other. Throughout the evening Hand seemed all the gentleman, hardly the sideshow oddity whose crudity is ever at least the product of his pitiable and detested station. His knowledge of the circus was surely welcome, particularly when we discovered he had worked with half-a-dozen of the performers before and secured our ability to stay abroad after the show was ended.

The three of us walked the grounds as the beasts were put to bed. Then ended up in the wagon of a friend of Hand's, who had relinquished it to us for the night and supplied us as well with a bottle of fine bourbon. He more than once expressed unseemly regret that this friend, the camp's contortionist, could not have joined us, and nudged Marie with short padded elbows of depravity.

The effect of alcohol on the dwarf was extreme. He began laughing excessively, and his already contorted features brightly glowed both red and orange. A strange green light seemed to appear in front of his otherwise black eyes as they sparkled.

I admit a kind of fear or apprehension, presentiment, if you will. It was the same spell upon the sturdy little man I remembered seeing as a boy, on those occasions when my father graced our household with his actual presence, if only as long as it took his beloved cider to whisk him away once again.

At this moment the bourbon took hold of me with a not unfamiliar power, bringing my courage with it. I looked toward the young Marie. But rather than share any of my malaise, she seemed not just the slightest amused, nay pleased. And with that look that I had known before in other women, regardless of their age, and an almost unnatural quiver of her lower lip, she reached for me with sudden strength. Her brow creased disappointedly as I withheld my hand.

"Touch me," she said.

But I could not. Only did I look back toward Hand where he seemed to gloat and stew in his snifter. He let out a cackle that gurgled down to his gut, and when he brought his head up again, another look at Marie forced it back down with a grin.

She was sitting there, as before, a quiet intensity possessing her entire mood, looking at me longingly as she rubbed both hands over and then down into her blouse.

"Touch me," she repeated imploringly, yet with an insistent tone. "While our little friend watches. Yes," she said with satisfaction. "While our little friend watches all!"

He is not my friend, I thought. Some agency of evil whose curse has borne its mark upon his charred complexion and withered his form that he might slither, as if limbless, enticing those whose spines were lost to temptation or supple as his own, but recognizable at a glance to any who held trust in God and his ways.

"Do you think I look better with my clothes on or off?"

"What?" I frowned warily.

"I have been told I am one of those people who looks better with them off," she said matter-of-factly as she stood in the middle of the room and removed the last bit of laced silk.

Altogether motionless, she merely looked to me for comment.

It was true, I suppose, although I had never before considered this group of people to which she belonged and wondered slightly who had, to term them so with some pretense of expertise. Had they then, by matter of course, detached themselves so far from passion or moment that they might analyze and catalogue for future reference or compliment? Yet one could scarcely deny her exquisite form, slender but buoyant, pulsing yet serene.

"I suppose so," I shrugged off with an adopted proficiency of my own.

"Suppose?" she questioned with the plaintive tone of a harlot judged a schoolgirl or commended for her domestic ability.

***

Tuesday, February 28, 1865. New Orleans.
The second- or third-floor boudoir of a brothel, a YOUNG PROSTITUTE, blindfolded, giggling. THE ACTOR, bootless and breathy with liquor, lies atop her, also laughing. On one side of the room French windows open onto a slender balcony overlooking the New Orleans streets during Mardi Gras. Rockets and bombs explode.

THE ACTOR (playfully): Who am I?
YOUNG PROSTITUTE (mock terror): I don't know. *(comically)* A rich man who does not have to worry for money or for work?
THE ACTOR: The greatest work is that performed upon the stage of life. There can be no money to pay for one's heart. Who do you think?
YOUNG PROSTITUTE (laughing still): Think? How may I think? I cannot even see!
THE ACTOR (sudden violence): Who am I?!

The Young Prostitute reacts abruptly. The Actor controls his mood, calms somewhat — makes light of his own temper.

THE ACTOR (cont'd): Who would you like me to be?
YOUNG PROSTITUTE (still intimidated, plays her part by stroking his arms): I am happy with who you seem to be. Strong, handsome.

THE ACTOR: You cannot see if I am handsome.

YOUNG PROSTITUTE (seductively): I can feel. *(kissing his neck)* And I can taste. You are handsome. *(still kissing)* Very handsome.

THE ACTOR: Perhaps I am a favorite lover. A former beau?

YOUNG PROSTITUTE: You are all of these—this moment. *(lustily)* I have you now.

THE ACTOR: But if I were a killer? If I hated—

YOUNG PROSTITUTE: Why, Johnnie!

He starts, confused, nervous, then—

THE PROSTITUTE (cont'd): Johnnie Reb! My poor young gentleman of the South. *(kissing his shoulders, arms)* But I shall heal your wounds—I shall kiss them clean and shut. *(unbuttoning his shirt)* Let me lick your battered limbs.

THE ACTOR (taken by her seduction): How do you know I am from the South? And how can you see which wounds demand the most attention?

YOUNG PROSTITUTE (laughing again): Only a Southern boy would be so foolish! *(quietly)* And every hero suffers from the same affliction. *(kissing down, well past his chest)* It is your heart, of course, that bursts to breaking. *(still kissing downward)* Your heart!

***

We left the girl Marie asleep on the floor of the circus wagon and walked back into the woods toward the cabin. Hand seemed not the least disappointed with what I prefer to phrase my indifference, and in truth seemed to revel in his advantage of me. Still, he showed a kind of sympathy which, after all, is the reason, I imagine, he could not see me leave alone and rather left Marie to wake by herself in strange surroundings. The sun was still some time from arising, but our way was half-lit and well-worn.

I looked at Hand across the plates of our finished meal and noted a glance I had never known before. It silently goaded me into declaration.

"I do not care of Corbett. What has he done? Shot some unfortunate imposter to satisfy the government reports and the accountings of the penny press. I must find the man who truly murdered me."

"So, you will not listen to me?" said Hand.

"I told you what I must do."

"Z'en you must listen to me. Go West. To Okla'oma."

"Oklahoma? West?"

"Yes. 'E is z'ere."

"Who?"

"Your murderer, Coh'rbett."

"How do you know where he is?"

"What does eet matter? What h'are you looking for—really?" asked Hand, sensing my preoccupation with the morning departure.

"I don't know. Myself?"

"You h'are dead!" he said with his gleeful cackle.

"Then I'm looking for the man who killed me."

I stopped short at my own simple logic. That was, after all, what had been bothering me. Haunting me the whole time. How should I be dead unless someone had killed me?

"Someone, a man, a stranger whom I daresay I never met, died at Garrett's Farm. Badin, perhaps, someone. Whether by gallant choice or unhappy accident, I owe him my life. It is his murderer, too, I must find. If only I—"

"*Mais*, h'all z'e world knows. Z'e sergeant Coh'rbett. 'E is z'e one."

"No. He was only the finger on the trigger. The tool of the hand on the gun. This was not the work of a single man."

"A madman. Z'at is what Coh'rbett is. *Coeur bête*! 'Eart h'of a beast! A very, very mad man. And not h'even a man any more!"

He let out another cackle, this one gurgling deeper than the last. His eyes flashed as he grabbed at himself between the legs and moaned like a wounded wolf during a full moon.

"A madman to kill a madman!" he cackled and howled again. "*Mais*, 'o 'ired 'im? 'O paid 'im for 'is deed and 'is devotion?"

Scene IV

How the flakes gather and laugh as they go!

Strophe

From deep within my corn-husk crib I had unearthed a leather satchel—the only possession of my former life—which had once served as my theatrical make-up bag. How many times had it aided my various transformations?

"I told you I wished no part of the past," I said to Hand, "the Christmas you brought this to me."

He smiled reflectively, surely musing that despite my oaths I had kept it well.

"'You will want it more, some day,' you said," I recalled. "But you could not have then known—could you?"

He continued to smile, looked straight at me and shook his head. Still I wondered.

Into the bag my journal, two drab shirts and a pair of striped serge trousers were stuffed alongside the spirit-gum and other theatrical effects. Leaving Hand and my needle behind, I donned my nankeen topcoat and was off.

It was not a cold wind that greeted my scalp that spring day. The sou'westers balmed steadily, but the sensation was cold, nonetheless. How could I travel then, back to New York where I might be recognized without some form of disguise? Booth was known for his raven curls, moustache and imperial—and eyes. But uneven strands and shocks of now stick-straight, salt and pepper hair and uniform silvery stubble seemed enough to change all—especially when aided by one patched eye.

The winds drew up draughts of moisture from the gulf to confirm the late afternoon. I had worn my hair and beard long for fully twenty years, and while it had begun of necessity as disguise, I shortly became rather fond of their appearance. They seemed to mask the eyes alone with a strange, reversed sympathy. It was still many months from the first before I felt secure in my new look, my anonymity, and I never truly felt safe from the eyes of any who had known me even a little, yet ever was. Each report that found Wilkes Booth at this location or that event, preaching from some Dixie pulpit or painting houses in several western settlements, was but another fantastic sighting. They affirmed the safety of my immediate asylum as well as its necessary refuge.

And now had I to chance whatever nature had in mind. But with a thought to safety still, and on Hand's recommendation, I chose the route of my return to be more secure than direct. After traveling by coach to the Illinois capital of Springfield I would begin my journey east by train, first going north to Chicago. From thence I would continue to travel somewhat round-about, lest any—but who should there be, really?—might think to follow.

I felt strangely calm about my errand. It was not an end to exile—my name and face were banished still—but it was a chance at a strange new future. A future I could once again help to shape. This time with certain informed hands, would I see the way to make of tomorrow, regardless of the acclaim of others, the place where Wilkes could know his name.

Arriving in Springfield with more than an hour on my hands I stopped at a certain Diller's Drugstore for a fruit-flavored soda water. It had been so long since this simple civility had been available to me that, I daresay, I relished it as if it were a shot of fine pale brandy. Upon leaving the fountain a yellow dog began to follow me and continued so all the way to the station. There he sat, as if to beg command that he should board the train with me, then barked twice when I mounted the platform without a word, without a command. A colored porter observed the scene and smiled at first on what he supposed my dog's loyalty. His smile soon turned to puzzlement when he saw the lack of attention I gave the beast while it yet stared ever-faithfully. Once on the train I thought I heard a single yelp as the station-master cried, "All aboard," and the great steel wheels began to roll—but that was all.

Installed and on my way, it was yet some time before I was

able to again read the letters brought to me by Hand.

The first ran simply:

Father,

Mother is ill. Unable now to travel to see her only daughter's marriage. Near to death. What joy she might have had is gone forever. I am a man and can not honor you with the foolish and careless heart of a boy.

What you have done I cannot forgive, thought until this moment to have forgotten. But then, it is only you I must forget.

Sebastian.

The second, somewhat longer:

Dear Father,

You have always lived within my intuition, now rumor resurrects a deeper instinct—truth. Mother's final wish was for my understanding. I believe I can grant her this, though she guards your "horrible secret" with her life.

But my life must have something more—hope. What had seemed even one year ago impossible is mine at last. The shattered fragments of a complicated youth, become whole. I will have a family. And I will be loved, cared for, and remembered.

My brother's torments are legion, if not unlike my own. Mine have found a power from without, yet he still struggles inwardly and finds no solace. But he has a strong will and shall overcome. I pray it may be soon.

I thank God our shame is yet disguised from the rest of the world. Thank my uncle for giving us the security of a home to learn our faith. It was not easy. Where my mother always found her courage, I can only guess. And be thankful.

Still, I must forgive you. I pray for you and hope we shall never meet.

Your daughter,
Viola.

***

In Chicago I switched lines and paused just long enough for a short walk along the river and watch for twenty minutes where a side-wheel steamer was having some difficulty pulling either in or out of its quay. As I returned toward the station, I passed McVicker's Theater, but the afternoon's performance was on the street corner. A gaunt and grizzled man, fixing his stare at all who paused, raised a haunted bible against a strong head wind and shouted hoarsely, "As your Father in Heaven is perfect, be ye also perfect."

***

"You did just right to wake me," I told the porter as we pulled into Michigan City. The sky was bright and blue, and my simple breakfast of eggs and whitefish in the small railyard diner seemed, at that moment, the most exotic meal I could ever have had.

Switching lines again, the storm I had found myself in at Indianapolis continued for the entire eleven-hour leg from state capital to state capital. It was a gray and weighted Saturday in Columbus where I chose to board the night at the Petersen House before zig-zagging north again. Not at all like the Georgia city of the same name, where I played in the autumn of 1860 and found myself the victim of a certain incident involving a small pistol.

The mood of this city seemed summed up in a single glance at the sober masonry of its Soldier's Hospital, upon which I rose to view early Sunday—regular and austere, and forever mourning what might have been could not have been helped.

Quite a contrast from this was the forest city of Cleveland. For, while the rain had begun again, the mood was

58

welcoming and fresh as the shore of Lake Erie. The Union Station too was handsome and gay, and outside, as I walked through Monument Square, I was entertained by my memory of loud applause on a summer's or winter's night coming from the Academy of Music.

Overnight from Cleveland we arrived in Buffalo, twelve or more miles along the Erie Lake. Here, thirty years before, booked for a fortnight at the Metropolitan Theater in 1861, I had received standing ovations and singularly creditable reviews in the *Sentinel* for my two performances of *Richard III*.

This day none gave a second look to the strolling vagabond as I limped past the Metropolitan and St. James Hall before continuing *en route* to Rome. From my pocket I produced the half-written letter begun I know not how many seasons before, now stained with chocolate from the only supper I had purchased in Buffalo.

My dearest Ella,

I have on many occasions begun this, a simple letter to you, with no success. I, who was once the master wordsmith, could find none. No appropriate message for one as you.

Forgive me, I have not found it still—

It is dark on the train. I wake to the sound of the whistle and wheels. A steady chant beckons to either wake or sleep. I fumble to release my fingers from where they rest knotted about the handles of my one bag. Reaching for my throat, I feel the silver medallion suspended from my neck. So long has it hung there that I have learned to ignore its weight.

"Merry Christmas, Miss Nash," it remembers.

"Merry Christmas, Mr. Wilkes," she smiles as I hand her the tiny velvet-wrapped box. "What on earth can it be?"

She giggled with the knowledge of a child fresh from discovering the cache of all her Christmas toys.

But she cannot know what it is, I think. And then realize why her eyes dance so lively, as her hands numbly pick at the ice-blue ribbons. It is the size of a ring box.

I worried, as she surely awaited some special words.

"It is nothing, really."

"Oh?"

"Well, of course, it means a great deal to me. And I hope—"

"Then it will mean even more to me," lifting the lid. "And on your hopes will I ever pin my own."

She picks up the medal. Her face changes. No longer the excited expression of a child, she looks strangely older, becalmed, fully loved and loving. She holds it to the light, turning it slightly to reveal its age.

"I want you to have it. It is for you."

She did not take offense. She knew what I meant.

She held it up again and turned around. I imagined she had fastened chains about her neck a thousand times, but here it was right for me to hook the finely wrought silver clasp.

Instead, I sat down and began to laugh.

"It is from Italy."

She cast an unbelieving glance over her left shoulder, her hands still raised, poised dumbly for the untendered aid. With a slight huff and shrug she walked to the mirror where I could see the reflected resolve and realization in her eyes for a moment before the sheer power of her femininity masked it with a flutter of well-placed distraction and cabal.

"Have you been to Italy without telling me, Johnnie? Amazing! Mr. Surratt threatens to go there one day, and you return from the same place the next. The two of you share more in common than I ever would have imagined."

"John. The Evangelist. My patron saint," I explain from the past, as I return to the present, afraid of an unknown and threatening future. "As a boy I had always regretted that it was he and not John the Baptist. I used to ask my mother every week to tell me for which of them she named me, always hoping for a different answer, as if I had misunderstood every time before.

"Of course, that is not as absurd as it may seem. Actually, I was named for a grandfather, you know. And the choice of this or that saint was only nominal. But I never understood why my mother preferred the apostle to the Baptist. John the Baptist was the rumored reincarnation of Elisha and the cousin of Christ, the bringer of redemption and light, and therefore somewhat more conspicuous—famous, if you will. But, "The Evangelist," the dark messenger, was the answer she ever gave me."

"And why did she make that choice?"

"I do not know, but I have always told myself it was for two reasons. First, because she thought his gospels to be the most stirring, most inspired works of the New Testament. I think I agree. As an actor, that kind of thing is especially significant, I imagine.

"The second is nothing, really. Mother's very superstitious. The Baptist suffered his death at the hand of a tyrant who had fallen under the spell of a beautiful woman."

Just now the sun begins to set as the engine pulls out from Albany. A scarlet shawl of sunset wraps the mountaintops with deep glens of chequered evergreen, and black boots their rocky steps as shadows of evening march east. My day sinks into jostled fragments of the earliest of dreams and scattered, half-planned itineraries for the days to come.

Scene V

Whirling about in its maddening fun,
It plays in its glee with everyone.

Strophe

I am a smuggler. I smuggle drugs as I had smuggled emotion—clandestine transportation of character, through my craft. The secret carriage of my own desires, when open commerce would surely have failed subsistence, exposed contraband.

It is my third career and progenitor of my longest love and affliction, the first having been, of course, that of my father and family: the theater. It had afflictions of its own. The second, I suppose, my short-lived if prominent post as assistant quartermaster for the Virginia Regulars. If I thought for any length of time about the way each had started, I would be very careful about ever boarding a train again.

***

Lutz and I gathered no more suspicions than our previous positions had recommended. He because of his enormous wealth and continued successes—for it was never luck—as riverboat gambler, and I still making a certain amount of headway as the latest member of my family's considerable theatrical destiny. Still, that part of my fate seemed less absolute these days. Often for periods of weeks at a time, I was beginning to lose my voice. During performances, during rehearsals. When I awoke in the morning, as I lay myself to bed. And always, I could find only one relief. Never a cure.

***

Before I continue, I must take a moment to tell you of something you may already know. My voice. While you may not hear these very words as I pronounce them into their scripted place, you have certainly heard the reports of the younger Wilkes. Of his dark eyes, his athletic countenance, his passions—as quick upon the stage as off. His voice. My voice.

Oh, do not think me terribly vain to occupy your time with these few notes. Do not accuse me of conceit or pride until you understand the object of my digression and the manner of its expression. For they are not my words that you will have heard time and again exclaim the beauty of the voice that currently mouths its last public utterance. Truly they were never my thoughts at all, except they had been given me too many times by others. After a first and brief introduction, after a single word—it often would seem—of greeting or inquiry, until the intended compliment appeared all but premeditated. Always the same.

How long was it before I realized the power of such a gift? Not very, I admit. In my early youth I discovered its—not my, you will notice—ability to readily charm any woman upon first entreaty. And here I would proceed as if I could explain it, but I cannot. No, nor imagine at all, but I can tell you that it is. It was. It always has been.

Forgive me again, for here I would recollect a first comment upon its strangeness. I was a mere lad, some seven years of age. What was said I can less than recall, but our Bel Air neighbor good Mrs. Stephens made first in my memory the remark that was to precede so many others—and with a chuckling smile of which I had less than any understanding.

Or the day my young classmate tapped upon my shoulder to whisper her difficulty sitting behind me in our Sunday catechism, that when I asked or answered questions during recital, the back of my chair abutting her desk, her table shook with the timber of my twelve years. She reddened only where she had meant to explain.

And that rain-soaked night at seventeen, when I fancied a kiss from one of the young ingénues in my father's company, though she was surely already in her twenties. A laryngitis brought about by the dampness of the evening and my foolishness during that day caused me to immediately deem as futile my chances for so much as a second glance. It is perhaps the only occasion I remember where, voice or no, my powers were received.

***

As I rode my horse Cola from Graysville to Gloryton one bright midday, the Union picket guards raised their arms, more ready and willing to fire as not. It was completely the opposite sentiment from those in the actual field.

"Hey, Edgar!" shouted the young guard on duty to his older companion. "It's Mr. Booth, Mr. Wilkes Booth!"

"What's that?" came the disinterested reply from an unshaven sergeant with jet black hair and gray sideburns.

"The actor, the great actor!"

"Never heard of him."

"Of the famous Booth family!"

"*Never* heard of him! You daft Edmund?"

"Sorry, sir," he said to me alone. "There were reasons some of us joined the army. Not all of us have ever had the distinct pleasure of seeing a theatrical performance. Less one with a gentleman like you. Don't you worry, he'll know who you are one day."

"Thank you," I managed to grin, glancing past the apologetic soldier toward his superior, who continued to ignore the two of us as he stoked a pitiful lightwood flame of campfire. "That is a great comfort," I conceded. "A very great comfort."

***

Lutz's trust of me and faith in my sentiments and abilities was borne out of more than merely my now-infamous vociferations. John Lutz was born in Baltimore and for that we were, of a kind, kinsmen. More importantly he had for some time been involved with the actress Laura Keene. It was in her acting company my brother Edwin had practically apprenticed those several years before. Lutz knew, firsthand

64

through Edwin's disapproving filial rants, the true nature of my sympathies. That which was once enough to make me claim certain treasons for my own, just to engender my brother's foolish wrath, was finally abundant to have me perform much more.

Can you imagine what it was we smuggled, or must I satisfy your curiosity before you have had time to comprehend my current state and ever think the worst? Or will you be disappointed to know I was no pirate, no true adventurer risking all for wagonloads of arms and munitions—merely the transporter of quinine. At least, that is how it began. Still, even from the first, it was not the less delicate and disheartening. War is ever war.

Within less than two hours I found myself in a Confederate hospital camp. The burgeoning acres of blue just over that last ridge had given way to an anaemic sea of gray in the little smoke-filled valley. It was dirty and bloody and ragged and ripped, but it was still a comfort to me, this gray. As I crossed the guard post, an audible murmur fanned out ahead of me. From amid a group of weary young soldiers someone asked if I would play Richard for them, "Or Hamlet, or Hemeya?"

"All of them, or whatever you wish!" I replied, struck by the difference of this reception from the northern one at noon. "Only first show me to Doctor Bickley's tent."

This was the name Lutz had given me as my contact, and I never put it together until I faced him for the first time. I recognized at once the man I had met on the train to Charles Town those years before to watch the hanging of John Brown.

There were no chuckles left in the surgeon's eyes to remind of my having once mistaken the doomed abolitionist whose fate we swore to seal with a slave-owning friend of Colonel Lee. He recognized me too, but was only as cordial as his situation could permit. At this point of the war that was not much.

George Washington Lafayette Bickley was stationed with Stuart's regiment in North Carolina. Stuart was forever at the front of every doomed foray upon which the South embarked, and the doctor had his hands full. He was no longer the lean and scrappy surgeon I had once met, still tall, but now gaunt and possessed of a personality as pallid as his bearded stubble. Understandably. There was little time for him to shave, less to be amused.

But I was crossing the pickets daily on a pass signed by General Grant himself. It was thought that ones as I might color and entertain the ashen troops. I, being part of an already traditional family, had even less problems at the sentry points. I could nearly have as easily smuggled arms as quinine and morphine.

***

Bickley had his own way of showing appreciation for my services, though I required none. Still, he was of the mind that we were somehow brothers in the Hippocratic craft—my supplying him withal—and so we had to share a smoke he said, that day we were re-met.

I unharnessed my horse beside the operation tent of a thirty-year-old man dressed in the white robes of a surgeon and the insigne cap of an officer. His hands and gown were stained with blood, his brow besweated. Unwrapping Cola's corded harness I produced quantities of quinine to which the surgeon reacted enthusiastically.

"If it were in my power to do more I surely would to see these children suffer and yield their boyish lives limb by limb," he said. "But better they should lose an arm or leg to need than to fraternal strategies as in the prisoner camps of our illustrious foe. Their surgeons, I am told, are instructed to leave no son of the South whole of limb, that he will ever be disqualified from becoming a Freemason. I would swear to save all but a few, for all their calls for expedience and supply shortages.

"Still, there is a limit to the effects of chemistry," choked the major. "And none know better than I. Come. To my tent," he suggested in the doubly commanding tone of physician and officer.

I followed him through the makeshift city of canvas, the bivouacked rifles, the stacked and leaning soldiers, some uniformed in gray or yellow or green, many lucky to be booted.

In the midst of the camp was the surgeon's tent. Taller, larger than the rest, the folded flap of its entrance wiped rusty with weeks of a doctor's work.

"Shall I prepare an extra needle for you, Mr. Booth?" he asked as he held back the dried bloodstains for me to enter. "It will help make it somewhat bearable," he suggested. "It will help."

We checked each other nervously while the camp's collective moans became apparent for what they were.

***

"Why are all them boys dyin', Mr. Booth?" said the powder-faced soldier with sleepless eyes, hardly seventeen, his lower body ending in what might have been two split branches of birch.

Bickley prepared the towels and hacksaw, and I considered administering to myself twice the dosage we had just given this brave and spirited youngster. Only his lower jaw was still capable of movement.

"Weren't tellin' nobody what to do four years ago. Weren't killin' nobody—white nor colored. We was happy. Me an' Sue Ellen. Times was peaceful. Now they's just killin' an' killin'. An' dyin'. An' Mr. Lincoln's jus—"

I looked up from where I'd been watching Bickley work with his practiced and studied discipline. He looked up too. The jawbone was now as frozen as the rest of the boy's face. Bickley lifted the torn swathe of bedding from where it lay across the lad's chest to cover the motionless eyes. He signaled me to follow him to the next cot, two aides left behind to silently smooth the ripples of our wake while a

67

third, lantern raised high, continued on with us.

"This is Mr. John Wilkes Booth," Bickley introduced me again. "The greatest actor in all o' these Confederated states. Famous for his pronouncements of Shakespeare and Cicero."

This soldier's eyes were bandaged with what looked to have once been part of a Union uniform. Yet that did not dampen the enthusiasm he held for a visitor of any sort, particularly of such a great and famous actor. Even if he could trust the report of the introduction, I doubted he had ever heard my name any more than many of the others. Likely not at all. They were simple boys who were fighting and dying, not the kind who spent evening after evening at the theater. Still, the doctor's charm had worked its desired spell.

"Would you like to hear a bit of reciting from *Oedipus* or *Hamlet*?" asked Bickley.

"Oh, yes!" beamed the lad in a muffled trumpet of a voice without choosing one or the other perhaps unfamiliar selections. "Would you—Mr. Booth?" he wheezed, holding out his remaining arm to the phantom but accepted player.

So I recited while the doctor worked and every movement of the boy's forehead showed his appreciation for us both. The one of pleasure as grateful as the one of pain. Bickley's sweat seemed salve to the wounds as it dripped steadily upon his work, stopping only when he reeled to curse the aide who unsteadily switched the lantern from hand to fatiguing hand. My own declamations were pitifully absurd as I spoke of ancient plagues and murders in measured tones. Fictions only in the face of such truth.

From cot to steaming cot we made our way, sometimes successfully, sometimes too late for even a chance at success. The vapors of sweating blood and perspiring fear mingling with the imagined shapes of souls set loose into what one could only pray to be a welcoming sky. At last we reached the end of the fifth row of makeshift beds.

Here our work seemed hardest still. Though some of these soldiers were old and seemingly full-worn before any of this had started, most were only boys, surely younger than I. Yet there was a certain ageless glance about all of them. Something around their eyes that made one think they had lived a long, long time. That same something made it easier to watch them when they faded once and for all.

But this last one was different. There was nothing of the others in his eyes. Only beauty. A deep, certain beauty—impossible to describe, but less easily denied. Bickley saw it, too. He explained it as a look that is often there to warn a surgeon from being too optimistic with his own work, confiding, "Those are the ones who always die."

But there was something else. How can I tell you? I do not know myself. I seemed to look deeply into this boy's still and glassy eyes, but could only see my own image. My reflection. Standing, helpless and somewhat full of horror, in the light of the one pale lamp, and with the plain effects of one simple needle.

"Am I all right?" Corporal Dunlap kept muttering, hardly aware of his own words, the silence upon which they fell or his clearly mortal wounds. The blood seeped from bandages over no fewer than four large gashes as he looked at and through us.

"Am I all right?" in cadent tones. "Am I all right? Am I—"

Although his last breath was contorted and sorely searched, at the moment of its letting go the lad's face became even more pure than his less-than-a-score of never-shaved years. And there I held him to have the purity and peace of a swaddled babe. A closed-eye cherub answering the final call, borne weightless by a sudden sprouting of the soul's wings, the breath of heavenly chorales full upon his parted lips. So must transfigure all men in death who die true. Not to return to the dust and ash, but to the first moment of gardened innocence, the mind's eye of creation.

I fancy even the oldest of them had half that look in the end. A second's recognition of the unseen and unheard, that which will be forever. The semblance of feathers in the air above and a sourceless wind to cross their brows and mouths and hearts one final time.

Harper's Ferry comes to mind, not just for Bickley, but the images of its residue, which read so easily on the tattered sleeve and torn and soiled face of Brown. The helpless sense of loss, the smoking heat of blaring arms. The futile screams of ignorant young men. The week-old stench of innocent corpses sent thither by an incomprehensible filial duty. Yet, all its mighty repugnance, its acrimonious sensations—the sights, smells and sounds that all the more greeted my hasty desire to have some share in what surely would become a historical event—could still not have prepared me for the fetid horrors of post-battle hospital tents. I marched into a score of them with similar, if more mature and responsible urgency. And limped out of each with something less than I had imagined taking in.

After a time, I knew my very soul had been so deeply stained with spurting limbs and fevered glares of the shocked and guiltless that I would never again feel an innocent, any less a murderer. One could not merely watch or wait without a sense of participation, complicity. It was as if I had fired every scathing mortar and carbine, plunged each bayonet.

If not I, then who?

Entr'acte
The Day

The bearded tyrant sat grim and still. I could not hear him breathe or snore, but I imagined he slept then, as ever. How fitting it would be to interrupt his sleep only long enough to send him to a lasting one. One where his actions, visions, fantasies, could be neither enforced nor expressed. Let him be as some memory only, or some chastened devotee whose vows of silence and prayer may inspire without influence. But let it be done.

The deed awaited me. The result was my arm's length away. All anticipated my action. The seconds and scene changes, the minutes and final exits, the ten o'clock curtain and the tolling of twelve.

The gaslights cast their first glories upon the gaily dressed ladies, the proud, blue-uniformed men, fresh from the celebration of their short-lived victory under a shorter-lived tyrant. All seemed joined in some hapless and misdirected dance of conquest to the strains of the orchestra warming its brass and strings, while I wondered in my heart at my own metal and pluck.

And I questioned the coincidence of my thought. Knew I had not planned to martyr him by spilling his blood on such a day, yet maybe by some subconscious reserve. Had he not proclaimed himself a king of kings? Had he not spun his fabled sermons with allegory and common device? And promised to feed the multitudes with loaves and fishes where only Pharaoh's empty coffers could be found and blood-stained rivers flowed?

With these considerations and reasonings, what could stop my perfect scheme? The horses waiting at every checkpoint. My escape ensured, my reception only slightly imaginable. His death will be less remembered than any incendiary dome. And my action that of Tell, or a much-debated and advised Sanhedrin.

And I knew the moment of my deed. The precise instant of the thing. Had I not rehearsed Taylor's scene a hundred times and played it full a dozen more? Had I not played here too, but one month before?

Mrs. Mountchessington exited in a flurry and a single player stood upon the stage. His cue well-met, his lines well-spoken, I crossed and played my business out. And it was done.

Act II

The Journey Home

Only one shot was fired in the entire affair—that which killed the assassin.

—New York Times, *Thursday, April 27, 1865*

As an officer was about placing the irons upon Harrold's wrists, Booth fired upon the party from the barn, which was returned by a sergeant of the sixteenth New York, the ball striking Booth in the neck, from the effects of which he died in about four hours.

Booth, before breathing his last, was asked if he had anything to say, when he replied, "Tell my mother I died for my country."

—The Star, *Washington, Thursday, April 27*

At first Booth denied that was his name, or that he had killed the president. Harrold, also, at first called him some other name.

—Evening Post, *Washington, Thursday, April 27*

He lived two hours after he was shot, whispering blasphemies against the government and sending a farewell message to his mother.

—Associated Press, *Washington, Thursday, April 27*

Booth had in his possession a diary, in which he had noted the events of each day since the assassination of Mr. Lincoln. This diary is in possession of the War Department. He also had a Spencer carbine, a seven-shooter, a revolver, a pocket pistol and a knife. The latter is supposed to be the one with which he stabbed Major Rathburne [sic]. His clothing was of dark blue, not confederate gray, as has been stated.

. . . Booth's leg was not broken by falling from his horse, but the bone was injured by the fall upon the stage at the theater.

—New York Times, *Thursday, April 27*

Booth and Harrold reached Garrett's some days ago, Booth walking on crutches. A party of four or five accompanied them, who spoke of Booth as a wounded Marylander on his way home, and that they wished to leave him there a short time, and would take him away by the 26th (yesterday). Booth limped somewhat, and walked on crutches about the place, complaining of his ankle. He and Harrold regularly took their meals at the house, and both kept up appearances well.

Booth and Harrold were dressed in confederate gray new uniforms. Harrold was, otherwise, not disguised much. Booth's moustache had been cut off, apparently with a scissors, and his beard allowed to grow, changing his appearance considerable. His hair had been cut somewhat shorter than he usually wore it.

—The Star, *Late Edition, Washington, Thursday, April 27*

The body of Booth has just been formally identified by prominent surgeons. From long exposure it has changed very much.

A surgical operation performed upon him several weeks ago rendered identification easy.

The left leg was broken, and appearances indicate that his injury was sustained when Booth jumped from the president's box to the stage at Ford's Theatre.

—Evening Post, *Thursday, April 27, 3:30 P.M.*

The statement heretofore published that Booth had injured one of his legs by the falling of his horse has proved correct.

—The Star, *Washington, Thursday, April 27*

The fourth edition of The Star *has the following additional details. . . . No clue could be obtained of the other two men.*

—New York Times, *Thursday, April 27*

New York Times, *Friday, April 28, 1865—Price Four Cents*

BOOTH KILLED
*Full Account of the Pursuit
and its Result*

***

*He is Traced into St. Mary's County,
Maryland*

***

*Harrold and Booth Discovered
In a Barn*

***

*Booth Declares He will not be Taken
Alive*

***

*The Barn Set on Fire to Force
Them Out*

***

*Sgt. Boston Corbett Fires at Booth
He is Shot through the Neck
and Dies in Three Hours
His Body and Harrold Brought to
Washington*

Scene I

Chasing,
*   Laughing,*
*   Hurrying by,*
It lights up the face and sparkles the eye;
And even the dogs, with a bark and a bound,
Snap at the crystals that eddy around.

New York had changed. Some of the changes were subtle, some not. There were new styles and new buildings and new newspapers with new stories, like Pulitzer's *World*, whose new offices were being constructed and would soar to twenty floors above ground, thereby replacing Greeley's *Tribune* in both circulation and height.

The men seemed taller too, the women larger, the children less young. The omnibuses louder and more frequent. And there were blacks—men and women—everywhere. Not merely at the lobby doors of the great hotels—of course, they were there too. And those hotels also were taller, bigger, more sophisticated, busier.

And the myriad lines of wire webwork for streetcars, telegraphs—and telephones, hanging like Spanish moss above the avenues, buzzing and snapping, playing at life. The annual flurry of post-paschal snow blessed the lively currents of air with an anointing crispness as I walked a long time around the area of Central Park and was pleasantly faced by the conclusion that I too had changed. No one gave me a second look. Nor did I need them to see me. I who had been one of the most recognizable of the city's visitors, even before my infamy and surely thereafter one of the most sought. I, who had now lived almost half my life in cautious secrecy and seclusion, I could very nearly have lived right in the heart of Manhattan itself, I thought. But I knew this was not so. It had no bearing whether the multitude could identify me. It had only to be a single person, of any station, of this sex or that, of my race or the other.

And I had the sense that it might not even be their recognition, but mine of them, as with so many things. It would not be their call, but the look in my own eyes that would prove my undoing. Like a child gleefully exposing the secret he wishes to keep forever, for the sheer joy, and with no thought of his own betrayal. How could I allow a moment with an old friend or acquaintance to go unheralded, if only with a look?

Where once I had taken cabs to go everywhere this day I walked to where I meant to be, being sure to maintain the limp I had affected, while occasionally changing sides as I turned corners, just to amuse myself. I made my way downtown to that fashionable area of Manhattan Island known as Greenwich Village, curious if my friend Samuel Knapp Chester still lived there. The house bequeathed him on Grove Street was a stately one with high-arched windows and a tall staircase leading up from the street to its large double-door entry, scarcely the expected scene of a board-balancer or bit-trouper.

And Chester was more than a passing acquaintance, more even than a familiar player, for we had been fellows since the 1858 season in Richmond. And was he not also there, so close to the end, the very night, mere weeks before, though truly it was some few months when the three famed Booth brothers played their first—and last—tribute to the legacy of a father and his dream perhaps to found a dynasty: *Julius Caesar* at the Winter Garden?

Many times Chester and I had used his house as a departure point for our excursions to the House of Lords on Houston Street—as we did that last, when I spoke too freely and invited him to take part in my cabal. And he found himself unable to commit to a friend the way he had always yielded without hesitation to a fellow player—brandy after brandy there, or a feast of oysters and beer at the Revere House down Broadway. This time, there would be no such outing. Instead of the hub of some great and colorful spinning wheel, Chester would be the small brass ring whose cold hard perimeter girt almost too tightly my movements.

But what was I thinking? Was not an anonymous hotel all the better? Was I safe at all, or, as much as I longed company, would any in my confidence be? And what was I thinking? I had trusted Chester once not to reveal my identity—and I was reasonably certain he had not—but how would I think to compromise him, or myself, again? Whatever might have been, the idea was soon dispelled as I approached a dilapidated ruin, long boarded-up and vacant. Oh, there were changes, if I might only see them.

**

Uptown, just across from the Gramercy Park, Edwin had recently opened his Player's Club on New Year's Eve, but one year before. Most of the members, as the name implies, were actors, but there were some notable exceptions such as the unionist general William Tecumseh Sherman and the satirist Samuel Clemens, neither of whom would I be pleased to meet under any circumstances, if my boldness drew me there.

And Henry Johnson was surprised as he opened the back parlor door to my gentle, but steady raps.

"Master—"

"Good evening, Henry. Will you not invite me in?"

I tried to be as genial as possible before telling him of his cousin's death and the loyal service he had given me up until the end. Johnson seemed only slightly disturbed by the news. His entire mien was singularly concentrated upon my return.

"By jingo! It was a long time comin', says I," he managed as he turned into the cookroom. "Something to eat, Master Johnnie? I was just fixin' up a hash for myself. Course, I suppose you'll want somethin' finer. Poor little Antaeus. By jingo, says I!"

He turned toward me reflexively and stopped with a smile as I replied.

"That sounds perfect to me."

***

Just off the chamber wherein I awaited my long-forgotten if self-estranged brother was a small balcony with hardly place to sit, but from where one could master a wonderful view of the fenced and private park and this corner of the city. The idea of it could not help but remind me of the same-sized ledge outside Edwin's room at Tudor Hall. The view there was, of course, not of wagons and carts and the endless bustlings of countless people throughout the day and night, but of our small woods and ivory lake with its several swans' graceful, feathered yawns the only noticeable activity of an afternoon.

It was Thursday and my brother's entrance well past midnight fairly startled me. I had fallen asleep in the chair next to the window. The cheval glass in the corner of the room yielded a second, truer image of his actions. From where I sat in the shadows I could sense his slight start as well. He stood still a moment, silhouetted by the hallway light, before closing the door and fastening the latch.

I watched silently as he relieved himself of a kind of scapula or pendant suspended from around his neck and laid it neatly in a bureau drawer before setting about to light the lamp. The object hanging from this choker glinted angularly for just an instant before finding repose in what sounded a fast-lidded box somewhere deep inside a top-most drawer. I was reminded for a moment of Corbett.

He felt in the pocket of his vest and casually struck a match to light the lamp on the low secretary, then shaking out the match with cool indifference, his back still to me. He was, if nothing else, always a quick study.

Without turning said, "Who is there?"

"Your brother, Wilkes."

He froze, before intoning evenly, "I have no brother, Wilkes."

"Is that how you justify it?"

"What?" he spun defensively.

If he had seemed indifferent before, even the consummate actor could no longer shield his surprise.

"My God—"

"Your brother, only," I quipped.

"If you mean my brother, John Wilkes, whom I accede you do resemble—if a great deal older and scarcely as hardy, he's dead. Else how could I have had his body exhumed full twenty years ago to have it laid rest in the family plot?"

"He lives!"

"Not for me. Not for any of those who once had hope for his success or admiration for the ability of the youngest member of America's greatest acting family. A single deed of bravado and indiscretion has ended it all forever."

"Yes, I heard you announced your retirement the day after the incident. But then you were never one for long-term commitments."

"What is that to mean?"

"As bold as my action may have seemed, it was planned. The northern president's box was primed for my entry and security. My flight from the stage assured. My crossing of the Navy Yard Bridge? I had the evening's password. My escape south was lined with friends and fresh horses."

"But then?"

"My allies in Washington were all arrested within twenty-four hours and my own route intercepted by some of the most inept detectives imaginable. One of them shot the man he supposed to be me—though, from all accounts, he had already surrendered."

"And?"

"Someone wanted me dead, despite all the efforts to usher me to sanctuary and even the North's insistence I be captured alive."

"You think I would do that?"

"Men will do many things for the love of a woman."

"If you believed what the society columns had to say about your Camilla and me—"

"Is she my Camilla again?"

"She is no one's. Nor will she be. She left Washington shortly after the event. I had escorted her on a couple of occasions to help bring her spirits up, but I could do nothing. She wept at the thought of you and what you had done."

"How fraternal of you. A familiar plot. Bury the brother, marry his queen."

"*Richard* is your play."

"I was thinking of *Hamlet*."

"You presume to play my seasoned part of the young prince?"

"I play at parts no more. Nor do I know who or how or why, but I intend to find out. Unless there is a reason you should not, I think you might help."

Dawn was sensed, even in the constant dark, and a milk truck was making her rounds in the Gramercy Court below, the steady hoofing of her faithful draft sounding every stop. A strange silence preceded the sound of a strumming instrument wafting down the halls.

"There comes poor Lester," whispered Edwin.

"Wallack?" I wondered. "I read he died some three years past."

"Not even two. But his automatic harp hangs from the door of the room that was to have been his and vibrates occasionally to the rhythms of the early morning."

He bowed his head meditatively and turned toward the fireplace as if to warm himself by a fire that wasn't there.

"You are not the only one who comes back to haunt me, dear John," he portended. "We never truly part with the dead. Our mother, our sister, our brother, even those we never truly had the chance to know. Sometimes Mollie visits me in the form of a lark on my windowsill. How else would a lark have gotten into the city?

"But until this evening I had never felt your presence so

strongly. I must have guessed it was your time to return. Oh, you have been ever with me, like the shadow that phantom follows—just out of reach, especially as I walk the course of the park after dawn or late at night on my way back from the theater."

"Brooding again, brother? You're too mature to still affect the Danish pretender to satisfaction. Your season of a hundred performances is long past. But mould your melancholy madness into rage and let us have a Lear, or a passionate Macbeth at the very least!"

"You question my right to be pensive? You had everything! Still, that was not enough. How I envied you. You had the home and childhood I never had. Papa was always dragging me about like some carnival attraction. His little puppet he liked to call me. How I hated that. So much that when it came my time to bail him out after some besotted evening, I actually enjoyed the sense of independence it gave me—ignoring the bitter hurt all the while as people sniggered and spoke in whispers about 'the drunken thespian.'

"And our mother scarcely recognized me each time we would return from St. Louis or Chicago. Or, if she did, it was only as some strange reminder of the man she thought she had married. I was the red-headed stepchild. I honestly don't remember her ever kissing me. But you! How she would dote on her *dear little Jack*."

His temper brought him sudden silence. Tears do not measure time as sands in the glass, or moons months, or rains the seasons and the years. When next I looked at Edwin, his gaze was far away, trapped it seemed within the persistent flames of his imagined fire. He looked that moment just like our father. It was a similarity I had not remembered. And suddenly I felt very much the image of our mother. It was her blood that coursed now through my body. Her fears and doubts, her faith and devotion. Yet my father's dark humors could manage to overpower all else, and everything my black eyes saw or would see was shaded by that.

Edwin spoke again.

"None of us believed that it was you they had shot and killed at Garrett's Farm. Not mother, not Asia, not June. Of course Sleepy must have prayed it was, and did his best to tell us all that it had been. But why else would they not let us near the body?

"And then, they told us of your dying words, 'Tell mother I love her.' How like you that was. And, 'Useless!' We never understood what that might have meant, but again, it was so like you—so dramatic!"

"But that's it! Don't you see? Someone knew exactly what needed to be done—and said to convince the world of my death. And what could I do about it? Deny it? Come forward only to then be killed for certain? But who, who!?"

"Who, you ask? Who was responsible for my forced retirement? My struggled return? The torching of the Winter Garden and my entire wardrobe? The attempt upon my life? Poor Vickie's insanity? My ruin? You can ask who?"

"Am I to blame for all of that?"

"For that and more. Here. I have something for you, John. A letter."

He reached into that same drawer where what seemed an eternity before he had placed the token of his late evening, and handed me the red-waxed envelope.

"But it is addressed to you, 'Mr. Edwin Booth and family.'"

"She knew better than to address it otherwise. And I knew better than to think it was mine. Open it."

I knew what it was, but could not truly guess what it meant. Only that I returned the purity of her love with recklessness and uncertainty. What was her dream, her prayer, but to be with me? And what was mine, but so much ether? What could I have truly hoped the outcome might have been? My urgers wagered that for all my cunning, I would not be able to see clearly from one end of the scheme to the other—and an eternal inability to ever again look anyone, including myself, in the face. They staked their entire plan upon that. And they won fitfully.

Do we ever understand ourselves? Can we know at any moment that we are making the right decision?

How much I longed to see her then I cannot say, but somewhere in my soul I knew that I must not, could not. Wilkes Booth was dead. It was time for him to let the living live. At least those blameless souls who had suffered more at his hands than he by the designs of the one whose death alone would cool my passion.

I left Edwin there without a word of parting and walked back to the Chelsea, then carelessly upstairs to my room without replacing my eye-patch or guarding once my glance, or thinking for an instant to avert my face from any passers-by. Still, I had met no one the entire way except that same milkman and his honoured steed. Even the denizens of the night, those local rowdies who call themselves Pug-Uglies were noticeably absent, and all the hotel was still in bed at the time of my return. It was as if I had truly entered a world in which I was nothing more than a shade. How appropriate, I laughed to myself, I should room across the way from the new Institution for the Deaf and Dumb.

The small bed lamp offered just enough light as I stuffed a favorite pipe with a brandied blend, then took the envelope from my waistcoat, broke its ancient seal and cried to read my name in that absent, but familiar script. It was dated January 1876.

Your son and daughter are now ten years old. Your daughter is so beautiful. She has your eyes, your lashes, your funny little ears.

How many times have I begun to write, search for perfect words, only to start again, yet never post a single message.

I write this to you, wherever you are, that if you can not read my thoughts from there, perhaps my placing words on paper will make it easier.

Surely you will have learned of our children. Twins, as you always desired. They are fine, strong, beautiful, and possessed of the same wild genius as their father.

But how was I to know, or how could I have ever truly guessed?

I had to rethink everything. The scene had changed. What had happened, and what was my imagination alone? Who had then urged that fatal shot? I had been busily engaged in answering this as if the solution was then at hand. My fingers held what I could not feel, what a callous mind could not believe too readily. I read on.

Perhaps, too, you have learned of your brother's and my relationship. It is not love. And it could never be a tenth part of what we were, you and I. But it had helped. Oh, he is to marry soon again, and 'though I was hurt at the first, I know it could not be any other way.

As for me, my family has disowned us all. My father sends money, but reminds that my family can never be his, so long as I am not married and he remains in elected office. I will not marry to win his approval, 'though I will respect his position. The children and I fare well and our needs are ever satisfied, but there is, of necessity, a great void in our lives. It is —

Perhaps we will move away west. I really do not know.

I thought to find it difficult to write at all, and now I find it difficult not to tell all. Better to stop now.

You have my love, you are my love.

Yours, ever,

Ella

Beneath these pages were those of another, older letter. It was dated April 15, 1865.

Oh, John,

How foolish you have been! To think that you must indeed give so much, and so dangerously — so recklessly. More the fool because you could not believe my vow.

You. You are important. None, nothing above.

I will find that man for me, if that is truly what you want. But how might I ever kiss him without seeing some part of you. Why should I?

Still, I will obediently try,

Your pet,

Ella

***

Time. Place.

"I entered through the library and passed your room on the way to the study. I saw the portrait over your bed."

"You saw nothing! Any intimation of romantic involvements will be flatly denied."

"But she is mine!"

"Was! What Miss Nash does with her life at present has nothing whatsoever to do with Mr. J. B. Wilkes, or J. Wilkes Booth, or any other man fitting the description of the assassin of our Union's leader. He was killed at Garrett's Farm."

"You knew! You knew I still lived."

"Suspected. Sensed. My God! We were brothers. Were!

"I loved you, and I have cursed myself a thousand times for seeing Camilla, whatever the event. She came to me for comfort, for strength. For love, from the one link she had with the man who owned her heart."

"And now she warms your bed! How will the columns read now about your betrothal?"

"On whose authority? A dead man's? Or that of a hunted killer?

"Oh, Johnnie, it wasn't that easy. It wasn't sudden or clumsy at all. It was slow, gradual. We both knew it was wrong, yet there was something—Oh! I can't tell you we did it for you, but strangely—"

"Enough!"

"With my poor Mary dead over two years—"

"Stop!"

What could I think? What could I expect or hope? Oh dear God, am I so damnable to be cursed like this?

"How did you get in? What are you doing here anyway?"

"I need your help. Henry let me in. Gave me a very fine supper, too."

"Must he always be your nigger?"

***

"I need to ask a favor of you—brother," I said, with special emphasis on the last word. "It is important. Very important."

"What will you ask of me now that might help in any way to right what has already gone wrong?"

"It is a simple task—"

"Ask, then!"

"St. John's. I need the roster."

"St. John's? Which St. John's? Why?"

"Number three. In Washington City. My reasons are my own, yet I need it. And you are the only person I could trust to bring it to me. Think not, if I could retrieve it on my own I would involve you at all. It is the roll from December of 1863 that interests me."

"During the war? Those records were destroyed."

"This is not Chancellorsville or Shiloh. There were no raiding parties into the capital."

"By the members themselves. No one knew how the conflict might affect the standing of the membership when it was over. It is the Order's habit to raze the structure in complete disrepair, rather than leave it standing and risk hazardous collapse. It was the same after our revolution. The names of many brothers—I presume there is a particular name you seek—are forever lost."

"Still, as a brother, you could access them if they were still to exist."

"Yes," he paused. "I travel to Washington Monday next.

89

Will that serve your purpose?"

"No. It has to be now."

"The trains have stopped running, Johnnie. It is nearly one in the morning. You expect me to leave now by horse?"

"The trains run again at sunrise. I have purchased your ticket," I said, handing him the return fare I had bought that afternoon.

"Were you so sure I would or could do this for you? Why should I?"

"Because, after all else, we are brothers."

"And then?"

"I will be here again tomorrow night. Waiting for you."

"And if I have an appointment in the morning, John?"

"I am sorry to interrupt it," I smiled simply. "How often can you serve the pleasures of the dead?"

***

I followed my brother at some distance as he left the station and just before we would have turned down Columbus, appeared to him from out of the shadows.

"This way," I beckoned, pointing across the park.

"I should say I am glad you did not risk my reputation again by going a second night in a row to the club," spoke Edwin in his usual, affected manner. "But I am afraid," he continued, "it was for your safety and not my own you have waylaid me."

"In any event, the result is the same."

"Perhaps," he nodded, deep in thought.

We continued on toward the rocky crests that border the lake in the center park.

"Most peculiar," said Edwin, as we arrived.

The split moonlight filtered hauntingly through the trees. A low fog clung to the black shrubbery with tangling fingers of ambush. Edwin handed me a folded document on which he had copied a list of names.

"Peculiar and most fortunate, brother. How would you

90

remember the name of his lodge after so many years?"

"Whose?" I answered almost protectively.

"Why, Surratt's. I suppose that is the name you wanted. And, it is there."

My eyes fumbled past my brother's fingers as he pointed out the name. It was not the one I expected to find.

Strophe

I

I've only myself to blame. Oh, I conceived it, sure enough. Was long-convinced of its method and course before ever being approached. But I compromised the very nature of my choice. I took their money. Denigrated my every action. Obligated my very soul.

It was arranged. Accomplices at every turn. The coordinated fusillade—a military term, not mine. The letters to the press—all mine. The calling card for the vice-president—yes, mine again. An elaborate imbroglio to simply affect—what?

Why then could they not let me live? Trust me to kill for them, but not to keep my word or faith? Their words are hollow, their oaths sworn upon faithless hearts. Poor Wilkes! Poor blessed Corbett who too would also do their bidding for an Iscarion wage.

II

Cara,

I wonder if you will recognize this poor script. Have you waited for it, wished it into your hands before this moment?

I am, of necessity, far away. My heart, however, is yours. I—

III

Today I decide no longer to try and tell my story with the aid of invention and imagination. What better romance is there than truth? Who would believe our love and my story otherwise, if at all?

Events are going too fast. I cannot keep up with them, or if they are meant to race, keep wishing there were something I could do to direct them. Something whole and sure, quick and healing. Instead I find myself, my thoughts, bullied about by these phantom occurrences, these causeless results, formless uniforms hung in the shadows of a backstage closet, playing their parts while I appear unrehearsed in the speechless nightmare, unaware of the role chosen for me. For I have read the names of thirty-two young actors whose final curtain has been wrung by a greater stage manager before which you or I have ever played. And I know now that here shall be the thirty-third.

IV

Today I am a hermit. Today I am so lonely that I would spill or speak to any Tom or Jack or Richard. I would tell them, any or all, that I am not Jack Harvey. That there is no—no, nor never has been any—John Lee Harvey. I would tell them that and any else they would care or be so kind to heed, for I weary. Weary of creating a past for an uncertain present and a less certain future. Weary of the lies.

Oh, I have known the opportunity and advantage of a lie, the well-placed fiction and reception of a lie. Have even enjoyed the occasional thrill of a lie complete. But even the schoolboy tires of the game. And so do I.

Still, I am a beggar. My hair short but uneven, my face bare but stubbled, as it were streaked with grime from an actor's trunk, my one eye patched, my clothes ungainly in their fit and style and condition.

I am not the dandy they would expect to see, paid to see, think long dead. Or do they?

***

I had long promised my mother I would not fight, nor join the ranks of either army, a promise not so very difficult for me to make, as I did dearly love my home, my South. She knew which side it would have been for me and might have feared the extended division such alignment would have caused within our family, as much as she feared the omen that had been forever in her mind, but you will hear of that.

Because I wore no uniform it did not mean I could not serve. It was that my service could be different from those others who flew the banner of our South on their caps as well as in their hearts. My profession alone had disposed me to hide that heart from my fellow man, even if I never could from the eyes of a woman. But I was not a soldier. My expulsion from West Point had made that clear. My jail room parlay with John Brown too. Still, I thought, there is work that can be done.

In April and May of 1862, I had been playing in St. Louis at Ben DeBar's Theater. Part of the schedule was that I should star with the noted T. L. Conner in a revival of our roles as Phidias and Raphael in Selby's *The Marble Heart; or The Sculptor's Dream*. I had played the two parts—a feat not so easily managed—since my engagement at the beginning of the previous year at the Metropolitan Theater in Rochester, New York, and several times since. It was as Raphael I would first play for the Union president—at John T. Ford's in November 1863. The whole of the first act spent staring at him with every opportunity, and found the perfect line in the second act to wag an accusing finger at him, as to assure we would play together again.

I welcomed not only a chance to develop the single role, but to work with Conner, a stout fellow with an appetite and excuse for just about everything. After our final curtain Saturday night—and we took several—we two went out for a whisky and beer by way of celebrating our successful run.

DeBar's had been for some time known in Union circles as a hotbed of rebels, and I discovered Conner far and away the most vocal of its constituents. As we were sharing stories in the local saloon, a large, drunk, self-styled mountain man pushed me aside. I am afraid I paled somewhat that I felt no choice but to yield. The insensible's swamper, a rather short but stocky man possessed of a frankly pleasant face, looked to both Conner and me with an invincible smile as he stepped up to the rail.

It never fails as great beauty will always ally itself with plainness in women, so do large men seem to pair with small. So it was with Payne and Atzerodt. So is it always. The exact reason for these symbiotic partnerships I shall leave to you in every case but this. At Lawrence's Bar it seemed self-evident. One craved protection, the other demanded guidance.

"You've taken my friend's place," insisted Conner with a hand to the shoulder of the interloper and a forced laugh calculated to expose prominent canines.

"I'll give it back when the keeper's drawn beers for me and my mate," he replied with a glanceless motion over his shoulder to certify he was not alone.

The overlarge accomplice seemed neither appeased nor amused by Conner's explanation. While looming and large, aside from having clearly unfurled the majority of his sheets much earlier in that evening's junket—or pub crawl as it was termed by hardies—he sported above one of his ethyl-eclipsed eyes a scar to parallel my own. Though no stage-duel, I was fairly certain, had been the cause. And on the back of his close-cropped scalp an acquired cowlick testified to a gash by which the direction of his entire face seemed to be determined. Here was a man not only fit for brawling, but also habituated to being blind-sided as an only means of being subdued.

If this Philistine was not enough we soon had another obstacle, when suddenly we were recognized by one of the play-going locals, who reminded everyone of the company's reputation. Swore on the bible he had personally heard the two of us wish the whole damned government go to hell. The saloon was momentarily churchlike in its quiet.

"And, sir, if tha' is true?" returned Conner. "Is't wrong for a man t'express his love and devotion for the land of his birth?"

"It is, sir," mocked our sermonizing detractor, "when those sentiments run afoul of everything that is decent and pure."

"Well said!" grinned Conner as he turned toward me. "Then, I accept your apology," he added before taking a deeply indifferent draught of his beer.

To say that I was laughing would not do justice to Conner's style and wit. In fact, he had borne himself with such mock-heroic charity that everyone in the house roared—even those whose feelings were only an instant before quite obviously contrary to ours.

This, of course, had the predictable effect on Goliath and his mate. Being the smaller of the two men he opposed, I was the first at whom he swung his fist. But any frequenter of saloons will tell you there are only three men with whom one must not choose to brawl: the man who, though your apparent physical inferior, yet takes issue—he knows something you do not; the man whose features are a repetition of disfigurements resulting from years of the like—he has no more to lose, though constantly seems to try; and the man whose speech and manners are both coarse and combative yet, well into his twenties, has smooth, unsullied features—neither fang nor claw has ever found its mark. This last alone can boast the courage to face an imminent mêlée, while sporting the apparent certainty his nose has never been broken. I was two of these men, and only if my opponent had been all three—which he was not—should he have felt a distinct enough advantage to engage me. Yet engage me he did.

When the local police arrived, our unionist had long been removed to a corner of the hall where his swollen face was sleeping off the indignations his drunken patriotism had suffered. Conner was entertaining an appreciative gallery with wide gestures of laugh-producing story-telling. The only witnesses to the fracas were the few broken stools and one crippled card table.

No one expected that a simple owning up to events should still result in our arrest, except that our snoring instigator was nephew to the long-embittered and equally anti-secessionist mayor. I, therefore, joined my companion in yet another sentiment against the impositions of the North for the sake of a nominative Union, and with a great flourish we were led away to a disappointed, if ultimately unsympathetic, mixture of laughter and applause.

***

Conner and I were not only charged with disturbing the peace but opposing the national government, and thrown into jail early Sunday morning. Jails of themselves were not altogether new to me, but being on the inside was. They placed us in adjacent cells within a compact maze of tiny passages at the rear of the police station, and Conner continued to amuse a new audience with tales of Southern humor and sensibilities that made us seem the forwarders of some benevolent new order for the advancement of humanity rather than the ignoble faction of separatists we had become. Ordinarily I would have joined in his verbal forays, but something inside me sanctioned I should not. Besides, I was tired—not the less for my drinking and battling. When I closed my eyes for the night it was Conner's ceaseless and ringing protests singing me smilingly to sleep.

Seven has ever been thought a lucky number. But seven by seven by seven is no luck at all, I assure you. Until this time, I would not even have recollected the spirit of poor John Brown from that combination. But ever after how could I not? For though my stay was not long—less than a weekend—I felt in those two cold and painful nights what it must be like for every man incarcerated—true or false—begging for sleep to come in the middle of the day, that time should pass more quickly. Or being wakened throughout the night by the swearing curses of some drunken heretic as he tries to make peace with the God he no longer sees to fear.

When I was released late Tuesday, my intuitions proved to have been valuable. Conner had been sent off post-haste to the nearby penitentiary as a token act of Union will and sentiment by the politically and nepotistically motivated magistrate. The otherwise silent and efficiently duteous guard who escorted me from my cell made two offhanded but telling comments. One was pointed at Conner's belligerence as a product of his Catholic popery, the other was to cursorily admire my father's signet ring, as members of the fraternity occasionally did.

Not just a little appalled at the report of Conner's incarceration, I went to DeBar and the rest of the company to organize a formal plea to affect his release. I even took credit for his remark that the whole damn Yankee government go to hell in order that his offense seem less particular. If the Union could not stand to the expression of opinion favoring any viewpoint, then perhaps it was best there was no Union at all, I posited. Some situations require the jarring of confrontational logic.

But actors and troopers are a different kind of people, and though they can declaim and rave and deliver enthusiasm on the stage, they are most of them less than effective when off. Everyone agreed that Conner had been the victim of an injustice, yet none was willing to risk the possibility of the same for his release. With whispered reminders of DeBar's hotbed, what guarantee was there the rest would not be similarly considered and the theater closed for good?

Ultimately I was no better than the rest. Conner's part recast and the engagement done, I boarded the South Western Limited for Albany to connect for Boston where I was to open at the Museum as Richard in *Richard III* the following Monday.

I was sitting in my private cabin, a luxury I had only of late been able to afford, nor was yet altogether certain I enjoyed, when a strange knock came at my door. Before I could make reply a finely dressed gentleman entered. He had gray and raven hair under a flat-brimmed and belted hat, and a conspicuously diamond-studded vest hung with two gold chains. Scarcely seeming to notice I was there, he sat without reserve or apology. He carried a silver-tipped cane, but no luggage, and waxed his whiskers in the style of a groomed frontiersman—that is, gambler.

His hands seemed dexterous enough to stack more than a deck or two of cards as he produced two cigars from his vest. With a gold-encrusted device built expressly for the purpose, he bored holes in the one end and clipped the other of each. Lighting them both with certain meditative ceremony, he offered one to me, kept one for himself, unfurled and arranged the newspaper he had brought in with him, and began to read.

While he held the paper with one hand, he spindled five-dollar notes around the index finger of the other with only his thumb. He was forever to be doing this, though it was some time before I understood the secret of his habit. At this point I only saw him depositing them into his coat pockets. Their future application as timely, quick and effective bribes was yet unknown to me. How adroitly could he slip them into the palm of some young and impressionable officer with only a handshake. And never a question—no—not in those times. They were, after all, never Confederate notes. Only the currency of the North could speak so persuasively and uniformly.

"Would you mind to open the window a bit wider," he puffed casually and without removing his eyes from the paper. "Not just for the smoke. I would like to hear what goes on outside if we should make a sudden stop."

"Why should we?" understanding as I spoke the words that I was meant to ask this question.

"Why indeed?" he returned, before I had scarcely finished asking, and with a sudden sweep let his paper drop. "We are at war, you know. And the rebels can be everywhere. Or don't you believe that?" he demanded pointedly.

Just then the brakes blew their steam past our car and I must say I was rather fearful. It was a comfort to see my companion even more so.

"We met two weeks ago at the beginning of your engagement in St. Louis," he said, rising to the window. "My name is Lutz. If anyone should ask, we spoke briefly one night after one of your performances and met by accident again just as the train left the Strand Street Station. Any questions?"

I sat still and silent and the two of us remained so when the armed patrol came mechanically into my—now our—compartment and asked to see our transit papers. The fair-skinned intruder produced his with a certain amount of expertise and practiced nonchalance, which satisfied readily. Yet when it came to mine there was much ado.

"'Mr. J. Wilkes Booth,'" read the sergeant. "The actor?"

I nodded.

"Look ye," he said to his sully-eyed corporal. "And signed by the general hisself. 'General U. S. Grant,'" he read with a theatricality of his own. "And what does a man of your education think, Mr. Wilkes?" handing my papers back. "Do you think it be true that those there initials stand for these United States, as some says?"

I smiled non-committedly as I refolded my papers into my pocket.

"Not these days, 'course," joked the sergeant, quite pleased with his own humor.

The corporal shared his laugh, whether out of sentiment or device, and the two of them left us with a cursory tip of their hats.

We sat there for some time before the engines started up again and I could see my visitor sigh a breath of relief. His look at me intensified. His eyes seemed fixed on their purpose.

"I have a proposition, Mr. Booth," he began, directing

himself in such a way that, if I had any doubts, I knew then it was no accident he had stumbled upon my car. "News of your temporary confinement in St. Louis has traveled far and not without purpose. You may also be interested to know that your friend, Mr. Conner, is this moment being released. And who do you think paid the fine that liberated you?"

He shifted in his seat, crossed his one leg high over the other and replaced in the boot of it a derringer I had not seen him withdraw.

"That is not all. I tell you this only so you will know I am sympathetic to the same things as yourself," he said, pinching straight again the creases in his pantlegs. The same cause, as a son of the South, Mr. Wilkes." He took me by my ringed hand. "A son of the South."

The train had come back to its full speed and was rumbling easily on the singing tracks. The endless beauty of the Illinois landscape floating past us with a repetition that never wearied—unlike, say, Indian Territory or Arkansas—but seemed now strangely uncanny, the rolling hills with their fingered rivulets anxiously pulsing where once they were poised and serene.

"Did you see the way they handled your papers? Quite differently than mine. If you had first shown them yours, they may well have forgotten to look to mine at all."

"You need a traveling companion?" I suggested. "To allay some kind of suspicions?"

He did not look like a criminal, but he did not look much like a businessman either. I could not imagine what was making him so cautious and nervous, but that he needed some kind of cloak or screen.

"Not for myself, Mr. Wilkes."

"For whom?"

"It is not who. It is what. For now, enjoy my cigar. It is the finest quality. Perhaps you would join me also in a spoon?"

Scene II

The town is alive, and its heart in a glow,
To welcome the coming of beautiful snow.

The night before I was to leave I went to say farewell. It being
a Sunday evening, Bickley had only worked until some time
after ten o'clock, but the orderly in charge of the hospital tent
instructed me that the doctor expected me to go see him. I
found him in his own quarters amusing himself at his desk
where he continued to view glasses in a magic lantern as we
talked. He had only some five or six, but exchanged them
throughout our brief interview as if each were being seen for
the first time. His smile flashed and his eyebrows raised on
occasion, but throughout our conversation his voice remained
steady. He did not offer to share his pleasure with me, only
extended his hand when at last I said goodbye.

Dearest Ella,
*   I wanted so desperately to be loved by you —*

Strophe

I

You know my reputation. Even before my present notoriety I
was, I fear, somewhat the scoundrel. Scandal knew my name.
Enough that I was my father's son—though for that Edwin
was forgiven. I could drink and curse and make love never,
but that my several sins were counted and compounded to
that original curse from which the other had been relieved.

    Leave Hemeya for Edwin, for he is that righteous sort, even
in his waverings, his fears to face himself and difficulties
accepting fate, cursed though it may be. I was created in my
father's image, and while an audience will ever shy from
Pescara, Iago, and Richard Crookback, still they know
somehow that these are, far above, the men to be essentially

101

trusted. Not in their dealings with others but with themselves. Men of purpose—evil or dishonest, of direction—hell-bent, but undaunted. And if the deeds were examined of all, it would be my brother's imitations that would first demand restitution. He meant to do or say the thing, but that was then. Yet is the public far more willing to forgive the flowery worded and apologetic hypocrite. What sympathy for a drunken libertine, and less his murderous son?

And I would kill again to raise the cup of any tyrant's blood, full-capable of wafting every draught from the deepest tankard.

Curiously, I never heard the story of how I drank, only how I was drunken. The particulars of my misbehavior merely that it was thus. Nor the single name of my lovers, but that the list was ever-extending. One hears not why, nor how, yet what I did, and just as crudely of my death.

I rarely drank in company that had not at least a great share in the cause. Never swore an oath that was not in response to one more fiercely put by another. Never made love to a woman who might not afterward be capable of denying all with less than protest or refutation from me. For in this case my father's indiscretions had taught me better on my own affairs. And while you have ever read that I cried *sic semper tyrannis* before or after the pistol shots—in serious drama the line always precedes the action, tripped on this or that and broke one leg or the other—I shall not there begin to indulge your time or patience. But that someone, I know not certainly who or why, should have been, consciously or no, readily substituted for my own person, I would pray make mention. Of him I can only be sure that he too was suffering from a torn or swollen limb. Or how can I express the full extent of my horror that he should have been gunned down so helplessly when his very action saved my life, allowing for my nominal escape and salvation.

Yet, I am as sure that his deceptive death was correctly assessed by at least one. He who hired me—and to do that to which I had fully resolved, informed me of the opportune time and place, assisted me in numerous preparations of the president's box, suggested my escape route, supplied me with my horse, money and rude provisions. Provided me also with the evening's password to run the capital blockade.

You would not recognize me today, if ever you might have. And not, but for my wizening, the miles of years that walk upon my brow. For I have grown my beard and shaved it—my moustache, too—a hundred times regardless of the season, deferent only to the times of men whose course across my path would they rather inscribe and I could not avoid.

Nor I am as coldblooded as you would believe. You, I say, because I know that is your wish to believe me ruthless and mad, an aberration. How fearful if otherwise, that my same blood might flow in your veins. Yet there is no shame in the possession of a patriot's heart.

Tonight I watched an owl make sure and easy prey of an errant pigeon, straying too far from the square. I wondered for a moment if my father would have approved—he who once called the undertaker to his New Orleans hotel room in order that six dead pigeons might be given a Christian burial. They thought him mad or hoped it was some attempt at giddy humor. But Junius Brutus Booth gave no specific indications of either.

Was it sickness that drove the female owl to feast unusually upon a member of her own species? Or did she have the concerns of a nesting brood at heart? Concerns made more pressing by the steady encroachment of progress and man's city-building follies? Was life not sweeter on the open farm and plantation than industry could ever hope to replace? Who are those who will use their strengths, talents and unfailing courage to do combat with even overpowering odds if they must be labeled mad? Then perhaps they are.

You do not know me, yet know me you will. Not today, nor in these woods where I am safe. Yesterday, when I was known for some twenty-seven years by name and face and

103

fame. And for tomorrow, when the truth of what I have done and do is measured, marked and balanced, doubted or believed.

Let us call them this or that, or what we will, it matters not. You shall know them by their actions as you know me by my deed. For what had I known of them, their schemes and counter-schemes? Less—if it can be believed—than they of passion, honor, love of country. What moved me was not some proffered promise provoking further than my own heart's desire. It was belief in what would be best. And if my Southern sympathies can today be seen as cruel and outmoded, if all mankind can sing, this day, that—black or white—men shall be free and equal, let this be my error, not that I delivered a tyrant to his timely end.

II

How might I have thought of them? Savages. It is so simple. I feel disgust that others could feel any different or less.

I would not loose my Cola, for all my love and respect of her, in my mother's garden and expect other than trampled roses and violets. She is a horse. Obedient to command, and strong of character, but a horse.

My horse, pleasantly accepting my choices, my orders, performing my will. And yet, spurred to a gait, whipped to a gallop, asks no explanations, expects no apologies or false sympathies. Why did those Copperheads need offer both?

III

What must be done? Not for the deed, for its completion. My heart, my soul, are ready to heave my hands well into this. There is no doubt of his merit. The lives he imperilled, the webs he spun to achieve his own end. And I, no scheming spider, only some mindless drone, obeyed and performed all before the very meshwork was drawn tight around my neck and those of my fellows.

There was no reward. There could be no redemption. No

reception for heroic deeds. What heroism is there in removing one tyrant to unleash another?

IV

Twenty-five years have passed. Every stroke, silent as ever to the Fabian multitude, has peeled ten thousand times within my shattered soul. And each of those armored, brutish beats pulsed its throbbing minutes like furious knells over this my living, if cobwebbed crypt, for the trifling of a life. One thread mercilessly snipped, the other recklessly, dizzily, dustily unwound.

What could have been is never known. And yet I cannot help but harp as if I might, through some clear vision and focused ideation, change all—rectify and restore my name. Or in more lucid moments, while I contemplate my fate, the result I alone have merited, still think to yield again to eternal perdition and kill once more.

This night I greeted with a pint of brandy where perhaps one swallow still remains. And so I cannot choose to hide from this my testament or any less, my imagined readers.

My desire to be a hero, fruitless and infatuate, is forgotten. If I worked and schemed and risked to avenge my South, or feel one-tenth part the accomplishment of my aim, how might I not the more forsake to plot and satisfy the vengeance of my honor?

I have been a fool before. Here is nothing new. Only how can I explain the sincerity of a fool's fancy? That at any moment, she might appear at my door. A smile on her pilgrim's face and forgiveness folded into the fingers that clasp lightly just below the buttons of her perfect waist.

V

I am her slave. And who will set me free, that now I have sinned the great sin?

Scene III

How the wild crowd go swaying along,
Hailing each other with humor and song!

It was a faultless day in mid-October. I tucked a loose strand of peppered hair over my left ear and squinted through the spectacles to which I had long grown accustomed. It was good to be old. My chest was tight but did not ache as it had even in my youth.

An Indian summer had bronzed the edges of so many red and yellow leaves and given hope to a young generation of new others. I had sported my moustache again, no longer fearful of its association or even my possible recognition. Somehow, everything seemed wonderfully changed in the course of a single night.

As I rode boldly into Hodgenville, it seemed all manner of transformations had occurred. People about their business returned my looks only to continue on their private ways. That one might nod, this one might salute a hat, that lovely other cast a coy and knowing glance somewhere between herself and me, perhaps at her laced boots, perhaps at my smooth ones.

I was no longer the renegade and fearful assassin. People's minds had changed. Seen through to the truth here, where the national frontier of Hardin County allowed more time and distance to survey that truth. What had been awful, even desperate, was become legitimate and comprehensible. Not that there had been a choice but that, in choosing, I had done more than many blind or wilfully disinterested others.

I hitched Cola outside Murphy's provisions and nearly had a conversation with Mrs. Purtella. That is, she said "Good day," and when I returned the compliment she went on by saying she hoped I was enjoying all of its benefits. Spoken by such a God-fearing woman, I understood her intentions to be of the highest character and felt I might have continued at some length had I not been pressed for time.

As I entered the emporium I suddenly could not remember what it was I needed or why, indeed, I felt so pressed. Murphy was behind the right side counter making some kind of inventory and addressed me by name without looking up from his tablet. I returned his hello upon which he demanded, "The usual?" Before I could think to answer, he completed, "It's wrapped up there under the front counter."

Instinctively I reached beneath what seemed a large stack of yet more balance sheets and withdrew a small, but weighty parcel.

Tucking it under my left arm I marked off a notation next to my name upon a small sheet of paper tucked next to the door and turned to say goodbye. Murphy was now some few steps up a ladder with his back toward me. I could see him smile without turning as I left him in silence.

Outside the shadows seemed almost to have lengthened even as midday approached. Cola was at the other end of the street, her post having inadvertently become the focus of a group of playing schoolchildren.

"Mr. Booth!" called one of my young students, grooming the horse with the edge of a pickaxe, while another conducted an imaginary symphony. "How are we to think of your lectures on liberal spontaneity when everywhere the theaters fill with those who crave only Zola's studied indifference and Belasco's mechanical perfections? Even your brother's style is today branded somewhat libertine!"

"Then leave!" I commanded. "I am master of this school, not of your life. There is nothing wrong with the approaches of which you speak. My father greatly admired Mr. Keene, though their audiences thought them bitter rivals.

"I am a Booth. And here you will rather learn to think with your heart and act with your soul."

"John!" came the voice from behind me.

***

107

And I awoke. An April drizzle was tracing wet forests on my window and the sound of a swelling river rushed up from the glen below. Hand was sitting aside me, just staring, as he often would.

"What were you going to do last night?"

I looked at him for a moment. It seemed fairly obvious. He looked back, knowingly.

"But where did you find eet?" he continued. "I z'ought eet was h'all gone—finished."

"It was cognac."

"*Mon dieu!*" he gasped, nodding. "Ah, yes? I suppose z'at would 'ave worked."

"Ah, yes?" I mimicked in agreement. "I tried. I really had tried. But I was sure you would never return. That I would stay here forever. And for what?"

"But I did return. And now, per'aps, you 'ave a reason. H'even I would not 'ave suspected z'is." His look of serious concern turned to a simple pout. "And yet, maybe."

***

That day, our father looked to us with studied grace from across the table of the palace car as we three trained to New York City for the first night of his new season. One hand tucked inside his gold-embroidered vest, the other poised about a too-thick cigar. The signet ring on the little finger of the one barely exposed, shining its trillium diamond ever bright, the thumb and forefingers of the other perfectly balancing their West Indian quarry between occasional puffs.

That was the last time he took me along, choosing my brother Edwin Thomas as better company and more fitful successor, perhaps, to his career. Certainly more proximate, with his fourteen years to my nine. Proud, confused, ever-haunted Edwin, the heir apparent. But that day father's pronouncement was to us both, that we should together follow him upon the course of his profession. "Trod the boards and find acclaim!"

This same injunction he had made only months before to our older brother, his namesake Junius Brutus Jr. But puzzle-faced June could never wholly see our father's drunkenness as a viable career, and acted as he might between his other vocations.

I still see the scene. The sweeping views of fields and towns brushing unrecorded past the car. My father's anxious enthusiasm. Feel yet the locomotive's steaming breath. Hear the rhythmed pistons and grating gears of the coal-fed engine, the tireless gait of steel-wrought wheels. Know its might and force and course.

And I am ever haunted by the resemblance of my father's black appetite and tireless propulsion toward an unknown station along miles of ever-widening, ever-disappearing tracks. Secreted, silent and anonymous, I should be thankful of my life. The simple, carefree woods, the steady, mindful brook, the pulsing heavens and guileless toads—they hold no comfort.

My father too was ever desperate. Of success when he was young and hungry, of fame when he was still unknown, of adventure at all times, of progeny when his instincts called, of freedom when his family and work consumed him. Twice only had I seen him satisfied, yet never with himself. Only with some vanquished bottle whose constant protests he had quieted. The device's final sobriety having insisted the deafening vengeance of a would-be conqueror. Alexander's empire was no less regretted.

The Sunday when the news of my father's death reached us from Cincinnati, Asia and I had spent the morning quarreling. Mother had expelled us from the house despite inclement weather suggesting, "A fresh rinse might cool our spirits and souls."

So when she called to us regretfully an hour later, we did not expect the reason for her melancholy humor. Neither my sister nor I had seen the messenger, nor guessed the letter

109

from the previous week proclaiming our father's victory over the New Orleans audience was to have been his last. The riverboat steamed all the way to Ohio, but Junius Brutus Booth had made the passage only as far as Missouri. Asia and I listened with the calm and acceptance only innocent youth can truly muster.

"It is your father," sputtered Mother, eyes swollen.

My mother's face, elegant, almost too simple. Watchful, unaware. Familiar stranger. Complete contradiction. Who she was, who she seemed to be. She was my mother, my suck, my eternal warmth.

And she was as cold to me as she was to my father and herself—with herself it was protection. My father and his erratic passions accounted for at least the better part of the need for that. But with me I would never understand. I was at once her favorite and, as a result, the least approachable.

I, who should have received her tenderest counsels and confidences, received only conditional comfort. I was held, occasionally kissed, and felt nothing. I was told I was loved and only longed for proof—more than words.

That next day was Black Monday, the day the school term began anew. There was already a certain understood anxiety about this day, and in my mind it would ever then be increased. Holidays had been so welcome, so full and yet over-short, one could scarcely believe classes had recommenced. There were ever those, of course, who seemed to have benefited only from their time off by further burying their noses and souls into hopes of pleasing their masters. A kind of sincerity one must ever study to produce. How do I think of my brother Edwin with my most insipid recollections?

This year, whatever soothing had occurred during the term break was forgotten in a moment as Asia and I left our mother to cry alone on the emerald green divan in the parlor. Recognition of the next day's responsibilities furthered our commitment to acceptance, but we were nonetheless loath to part, and our affections for each other increased according to the proverb.

Monday morning, after Asia had already left, I lay half-waking in my room as Mother opened the door and wondered was it not time I was about. She scolded me with the same look that proffered a mug of strong coffee and in that instant I felt I had never loved her more.

***

How was I ever to think that I, the son of such a man, might be different? Or, if God's graces had fallen upon my family, assuredly on the forms of my brothers Edwin and June, that there would still be more of it at large. Enough to carry me into some light or favor.

What I am I have inherited largely from my father. I could no sooner be a surgeon than he could be a solicitor. Still, had I studied medicine as my younger brother, I could have known how the missile had penetrated this or that tissue, had entered the cerebellum, having left some occipital or other skullish plate shattered clean. Oh, would that I had never dreamed my father's mad obsession, but left it to June and Ted alone while I joined young Joe.

And, as if my waiting knowledge could stay the life that, though still I hate, has long since ceased its madder movements. Or reverse that wound that a thousand dreams have seen these same hands inflict to satisfy the gracious multitude of promise. A greater ovation would I have received to tender my time on curing a cold.

Yet I will not content myself to be seducer nor wastrel. If the neighbors should nominate me Farmer Booth, the Lunatic, the inherent eccentricity of that remark—as it places me far outside their humdrum world—should please me thoroughly.

If I have inherited my father's madness, I can own it without assuming the adultery of an entire family. His first wife Adelaide, whom for the sake of my inconveniently pregnant mother he unabashedly left penniless and broken, or

111

June's slighted Clementine, and Edwin's neglected Mary, still dying in the belief she was the only one. Why would I go on?

The theme was so the same. If I had not seized that life for whom you otherwise might grieve more, admitted Atropos—she who cannot be turned, to his porch and cleaved the scriptured spool to still the clamor of so many cutthroat hearts—if I had lived out my life in careless comfort and relative renown, would I not have rued the mediocre coward I should have been? Remembered for the career that dared not soar, the flightless child of legacies lost, the man who would not act upon his one invention, forever confounded by his other?

Strophe

I

This was not murder. It was justice, vengeance, retribution. Sacrifice. Glory for the South. If not an exchange, the purchase of one unworthy life as payment for the loss of so many brave and loyal others.

This was not murder. How could it be? This man's appearance, his pedigree, his coarse, low humor and home-spun anecdotes, his vulgar similes and careless frivolity were a disgrace to the seat he held.

It was not murder. It was deliverance.

It was as if someone or something—some universal power—desired my simultaneous success and failure. Some law of God or nature or both, cried for the supreme justice that could only end with his death and my ignominy. Compelled me, the flawed and cursed champion, to perform its will—despite the cost. Was as unable to reconcile my valiant act as to suppress its own egoed enterprise. Better I should fall than it fail. Who, what, might I imagine, could possibly own to such power, responsibility, contradiction?

It was ritual; and the sacrifice was mine to make. Was it

not, after all, my own soul that gave of life and meaning?

Still, once a man has murdered, once he has taken the life of another—particularly an innocent—what would he not sacrifice or risk to satisfy and avenge the loss of that life on its truest thief. While the villain lives, I will not rest.

Our country was at war. And war, as ever, her separate heroes had made. Strangely, they had changed from those who had pursued and hanged the villainous Brown to those who two years later hailed his martyred act. For my own part I was later content to feel that I had done some good by supplying my brethren of a poor beleaguered South with what comforts smuggled quinine and morphine could provide. But there was a time I thought to share in what I imagined as the inevitable and was where you will know it all began. For war, like love, springs forth from design, even to the smallest action that is as a wrinkle upon the brow of God, or the furrow of his deepest thought. It is no chance that I too am who I am, have done that which I have done, and know you are no less a part of what was meant to be.

***

I know if I were somehow to look into their eyes I would recognize them at once. If on some city street or public garden or town square we should happen upon each other, they would recognize me too. Recognize the depth or peril, confusion or insanity or misdirection that inhabits all our eyes.

There are those things that time and life and even generations cannot change or disguise. Blood is one of those things, perhaps the most powerful. The blood that swims inside the body, and the blood whose scent spurs the mind to imagine, create, accomplish.

We toss from Springfield into Chicago, that loveliest of three-rivered and be-smoke-stacked vessels, thence to the lagan that is Harrisburg, and lastly to the improbably afloat Philadelphia. Everywhere the results of a twenty-five-year-

113

past conflict are submerged in the waved progresses of a reconstructive sea. Quiet, implicit, echoing, unknown, but felt, unseen, but heard, unfathomed and treacherous for their shoals. But this is North. Here the tides of fortune return with currents of kindness, though their shores are no less littered with wreckage and debris.

Still, the train ride from Springfield to New York is not without its comforts. Even for those who must travel in what is courteously referred to as third class, or freight. Gone are the days of my extravagance and pretense. Hail these times of truth and simple vision.

Fortunately, the railway is no worse for the passing winter, for the alternate route by river is still closed with the ices of a lingering season. And though much of the country is yet cold and stony, one can manage a pleasant journey—providing one enjoys the study of the human character, for its representatives are legion and varied on such an excursion.

I particularly enjoy the spinster twins who embark at Pittsburgh, each the image of the other, from hat to clutch to dress and shoes. Their over-pleasant faces given to the porter mask the looks they share between themselves during the course of their overnight travel.

In the early hours of our collective morning, I switch my eye-patch from the right eye to the left, knowing, though they never so much as hint a look in my direction the previous evening, they would not fail to notice something remarkably different about me. I pretend ignorance to their resultant yammering, as they do not cease to exchange looks at me, and words between themselves. I chuckle to wonder how precise those words might be.

And when I learn their conversation is indeed occupied by a particular subject this morning, the little boy who sidles with his mother on a bench in front of me and last night kept the entire car awake with his snoring has been wholly vindicated by the spinsters' conclusion—and conviction—that I, not angelic he, am the culprit. Once more I find myself a convenient victim of a somewhat inconvenient circumstance.

Still, what do I care of this blame, so long as his mother knows the truth? And so she does. It is she, in point of fact, who conveys to me the elderly censure.

"One day my son will be a fine declaimer," she continues in a whisper, with a proud smile and a handsome turn of her head.

"Actor?" I puzzle at the happenstance and hesitate to raise or avoid the topic.

"Politician," retorts this proudest of parents. "Perhaps even president!"

She turns to the boy who has his eyes only fastened to the constant stream of passing fenceposts and the trespassable fields they pretend to protect from his slingshot eyes. Not a thought of future, less of law. And yet there is something familiarly likeable about him, and he waves farewell good-naturedly as his mother scoops him and their baggage away at the last though briefly sunlit stop of the day. The spinsters had quitted us just before midday.

***

Friday, November 1859. Richmond Theater, Richmond, Virginia. Afternoon. A TROOP OF ACTORS prepare an adaptation of Charles Dickens' Nicholas Nickleby.

***

One afternoon in late November, I was preparing my part for the Richmond Theater's production of *Smike*, an adaptation of Mr. Dickens' *Nicholas Nickleby*. As we rehearsed our lines and set our marks, we were suddenly aware of a great disturbance on the street outside. We often practiced our roles at volumes that took the sounds of racing steel, locomotive engines, passengers, and merchants into consideration. Those sounds were there, but this time the very sense with which our ears received them was remarkably different. The train whistles seemed to come from a different station, signal departure for a very different destination.

Without a word the entire company stopped its work and walked to the front door of the small foyer. Outside, a detachment of local Grays, under the command of a certain General Lee, then in the service of the one united army, was forming ranks and readying to board the steaming train like fledgling angels at the cloud-caped gates of paradise. Hardly aware of the moment and urged by a hand I felt, but knew not, I turned to one of my fellows and expressed my resolve to go with them.

"What do you mean, Mr. Wilkes?" came the obvious, if somehow unanticipated reply from the over-practiced rustic, fancying himself rather comely as he found the spittoon on the corner of the porch. "This cannot be one of your famous Booth family larks. We play tonight."

"Smike is a very small part," I assured him, "and any supernumerary who can hunch, look humble and diseased, can surely fill the role. Perhaps yourself?" I suggested.

I did not chew tobacco—smoked it only on occasion—but was in command of my throat to the extent that I could instantly summon a sufficient insult for the quite taken aback Norris as I turned to join the company aboard the train for Charles Town.

"But, Wilkes," he called behind me. "The play is Smike!"

"Congratulations on being cast in the lead," I grinned.

At the moment I stepped outside the theater the commotion increased, as if I had suddenly entered a forgotten, fully sensible world. Gone were the drilled and practiced mechanics of the play, the familiarity of cue and cross. Still, I was fairly amazed to see and hear the coincidental precision of the day's choreography and orchestration, and the expertise with which the city's inhabitants performed their unrehearsed parts. Bustled mothers with parasols and zig-zagging broods in tow, coatless porters of high-springing, gaitered and salaaming steps, yah-sah-ing and yahs-ma'am-ing with perfectly compliant smiles, and all nature of cherooted salesmen, tradesmen and slouch-hatted dandies, each as particularly uniformed as the Grays themselves.

The buzz on the street was that a large group of mercenaries in the employ of a foreign power were being landed, along with heavy artillery, outside of Charles Town, Jefferson County, West Virginia. The Grays were to confront the faceless foe and be praised for their courage, laughing and joking as in preparation only for color-guard duty in the following week's parade. I sensed my fellow actors standing at the theater door, shouting to recall me as they whispered among themselves, still I moved forward, and by the time I was halfway into the street the simple facts of the regiment's duty had surfaced. They had been called to Charles Town to guard the captured abolitionist John Brown.

People had been arguing about the issue of slavery for as long as the Union had been around. Longer. But Brown had been lately making the headlines with a bold attempt to enforce his beliefs in the inherent evils of the slave trade and institution. What started the previous year as bloody confrontations in Kansas had moved into our heartland. He holed up at the armory in the small town of Harper's Ferry, demanding immediate attention to his desires on threat of either controlling or destroying the river crossing. For a time he was actually rumored to expect support from other nations – from exactly where was unknown and unlikely, but not altogether unreasonable, as the circulated stories attested. Any man with the courage and daring to hold an entire town hostage could not be underestimated.

After hearing descriptions of Brown's wildly prophetic features, accounts of his divine inspiration and the tragic sacrifice of his sons, I was even more resigned to go, but met with a modicum of opposition. Three of the officers in charge, while insisting they had much else to do, yet stood long enough to make an exaggerated fuss over my desire to travel with the regiment, said the train was strictly for military use. I had begun to speak of my many years as a cadet to very little effect when one of the officers excused himself after commenting on my father's signet ring. It bore the initials HTWSSTKS in a circular fashion around a broad cross and had once belonged to a great uncle.

I imagined it had some sort of theatrical significance, and when first given it as a boy I pored over volumes of my father's plays and poetry seeking the title or selection to which the letters referred. Week after week I searched to no avail, but committed it to memory as "How the weather starts, stops, then keeps storming!" The only help my father volunteered was the key to his library trunk, a chuckle and news that it would come in handy if I ever took to travel east. But at the moment, south by south-west was my proposed direction.

Inside five minutes' time the young officer returned while the other two continued to engage me, still protesting the urgency of their mission and the limited time they had to argue with civilians. He handed a packet and uniform to me saying, "Compliments o' th' Co'nel," and I was instantly, if temporarily, appointed assistant commissary or quartermaster.

"Which colonel is that?" I wondered aloud.

"Why, Co'nel Lee," he answered with a deep and toothy grin. "Th' Old Man, hisself. Co'nel Bobby Lee."

It was some time before I understood the significance of this officer's recognition of me, thinking at the moment it was only my father's name that recommended me to his favor.

On the ride down to Charles Town I met another soldier, no older than myself, who acted as both surgeon and chaplain for the regiment. He too was intrigued by the stories about the Harper's Ferry incident, and we shared our feelings that, regardless, the now-caged beast named Brown was a man of dedication and purpose. An abolitionist—a word that would shortly gain much more attention than any other in our nation's history, he and his sons and the handful of zealots who felt their passion held the crossing at Harper's Ferry hostage to a demand for the end to slavery. This was not a new idea, but his passion gave it a fire and authority it had never known. Still, there were laws that men had vested with authority and power, and by those laws the wretch and his righteous renegades were confronted, and by those laws they would be put to death.

"But what are they doing?" I asked the doctor as we stepped off the train together. "Is he going to be freed?"

"Wha'? Who?" he answered, flustered by my choice of words.

He followed my eyes to where Colonel Lee apparently spoke to the very object of our mission. Several inches taller than the colonel, his hair and beard were not as hoary as I had been led to believe, but every bit as wild. Yet it was not purpose I saw now in his otherwise decisive brow. It was laughter. The two of them laughed and caroused like old schoolmates, as they engaged in a prolonged and double-fisted handshake.

"Tha' ain't him!" chuckled the doctor. "Tha's Mr. Pike, a good friend o' the colonel. Though, them frontier boys all looks 'bout th' same. Mr. Pike shows up at some o' th' queerest times." He laughed again. "Tha' man ain't never loved no niggers!"

"Who does?" I remarked distractedly, wondering where or if I had previously heard Pike's name.

"Truth be told," he answered seriously, "rumors are th' Old Man! I don't know for certain. Only wha' I hear. But one thing's sure—he don't keep none at Arlington House. An' they say tha's cause he don't think it's right."

I looked again to the two comrades, trying to make some sense of it. Something was happening already. I could feel it. But I didn't know just what.

My turn at guard duty came the evening of the third day. Not turn, really. Thirty-two dollars I paid for the privilege of overseeing him for one hour of a particular private's watch.

"Don't let 'im scare ye'," said the young private as he counted his money with a smile. "And don't be disappointed when he won't talk to ye'. Outside of mumbling a few prayers, he hasn't said a word since 'is arrest. Remember, nobody can know I've gone—'ceptin' you has t'. And then, jes' tell 'em I had t' get sick."

A bright sun shone its last rays forth through dark gray clouds as the soft rain continued to fall. "The devil's beatin' 'is wife," said the private, looking skyward. "But I don't think it's with no leg o' mutton! It's with the promise of this man's two legs swingin' in the wind," he nodded and grinned as he sauntered away.

Then I saw him, the man Brown, slouched in the corner of his cell, his body stripped to shirt and trousers alone. Scarcely acknowledging our actions, he yet seemed fully aware as he closed his bible with a lover's fingers.

The cell in which Brown was kept was a familiarly hollow gray cube, seven feet wide, seven feet tall and seven feet deep. It had a barred door at the front and a small barred window at its rear, and Brown looked every bit the prophet of yore to which he had been likened in the *Tribune* and *Post*. His savage white hair fell in plaintive waves to his shoulders and his beard was snowy with implicit wisdom.

He was not a huge man—though quite tall, yet he filled his cell in a way that made his shoulders seem to hunch and his head bow with a forced obeisance, which withheld an attitude of defiance. I, who was never at a loss for words and had insisted I should take watch for the chance to speak alone to the possessor of such an undeniable presence, found myself awed by the very look of the man.

As soon as the outer door clapped shut he began to speak, but not in quiet psalms or verse or parables. His words, if uncommon, were clear, his voice quite like thunder, matching his grave and stormy look.

"Do you know what you are doing here?" he asked with a tilt of his head, directing an ancient gaze out the moon-split

120

window.

Although it might have been addressed to any issue and any one, there was no doubt in my mind to whom and what he referred.

"Why the mysteries of life have called your name outside of sleep, so that you might respond while waking to their call?"

He turned his stone-etched eyes to meet mine and answered before I said a word, the foremost, if unframed question in my mind.

"Our lives are not our own, not really. Their purposes are ours to find—as Mr. Emerson says. But, once discovered, what choice is there? That you or I should live and die without some end accomplished is hardly worthy for the mind of God to have conceived."

He walked toward me, his giant form and oaken features gaining in their majesty and effect, the seeming fire above his grizzled brow, a living forge for the laws of men or every one of my curiosities. His body was like the fabled pillar of smoke, his eyes reflections of the pillar of fire, and upon these two columns the strength of the man Brown rested its trust.

"Will you pray with me?" he asked, sinking to his knees and closing his eyes as if there could be only one reply.

"Great Heavenly Father," he began with commanding humility. "What are we to do—I who have these many months been the servant of your will, and this man, whose journey just begins? I am chained, gratefully by your most ferocious will. His chains he scarcely feels —yet knows they are but part of your design."

His eyes were still closed, but I could feel their watchfulness, as if many others were present. I looked around to see we were indeed alone and realized I was not only kneeling, but my hands, as Brown's, were folded in prayer.

Suddenly his eyes opened with their kindled fury, and he reached through the bars, enormous fingers wrapping like pulsing manacles around my wrists. Drawing me as close as our barred barrier would permit, he stared intently at me with the vast honesty of a fasting wilderness.

"These hands," he said, looking at his own knotted knuckles. "These hands have wrought the Tempest's soul. Those hands," as he shook me with a horrible power, "Shall free it! Those hands have not seen their day. There will be a time when they would rather fill an endless cup than sip the waters satisfied.

"What will come, all men must fear, though none can say."

Ten years earlier, my father had taken our family to New York at my birthday to attend a performance of William Macready as Macbeth. Edwin, at 16, was just starting to accept roles, Asia was 14, Joe 9, and I was turning 11. Junius and Rosalie were to meet us at the theater, but could not get close, because that very night the tragic Astor Riot took place, claiming a score of lives and injuring an hundred others. Both Macready and Edwin Forrest were playing the role of the Scottish lord at the same time, and a theater-going city could not reconcile who was greater. As it was my birthday, and in typical fashion, my father, just as typically drunk at the time, blamed me and my birthday for interrupting the season of the world's finest actor. He meant neither Forrest nor Macready but himself. Was it not ever so?

And now another self-proclaimed scion was again proclaiming my defect.

Brown turned to look at me, showing a kind of luminescence. I felt a strange foreboding and was reminded of yet another time—of family, not my father, but my own dear sister. The following year, two or three weeks before my twelfth birthday, I had my palm read at a traveling carnival for sheer amusement and came home with the fateful news I had been born to cause great misery.

And now, all my life seemed fluid in front of this Brown's vision, and every image, recognizable or no, was sure and true. So penetratingly did he look into my eyes, I could not doubt his second sight.

"The gypsy said, the gypsy said," repeated Asia to my deep, stump-seated afternoon thoughts. Her impish smile and glistening forehead mixed with the scent of early magnolia to tilt my credulous senses.

"Pay no attention to that old hag," she dismissed. "She is just some circus stroller who will have her dollars by scaring young and trusting boys into believing she has their answer to 'life's great mysteries.'"

"She knew I was born on a Thursday!"

"You told her your birthday, didn't you?"

"Thursday's child has far to go! How did she know?"

"It is not that difficult to calculate."

"Can you do it?"

Asia gave me half a smile, but I knew she was struggling to explain.

"She was right!" I concluded, staring directly at her.

She lowered her brow and squinted her eyes with a mocking intensity. Rolling her arms conjuringly about my head, she adopted the drama of a Slavic accent as she circled the tree stump on which I sat.

"Fvadt she fvas rhighdt aboudt fvere youhr eyes. Szey shall charhm fvone szousand unlucky szouls."

"If that is to be true, I must do it deliberately," I dared to boast.

"No. By accident'al," she exceptioned with a haughty air, grabbing my arm by the wrist and pointing to the criss-crossed lines. "By accident'al. It isz much more sze gentlemanly szing to do fviszout trhying." Making again to swoon, she released my hand and looked deeply at me, "Oh! Sze moszt handsome of men in sze countrhy, in zse fvorldt." She sidled next to me. "Ahndt szose eyes. Youhr eyes! Szey shall charhm fvone szousand szouls ahndt break fvone szousand hearts. Szey fvouldt breahk mine—ifv I fvouldt ledt szem," she pulled herself away, as if to break her own charm.

"Ahndt ifv I fvas not—"

"Not what, not what?" I called to her, half angry, half laughing nervously, as she broke off and danced into the budding hickory of the Cockeysville woods, her arms still twirling poetically, her body spinning a favorite summer dress into calico waves and hoops.

"Your sister, silly!" she replied in her own sweet voice, tripping backwards over a broken branch and giggling as she fell.

She continued to laugh as she got up and skipped off gaily. I, of course, followed.

I tried to forget the incident, but there was a lingering uncertainty to Asia's mockings and the cautions of the old gypsy woman, and April would ever after hold promises of more than merely nature's spring fulfilled – but of mine own hands, and mine own eyes.

"This is where you are coming from, this is where you are going," said the hoary old woman as she balanced my two hands in her own, weighing them together and separately and leaving me with a sense of wanting. "This is what you are given," looking into my eyes as she raised my left hand slightly. "And this is what you will make of it," now lifting my right.

Her voice had not the Romany lilt Asia imagined, sounding rather like the one or other grandmother I had never known but who knew me completely—always. She spoke in clear, unmistakable English, at once distant yet connected.

I dreamed out over Tudor's acres, my family's lands, the rambling greens running into one another, the rolling hills and jagged crests of Maryland. I did not watch them alone. A quick look over my right shoulder. No one. My left. Still. And yet I heard a voice, his name, the sound of his soul trapped within those woods. The gurgling of his last breaths. Some one bathed his feet just below the bend in the creek.

***

Brown seemed to see the same aspect of grief in my features. I could nearly see the tears welling up in his eyes, like those of the boy who makes his first kill at the hunt. While knowing that he must eat, still he wonders and despairs that it should be the flesh of another living being. The motionless form with still-wet eyes incomprehensibly panicked in its last moments upon the grass.

"Blood," he said without bending his brow. "The crimes of this guilty land will never be purged, but with blood. Your time will come, when you must do that for which you were designed, despite the cost to your life—and soul, despite the disapproval of those whom once you loved, but may not see. Even I might hate you for it—if I were not dead."

"You will die in the morning."

The words escaped without my knowing how or from where, except that it was a place of fear. His reply did nothing to ease the feeling.

"In the morning. Or on the evening when you fulfill my dream."

"What dream?" I wondered, but could not speak, only watch him as he once again turned his eyes to the dark gray corner.

At the end of my hour, the private came back to relieve me, fastening the brass buttons of a brown oversized redingote.

"Gave me just enough time to win his jacket at dice. No one questioned that a quartermaster should be doing the duty of a private, I suppose?"

"No. No one."

"And no word out of him either?" he added, expecting only a single answer.

"Just some mumbled prayers," I replied and walked away.

Scene IV

How the gay sledges like meteors flash by—
Bright for a moment, then lost to the eye!

I suppose I was a handsome youth. Beautiful even, if I may dare to use that word—for it is not mine own. My sister Asia would often tell me so in a way I never fully understood and also truly frightened me somewhat.

"Oh John, those dark eyes of yours will surely be your undoing," she would say playfully. "If you were passing clever, they should be the same for all the world. And your ivory-sculpted arms—what would I do if I were a stranger woman?"

And though we might imagine it betimes, it was but one more thing that could not be. Then she would laugh wickedly and walk a careful circle around where I might stand or sit, fetch a curl or two from its place upon my head, tug playfully, and laugh again. Being only slightly more than two years apart in age—and with no other relations in America—we were as much cousins as brother and sister. At least to our minds.

"We might well be sprung from different mothers—or fathers," Asia would hint, before either of us understood the possibility of that truth.

Our time together seemed always an event, a holiday. So it was whenever I came home to Tudor Hall between the spring and autumn sessions of the St. Charles' Academy, we would rise early each morning with a child's yuletide enthusiasm and read late into the nights from Poe or some such latest entry in *Burton's* or *The Messenger*. Each would try to wring the fullest effect from the delightfully macabre words, to outdo the dramatic tones of the other, until we would fall into a rolling contagion of hushed laughter that our mother should not be awakened.

My sister's name, anything but Christian, had ever

influenced her desires to study the Eastern philosophies and even those of the pre-Columbian American continent. She seemed to read constantly and was, from childhood, somewhat the family expert on primitive societies and religion. Her middle name, Frigga, for the Scandinavian goddess of love, tempered all her research with a kind of icy maternity that at once understood and yet held all at a distance more worthy of reason and realistic perspective.

But when she laughed it was the knowledge of that most primal part of herself that glinted unashamedly in her dark eyes. That same strange knowing that led her one day to kiss me more fondly than even cousins might.

I never had to kiss a girl, to beg or ask or plead for favor. As with Asia, they kissed me. First, last, always.

What clever joy was mine to watch the other boys trip and flatter for the courage to crave a soft hand. Their own full-drenched by the final moment of request and possible acceptance, only adding to their shy discomfort.

Yet I, whose dreams were surely no less agitated than those around me, seemed ever courted, wooed and sneaked upon. First by some scheming, winking, wicked eye and soon by lips that presumed to follow. When finally I was ready to commit my heart, it had long before been plucked and plundered. Still, what was left—and it seemed enough, if not overmuch—I gave to her, to Ella.

And she had also kissed me first.

My promise to my mother that I would not allow my passions or bachelorhood to persuade me to join the army was balanced by the contentment that I did my part by supplying my brethren of a poor beleaguered South with what comforts smuggled cargoes of quinine could provide. For fourteen months I rode vast quantities of the same past Union blockades with—as he liked to be called—United States Grant's own signature pass. My tentside orations and fragmented scenes were the alibi of my movements, but my greatest performances were those delivered to the blue-vested picket-line sentries who never guessed beyond my practiced calm to search the over-stuffed harness, the reins of which I steadied with sweating hands. Nor shall I say I did not find, upon the advice of a friend, quick and reliable strength in the ingestion of another such medication, which, though more rare, found great purpose to my deed.

"Really, Johnnie! What is so difficult to understand? I cannot imagine anything more difficult than a mother sending her sons off to be killed at war. Maryland has no part in this conflict. And you have no duty to either side."

"I have my opinions. And I have my sense of truth and honor."

"Pooh!" she scoffed.

"And I don't wish to hear how I am her favorite," I told her. "She has other sons. And each of them holds a special place in her heart."

"Don't let us talk about it then. Because you know it's true. Though I can't for the life of me imagine why," she giggled. "Still, I must say, I have fallen prey to your spell as well." She stared mock-seriously, as if entranced, and recalled the gypsy woman. "It must be your eyes."

Asia played the serafina with vacant gaze and mechanical steps across the slope of lawn, habitually tripping over some unsuspecting shrub until I joined her laughter.

"She has other sons," I continued, fishing in a well-stocked pond.

"That makes no matter. Nature provides our spirits with some kind of precognition, prepares us for the day our parents will leave us. We had one father, but it was no surprise to have him die."

"He was overdue."

"For us perhaps. Even still, when mother dies, what will we say except that it was to be expected?"

"Do not talk like that!" I snapped. "I am not sure I could bear it."

"You see. Still, it must be." Her intuitions were rarely

understood, even when correct. And often, as in her choice of husbands, no less unacceptable.

"I, for one, will grieve," I sulked.

"And so will we all, sweet Johnnie," she caressed me with her words. "But we will say she lived well and long."

Her glance was as far away now as the oriental shores of her christened name.

"Don't ask me why. Somehow we understand life's pattern. That is why so many societies exalt the notion of patricide. Yet of the killing of a child or sibling there can be no tolerance. It is the true horror of the present conflict. Nothing in nature is more offensive, more truly onerous, or anathema to our hearts and minds."

"Perhaps it is the parent who should perish, then," I suggested. "The sire of this bloody business."

"But of course, he must," she replied. She could not have known my thoughts then. Or, if she did, she made that they were mine alone.

***

Perhaps it will be necessary to explain some several other incidents, which, having occurred brought me not only to this woodland but also to this point of recounting my life. What my name is you know already. How I received that name is part of my family history and you may easily ask your uncle if you wish an accounting of the same. Let us start then with a similarly familiar story, yet which, because of the teller, must needs be different.

The war had dragged on those many years and the end was about. Yet for those of us who had not asked for war, nor could not settle for a peace that meant to finish what had no right to begin, there would be no end. Things were then what they always had been despite the appellation of this or that condition. Dissatisfaction would not be satisfied, nor argumentation resolved because some martial tyrant willy-nilled it should be so.

Strophe

We were not satisfied and could not forget the cause of our unrest. If they meant the war was over, what did it matter to a civilian? If they meant that all was repaired, how could they think the deaths of brothers or the tears of widows and the unborn might find appeasement in the ceremonious yielding of a sword, the futile language of some engine-wrought eulogy? Four score and nine years later our nation was torn, our spirits were ravaged, our principles rent, despoiled, profaned. Was this peace?

I may easily state that this was in more than one way a difficult and transitioned time for me. Edwin's widely circulated fame was also thorning its way into my side. His earnings were reportedly excessive, at least for his talents. It seemed overtime for the family name to recall its former genius. Or what was I? Not merely a descendant and namesake of his excellently rebellious Lord Mayor.

***

That was all before I met your mother. Even in those most unsteady times, there was that separate, if grotesque, peace maintained in Washington. The White House itself had set the pace and busily maintained its languorous lead. Expensive gowns were bought, expansive preparations made, indifferent balls and dinners given. While Pennsylvania farmlands bleated and bled, Missouri and Kansas stretched and suffered, and all of Richmond wept, the federal capital dined and danced.

When I received my invitation to the 1863–64 New Year's Eve gala at the home of a certain Senator Nash, I was somewhat surprised, yet thought little of going. My brother Edwin, finished with his New York season, was in Washington for a dinner given in his honor by Secretary of State Seward. This the result of the Union tyrant having seen Edwin's performance of Shylock in a current adaptation of the same name. Seward, forever trying to put himself in everyone's favor, particularly the northern president's, had heard of this new affection for my brother's work. A man who rarely missed an opportunity to go to the theater, the tyrant had never stayed awake through an entire performance—until seeing Edwin. So my brother had received the invitation to the Nash home and urged me to attend with him.

"There will be many individuals by whose introduction you might benefit," he added.

Not only because it was unusual for Edwin to ever take an interest in my affairs, much less in our doing anything together, I conceded. There were those rare occasions when our lives seemed less complicated than the times and our contrary dispositions generally insisted. Yet there was then a greater need in my system than that of a brother. Nor could I pass up an opportunity of cementing our relationship beyond the mere fact that we were family—especially as my sympathies for the South were already well-known, and Edwin was busily and forever trying to disassociate himself from any ideology that might be construed as harmful to his career.

But things with Edwin had been greatly changed since the loss the previous February of his wife of less than three years, the actress Mary Devlin. Not even 23 years old, she had left him his one great remaining joy, Edwina. Strange, dark and haunted, she was yet a loving and devoted daughter and bore constant witness to her mother's lasting impression upon my brother. When some years later he married Mary McVicker, he could bring himself only to call her Vickie, rather than summon once more the memory of his first marriage.

The previous summer I had paid a visit to New York as the dutiful uncle at the moment when a friend of Edwin's, a writer named Adam Badeau, had been wounded in the city's anti-war riots. I helped carry the man into my brother's house where Edwin and I nursed him back to health. Badeau was a sometime journalist and state department clerk who, at the outset of the war, cast down his pen to take up the Unionist sword and was presently on staff for a certain General Q. A. Gillmore. Prior to that he had been an *aide-de-camp* to General Sherman, a position recommended him by his enlistment and state experience — and rumors were prevalent of his upcoming appointment as military secretary to General Grant. From camp to general's camp, Badeau's assignments increased in honor and prestige without a hint of effort. How ironic that he should become the innocent casualty of a freak accident from a dispute over the irregularities and discriminations of mandatory inscription.

Edwin was surprised that day, I recall, to see his young and fiery brother forego his passions long enough to recognize a man in need regardless of the color of his uniform. Still, something underneath the situation seemed to recommend to both of us that we were brothers, we were Booths. Edwina's sweetly clinging, year-and-a-half-old affections for her uncle were in no little part responsible for this new-found filial amity.

Edwin had wired home to assure little Edwina's well-being in her grandmother's care and explained to me the source of our invitations to the New Year's party to be his friend Badeau. When he told me of the expected attendance of Generals Sherman, Gillmore, and Grant, he paused to check my reaction, as if I might be as vehement in my company as my opinions. But that was his persuasion dictating a perception of how I might also be.

The New Year's ball seemed an opportunity for us to complete the mending of our long-standing rift and Edwin's estrangement toward me. His recent widowing made him seem almost desperately in need of friends and family, and I felt our bond more strongly than ever, in spite of growing political and ideological differences. In addition, I had always meant to thank Grant for the courtesy he had done me by extending a pass to me solely on the recommendation of my name. I could not help but laugh to myself that I had taken such advantage of the general's generosity. The man who was routing our Southern armies was inadvertently seeing that those same routed armies were receiving the medical attentions they needed to continue their fight.

Scene V

Ringing,
     Swinging,
          Dashing as they go
Over the crest of the beautiful snow:
Snow so pure when it falls from the sky,
To be trampled in mud by the crowd rushing by;
To be trampled and tracked by the thousands of feet
Till it blends with the horrible filth in the street.

John Harrison Surratt Jr., according to the record, was living in Baltimore in 1890, where he had accepted a position as auditor for the Old Bay Line of the Baltimore Steam Packet Company. Of all of us his story is the most fascinating. Yea, more than mine own.

Harrison, as he was called by the others to avoid confusion with references to his mother, I suppose, or Jack, as I knew him, had left Capital City the day of the deed, ostensibly to follow the departing Grant but truly to flee his own cowardice for the plan he himself had helped to conceive. I can forgive him for his fear, but for his treachery, never.

Indeed, Surratt had boarded that same train upon which left the Union general, but rather than perform his part, continued on to Canada, from where—prudently, most prudently, then—he boarded a packet to the continent of Europe, where he accepted an appointment in the papal zouaves at the Vatican City. There was the truth of his promises to my own Ella, and the jealousy, which I justly bear as a result.

Somewhat over a year later he was appropriately betrayed by one of his fellows, and brought back to the United States for trial only after a daring attempt to escape that saw him leaping—if not as gracefully, somewhat more successfully than I—over a hundred-foot cliff, only to be washed ashore and apprehended on the coast of Egypt.

Surratt's trial, though it did not serve my vengeful heart, was a triumph of our cause, as the jury was hung—four for conviction, eight for acquittal—and dismissed. His subsequent lectures (Yes! I said *lectures*) on our association and the plot itself drew crowds and sums as large as any actor's debut. Throughout all he conveniently omitted any reference to his knowledge of the plan to kill the union leader. This, perhaps, no less than I would have done by then.

His implications of the weasel Weichmann for the latter's denouncing of our plot to save his own skin, while just could only have been half-hearted as he surely sensed his own betrayal of his one true friend. My only solace was that despite any efforts I might have imagined he should have made to reconcile with Ella after his return and acquittal, he was a reported bachelor who had never married. I prayed and thanked God it was true.

It was neither difficult nor particularly fruitful when at last I found Surratt on the fringe of Baltimore, in Ellicott City. Oh, he recognized me immediately, and reacted as strongly as had my brother, but had nothing of much interest to say either to me or in his own defense. In short, and for all his past adventures and exploits, he had not really changed. Except I discovered he had in fact wasted little time in marrying and had seven children, the youngest being five years old at this time.

"Still delivering your lectures, Jack?"

"Lectures? No, no more lectures," he said, stopping short and checking the street in both directions before turning around with blunt reply. "And you, Wilkes? Are you still in the habit of delivering yours?"

"Jack, poor Jack!"

"Wilkes, ever Wilkes," he replied.

"You recognize me so easily? Without my name, without my fame—my face too so changed?"

"Who else would call me Jack? And your eyes, Wilkes, your eyes. You cannot change the eyes."

We walked for a moment together—he continuing to look in every direction for the unwanted eyes, and he admitted seeking out Ella as soon as he could—to bestow a favored fez, no doubt—intending to invite her to one of his lectures—but had no luck whatsoever in finding her. Could not remember the precise excuse offered by her father upon inquiry, but recalled never having received a colder reception, "No, not even by Judge Fisher, himself."

Apparently, Surratt could view me only as one more likely audience member to hear the recounting of his exploits. I had no such desire and resigned to take my leave, swearing him to a secrecy I was not sure could be trusted—even after he acknowledged he had become a family man, had a wife and children—until he briefly accounted the circumstances of his narrow escape from hanging those many years ago to a lack of evidence for the extent of our association. The story could not be changed, even twenty-five years hence. He was right, I had nothing to fear from him.

***

"A little education will lead to atheism," Edwin misquoted. "A lot of education leads to true faith."

"Brother, you know I have never had even a little education," I replied, smiling. "Still, I have ever tried my best to be the most devout atheist. But the deity keeps getting in the way."

He tried to return my smile, yet could not.

Henry drove us up the tree-lined drive and waited in the front carriage court with the other livery servants and lackeys. The stately brick home, with its exterior gaslamps, curved and tiered portico and symmetrically columned design, was much the impressive image of a distant capital or foreign embassy. The air about seemed almost perfumed as pure white smoke billowed out of the three visible chimneys, and a light snow began to fall, furthering the candelabra-lit entry's glowing allure as we laid the evening's first bootprints in the newly fallen snow on the red brick porch stairs.

Inside, costumed menservants with powdered wigs looked out of place but took our capes and hats and canes and led the way to the reception room. There we exchanged salutary greetings with a group of masked and anonymous hosts and certain sober men by the names of Crowe, Jones, Kennedy, Lester, McCord, Reed and others, then left to our own. Dutch-capped maids bustled about, attentively serving sparkling Catawba and Cornish pasties.

"Why were we not told this was a masque?" I asked Edwin almost nervously.

"Oh?" he said with half a smile. "I thought you knew. But what need have we for costumes, brother? Effortlessly, we shall change our parts every half-hour, according to our whims."

We stepped into the grand salon where Edwin was greeted by this and that admirer or consoling friend, all quick to also wonder why we had not arrived in costume. His answer being that, as theatricals, we found more disguise in our natural state. Soon Edwin was off with these others, leaving me alone to contemplate a poised and easy posture.

I recognized Lee's old friend Mr. Pike standing in one corner, his powerful stature towering over the others. He was becoming my personal landmark—if he was in attendance, I somehow knew I certainly belonged. When last I had seen his granite-featured face, it had been chiseled with lines of laughter. Here, as those of the men he addressed, it was uncommonly grim and recalled Chappel's painting of Washington's farewell to his officers. They were all talking loudly, yet from where I stood their voices mingled with those about the room into a strange, almost coded language, somewhere, perhaps, between the Portuguese of explorer priests and another less-familiar tongue.

In another section of the room I saw Lutz, on whose arm was that other long-time friend of my brother, the ringlet-tressed actress Laura Keene. As we, she wore no costume. A knotted strand of Indian beads about her neck and short black leather gloves commended her eccentricity. She and Lutz were gathered with yet another group of seriously demeanored men, including two of those who had greeted Edwin and me at the door, but no one seemed to be talking. Lutz stood with one arm propped upon the mantle, according to his habit. Whether he stood or sat, he always had one arm raised to lean elbow-first against a wall, or over the back of his chair, always in readiness, wherever, rather than easily rest both arms at his side.

Lutz saw me too, but his expression remained unchanged and the idea of our having never met was implicit in his avoidance of me, and so I pretended. And though I might have prevailed upon Ms Keane, instead I enjoyed a rare, footloose moment. Nestled under an archway, as a small orchestra played a waltz the entire room glowed with the colors of seasonal draperies and candles, whirred with the rustlings of pinafores and coattails.

Among the flurried pageant of capers, curvets and caracoles, the occasional jig or even minuet, I straightaway noticed a beautiful young woman. Auburn hair, emerald eyes, a carnelian-and-pearl dress accenting her complexion, and a smile that glinted as she danced. She was herself the picture of the season. If I had not immediately known better she might have appeared the kind to be biding her time until her inheritance. Hardly more than a girl she noticed me as well, seemed somewhat surprised with every turn that I was watching her, and very forwardly took advantage of the first opportunity to escape her dancing partner.

Retrieving an *hors d'oeuvre* from the banquet table she was soon alone in a corner of the gallery, continually nodding apologetic pardons to disappointed dance suitors. There she stood, somewhere between a fidgeting girl and swaying enchantress, lost among lacy billows of ruffled silk over hoopskirts delicately hung with rosebud garlands, when an unexpected yawn brought me instinctively to her side.

Here was a romance. No crash of symbols, rolling flats, flickering lights, hoisted or descending backdrops. No exotic locale, time-pressed moment, glorious protestations, and oaths. Simple, careless, conversational romance. We stood hardly aware of our surroundings, lulled by each other's breathless harmony. She so much so that, indeed, she spilled her favored canapé onto the parquet floor.

***

Thursday, December 31, 1863. Washington City.
New Year's Eve. A flurry of motion, a pageant of costumes and color. THE ACTOR moves to address a YOUNG WOMAN with patronizing interest.

THE ACTOR (whispering rebuke with a smile): Cover your mouth when you yawn!
YOUNG WOMAN (with certain exception): I beg your pardon?
THE ACTOR (facetiously): Having a good time? *(still humorous)* When I was a boy, I often wondered what kind of life the people in these houses lived. I convinced myself it was really not so very different from my own. Now I see I was wrong. There is, for example, such excitement it takes one's very breath away.

***

I was not aware until much later of her distress. While I spoke to her with affectionate humor yet, I had discovered something she had always hoped to conceal. A measured if definite boredom of her very life. This discovery she at once despised and adored. And of my having drawn attention to it said she could never remember a gentleman treating her in such a manner. Still, her ability for recovery was remarkable.

***

THE ACTOR (approaching confidently): Would you like to

dance?

YOUNG WOMAN (sincerely): With you?

The Actor looks confused, then smiles and leads the Young Woman by the hand. They make their way across the dance floor for the dance, and at the end of the selection, find their ways back to the edge of the room. Retrieving two champagne cocktails from a passing MANSERVANT, The Actor offers one to the Young Woman.

THE ACTOR (with well-rehearsed brashness): Is it my imagination or have you been hoping for something more than our introduction?

YOUNG WOMAN (parrying expertly): A kiss, perhaps?

THE ACTOR: Perhaps. (laughing slightly) But we are strangers.

YOUNG WOMAN: Have you never wished to kiss a stranger? Just once? No preview, no past, no pretense of future – no expectations or regrets?

The Actor tries to remain composed yet is surely caught off guard by her matched forwardness. A moment's silence is relieved by THE SENATOR, a somewhat corpulent man in his fifties. Dressed in a gray tuxedo, he forages his way toward them through deep bows and nods from across the room.

THE SENATOR: I see you have met my daughter, Mr. Booth. (with a grinding smile) Please excuse her boldness. Saw your Hamlet in New York one night last autumn when you drew a substantially larger house than Mr. Frederick Forrest.

THE ACTOR (correcting): Macbeth?

YOUNG WOMAN (nodding): A splendidly sinister Macbeth. (pointedly) Not weak as the others. Drunken, perhaps. And crazy! (continuing ardently) Sinister. Strong—not feeble as he is so commonly and horribly played. I am afraid that, for all the beauty of the Bowery and the Park, New York will ever after have only one theater for me—Mary Provost's.

THE SENATOR: Insisted on meeting you, despite my refusal to introduce her to a man I did not know myself. Still at the age where she assumes everyone in Washington knows her famous father—even strangers.

THE ACTOR (to the Young Woman): Strangers? (to the Senator) Are you famous?

The Actor smiles, takes his eyes from those of the beautiful daughter for the first time.

THE SENATOR (with unfamiliar modesty): Oh, no! Not in the sense that you and your family are. Your late father was known all over the world. (motioning to where The Actor's brother Edwin stands surrounded by admirers) And your brother is surely destined for the same. Not famous like that! Though I imagine in political circles my name carries a certain—shall I say—familiarity?

THE ACTOR: And what of me? Will I ever share my family's—and my brother's—greatness?

THE SENATOR: What? You? (laughing) Oh, of course! What do I know of such things? You will become what you will. I only know what people say, and today they say the name of Edwin Booth will one day match his father's glorious memory. (walking on to meet an ASSOCIATE) Tomorrow they might change their minds, if he were not considered loyal to the North. I have seen him play a dozen times, and I declare I can not tell the difference.

THE ACTOR (wondering): Between—?

***

Despite his having confused for a moment my playing with that of my brother, I found the senator an amiably countenanced man with the showily exuberant nature of the purest politico. At some point or another, in recognition of this perhaps, someone bestowed upon him a signet ring, not unlike my own. It held no initials but had a representation of the sun encased in a kind of sextant.

Never long for serious conversations, the senator's response to any subject, even upon extended inquiry, was always as brief and inoffensive as possible, despite the risk of merit, meaning and credulity. Yet could he continue for as long as one would listen, changing trifling topic for trifling topic and always with a concluding smile as if he had just said something worth noting. And in all he seemed to chew his thoughts so carefully that by the time they arrived you knew not really what they were supposed to be.

Often his diversions seemed less device than I am sure they certainly were. Asked about his politics he would speak of his career. Asked about the state of political affairs he would go on about the fraternity of man. Still would he flash his ruminating smile as finale and nod certifyingly as if he understood your contentment and resolve to be as sure as his.

***

THE SENATOR: You consider yourself an artist, do you not? You acting people consider yourselves artists. I was once an artist. *(teeth chattering silently)* A real artist. An architect. There are men, and there are monuments, Mr. Booth. Things of stature. Things that last. If my family hadn't been involved in government, I fancied myself the next Christopher Wren. You know that name, do you?

THE ACTOR: Excuse me, I don't believe—

YOUNG WOMAN: Oh, Poppie is always preachin' to the choir.

THE SENATOR *(magnanimously)*: I beg your pardon. 'Bout time I introduced myself. I'm Senator Nash, Pop. Everyone calls me that. You might as well. *(turning to his daughter with a smile, his lower jaw sidling back into place)* My daughter Camilla, Ella.

THE ACTOR: Senator, Miss Nash.

Kisses the Young Woman's hand, but it is The Senator's eyes into which The Actor looks.

THE SENATOR: We are simple people, Mr. Booth. Ella was reared here in the capital, but she was born, as I, in dairy farm country. Dare I say, like Mr. Lincoln? Her roots are simple, though her ways, I admit, are often far too mysterious for a simple boy like me to understand. Just as I never fully understood her late mother. She favors her, though Ella was truly christened by the baker, I fear. Has freckles. There's no question she has her mother's citied manner. Still, deep inside her, there's the pure majestic beauty of open country. And that will never change. Not for anyone, not even her. No, my Ella once dreamed of being a diva—an opera singer, you know. But it did not take her long to realize that was an unfit life for a senator's daughter. There is a certain duty, would you agree, that is attendant to every man—or woman—according to his or her station? Things within or without their realm of ability or pursuit. Limits, man. There must be limits. And where the physical stops, it is the duty of the moral to begin.

THE ACTOR: I still do not believe—

THE SENATOR: Now me, I'm no member of the breast fleet. My chest would be sorely bruised with the penitent confession of all my sins, and any priest would shortly be hard-pressed to hear them. Though, I've always thought that this country needed a great cathedral. If we could only build and support it outside of any traces of popery. But, even the Anglicans are not devoid of such seductions. *(looking to Ella)* I should be careful. My late and beautiful wife was a devout Catholic and, true to form, Ella often scolds that I am not more reverent in my observances.

YOUNG WOMAN (seemingly unaware of her father's latest digressions): Do you play at whist, Mr. Booth? Whitechapel fashion, with the aces and kings first? Oh, but you would know that. It is rather a tradition in our house that close friends should stay on after the rest of the party leaves and

143

play rubbers until dawn. Or are you afraid to be lurched?

THE ACTOR: I am afraid, Miss Nash, I do not play at all.

YOUNG WOMAN: Good! Then it is arranged. Neither do I! *(beaming with a conspiratorial smile)* I find gaming at cards so very tedious. Really pointless. *(pauses)* Except Scopa; it is Italian. I do so wish to learn it. *(turns to him)* Of course, then you will go with us to mass in the morning and stay on for dinner. Do you prefer eggs or rolls—in the European style—for your breakfast?

THE ACTOR: I beg your pardon?

THE SENATOR: I'm sure Mr. Booth will enjoy whatever you set out for him, my dear. *(he grins with one arm about his daughter)* Isn't that right Mr. Booth?

THE ACTOR *(forcing with a not unsteadied purpose):* I— I believe it is.

***

Not Elizabeth, not Etta, nor Effie, nor Emma. It was Ella. Ella and only Ella. It wasn't immediate. Not for me. Although she may tell you differently. Then there were those things that began to quickly add up, amounting to—I know no better name for it—love. Slowly, the graceful shape of her hands and fingers, her tiny waist, the piercingly holy smile and eyes, candid posture, honest gait, delicate ears, mysterious lips and, Oh, the haunting diminution of her princess feet, became indispensable.

There are those actors who are said to step into a part, whose personality and disposition are perfectly suited to the role. This was how Ella seemed for me. What I had longed for, desired unknowingly and strangely lacked, while ever so certain I had all.

Oh! anything, of nothing, first create!
Oh! heavy lightness, serious vanity,
Misshapen chaos of well-seeming forms!

From the time it had been decided I made myself sure. Sure that she and I belonged. Sure of the way our arms wrapped so easily about each other, sure of the reckless precision of a sleep-breaking kiss. Sure that I would always be sure.

It was as if I might abandon her at any moment for any unreasoned whim, yet know that she would ever wait or find our way once more. Or, if I could fall again—and I cannot imagine how—still, I would rather not, but prefer to live my life alone in the memory of the love I once held for her.

I miss her strange, graceful almost flawless body. Her thin ribs and naked shoulders silently beckoning to me from beneath her gowns, that our legs should be entangled with unbearable heat, even in our sleep. The breasts and woman's hips that forever breathed a yielding promise, if only I might fulfill my part of the dream before they were returned to rough stone by the curse of some midnight sorcery.

And now it is her mouth that I am missing. The soft, full shape of it. The curve of its questions, the steady smile of its understanding. Her perfect teeth, the constant blush of chin and cheek.

If she will remember my hands or ears, the profile my *carte-de-visite* whispers only, I must say it is her neck, her throat, her voice, which haunt my silent darkness. The suppliant cries of the children we had dreamed to life, lost to wander stygian depths.

And what of all will I last forget? Of every virtue, grace, refinement? The Florentine mole behind her right ear.

The greatest joy, I cannot express to you properly, having once awakened next to her to find her wrapped within my arms, smiling absently in her sleep. To rouse her with a kiss to which she just as automatically responded with parted mouth and increased caress, then to fall asleep again. And only sleep, I must stress here, only sleep. Yet what could ever have been more satisfying, I cannot imagine.

And I have heard it said, though miscreant I might have been, I should never pluck the flower from any maiden. I may tell you now, or you could find it difficult to imagine, that I had never faced that choice.

What brand of woman would you think might seek an actor's parlor after curtain's wringing, the muse's portal at the instant of the wagon's loading or unloading. Only one who had yet attended the Bacchic rites, was already fallen lame. No, I had never met a single maiden at my dressing room door save one, and that time my heart gave to me no choice, but love. And I will cherish her a thousand years, although her love was false.

Thou art woman! That's another name for falsehood, treason, perjury, and hell!

Yet I have plunged into the bowels, either to resurrect my own integrity, or to have the villain slayer of it suffer with me.

An honest tale speeds best being plainly told. . . . My conscience hath a thousand several tongues, and every tongue brings in a several tale, and every of those tales condemns me for a villain.

Lest I am the relenting fool, while she the shallow, changing woman. Still,

I have set my life upon a cast, and I will stand the hazard of the die.

There were little things I might have noticed at any time, and did not. Indications of her waning, failing love. Messages she delivered whither knowingly or of an instinct, which spoke one half of her mind against the other, warned her good sense to resist her impulse, even if that impulse was purest love.

Where was I when these notices were posted? If you had asked me, simple months before the eventual realizations, of my strongest asset, I would not have named my eyes, my hands, nor any other likely part. My answer would have been only my intuition. It was this that celebrated my performances, this that reckoned my unschooled talents so formidable. This, too, that abandoned me, or was abandoned, when most needed.

Strophe

I had surely slept as she had questioned our belonging. Dreamed fantasies of comfort and assurance while she spun tales of caution. One night she would risk all to sleep in my arms, the next she craved some solitude for fear or fever. One day she loved the things of me for which the next found fault, the difference having been previously termed unique.

SHE: I love the man that cannot be sequestered, pinched or pulled along with the rest, only because the rest would not be lonely or alone. I love you.

Then, later,

SHE (cont'd): Oh! you are a fool! A weak dispassionate fool! The depth of her eyes seemed veiled by some shallow, yet unyielding curtain.

SHE (cont'd): How could I have ever given my love to one such as you? Is there nothing outside of a role to which you are willing to commit your courage?

HE (feebly and full-knowing it): I am committed to you.

SHE: Not really. Not with your soul, not nearly. Maybe not even with the heart you claim is mine. Oh, your declarations are pretty enough, but where is the fire, the purity? Where is the man with whom I fell in love?

Where indeed? He was not here, listening to her fool's tongue rebuking me for situations and circumstances over which I had no power. Certainly there were many areas wherein I had failed, shown no resolve, no courage. Of this I was aware, and told as much to her, my mirror, my confessor—as they happened, always as they happened. And did she use those same inadequacies to question my merits and the merits of my love? If she had not before enjoyed my soul, then she would dine upon it as it was offered up in some Phineal feast.

But who will mourn me at my death, if not she?

Who will sing the praises of my work, recollect my name or kisses like no other in the middle of a dreaming night, if not she?

Who else will understand my claims to passions unrehearsed, tantrums unrestrained and feelings scarcely understood? If not she, no one.

She was with me there when first I cried as a man and last wept as a boy. Her tears I shared as her lover while my dreams she became, as my love.

There will be no other—no first, nor last, nor any more, to hear or feel or speak softly again to me, and fear not my occasional symptoms and sympathies—if not she.

It is difficult to think I did not deserve her, more still that I could not confide as much to her when she fully gave me warrant to do so. I loved, yet feared. Could not abandon old troubles to new joys, which surely otherwise would have surpassed all.

I am a soul tormented, and those eyes of hers yet pierce the fiery armor doubly wrought, once by fate's own fiendish claws and then by my own poor hands that chose rather to submit to omen's disaster than freely struggle with defiant strength. And when she begged to make me strong and perfect, I laughed at the one, scorned the other as illusion.

Yet it was no dream.

It was her gift that I took so for granted. I forsook the courtesy to thank my god and praised instead the weary mirrors of the stars. For I would forsake on the moment and exchange my god for hers. Reconcile the irreconcilable acts, reversing only my outlook, not a single expression of my new or old religion.

If a heart must needs have been broken, am I foolish to say I am glad it was mine? She was so fragile, so giving, so loving, so sure. Was I even cruel to have loved her from the start? Where was the wisdom of my years and experience, or was I merely selfish to ignore the obvious signs of what could never truly be? Still, I think I loved her best I could, if never wholly, never holy, never enough.

***

Time. Place.

A theater backstage. A narrow corridor ending in what appear to be stacks of set fragments. High, black curtains, moving in a waving motion as with a constant wind, form one wall. The other is a row of doors interrupted by a single, low-turned sconce. Inside a dressing room, THE ACTOR begins to peel off a costume and sees a fresh bouquet of a dozen white roses. He looks for a card. There is none. A knock on the door. He opens it to an extended thirteenth, long-stemmed and very red rose. It is held out to him by the YOUNG WOMAN. She wears a lace-trimmed, wine-colored taffeta gown and has a seductive if playful smile upon her face.

THE ACTOR: They are very beautiful. *(the Young Woman smiles wider)* I cannot accept them.

YOUNG WOMAN *(still smiling):* Why not? What do you mean?

THE ACTOR: Exactly as I said. I cannot—

YOUNG WOMAN *(interrupting with a serious frown):* Is it not acceptable for a woman to give flowers to an appreciated player after his performance?

THE ACTOR: Of course. I just thought—

YOUNG WOMAN *(interrupting again):* That they meant something more?

THE ACTOR: Frankly, yes. *(pointedly)* And it is somewhat unusual for a lady of any age to visit an actor in his dressing room.

YOUNG WOMAN: Well, they do not. Thank you, again. *(hands the red rose to him insistently)* You were quite—charming.

The Actor takes the flower dumbly. The Young Woman smiles again, shrugs and leaves.

***

I ask myself why we ever met. Did we belong together? Were we somehow destined? Or was it simply so that I could meet my fate by insisting another man meet his?

If it were that we belonged—she and I—then why? What did we inspire in each other—love? What good did I ever bring out in her, or to her? I will assume that the brink over which she took me was for the best. This must be the assumption. But then how so for her? What was the reason, the purpose of her meeting me? I would like to think it was for love. To know the pleasures, questions, reminders, even sorrows of its face. But it is not enough.

***

Time. Place.

THE ACTOR's dressing room. The door is open. He dons make-up in front of a small but adequate mirror. The YOUNG WOMAN paces between him and the door. She wears an emerald-green gown not unlike that of the previous scene for its style and richness. The Actor seems almost at ease with her presence. There is a small bunch of pink tea roses on the dressing table to one side of him and a chess table set to play in one corner.

YOUNG WOMAN *(picking up one of the white chess pieces)*: Father will not let me play at chess. He says its strategies and intrigues are neither feminine nor modest. But I do, at every chanced opportunity, and I wonder to which member of the species it could be better suited *(putting the piece back down in a different position, turning)*. My father is rather taken with your brother, Mr. Wilkes.

THE ACTOR: Yes, and always has been. He is not alone.

YOUNG WOMAN *(smiling)*: He would be if I were the only other person in this city. *(with a sense of boredom)* And sometimes I feel like it is just the two of us.

THE ACTOR: My brother is one of those men who moves with equal ease among both men and women. An affair such as you hosted the other night is completely natural to him. I envy his ability to be so familiar with strangers.

YOUNG WOMAN: And I find it tiring. The reason I prefer a man like you. One need not question your sincerity.

THE ACTOR: Don't misconstrue. There's enough Booth in me to lend more than a fair share of ruthlessness.

YOUNG WOMAN: Is that a warning?

THE ACTOR *(humorously)*: Perhaps a challenge?

The Young Woman beams.

YOUNG WOMAN: You have plans this Wednesday?

THE ACTOR: No. I have taken the week off. Why?

YOUNG WOMAN: Then there is no reason why you cannot accompany me to church.

THE ACTOR: I suppose not. Wednesday?

YOUNG WOMAN *(starting to leave)*: Wonderful! *(turns)* It is the feast of the Epiphany. You know what Epiphany is, I presume?

THE ACTOR *(aside)*: The Festival of Fools?

YOUNG WOMAN *(startled)*: What?

THE ACTOR: Nothing. Of course I do. My mother was a Catholic. Although she forsook her faith to marry my father. He had been married before—and was still married to a first wife when they met, and continued to be until the last of us was born. In fact my parents did not marry until my thirteenth birthday. The very day! *(responding to the Young Woman's apparent concern)* I am not going to try to justify it, but I find it somewhat romantic. *(the Young Woman forces a confused smile)* Or, do you not believe in love—and passion?

YOUNG WOMAN *(visibly affected):* Of course. Very much so. But then, you were not baptized?

THE ACTOR: As a matter of fact, I was. Of all my mother's children only Edwin and I were—a fact our sister Asia uses to tease and taunt. Something about the midwife having once been a Sister of Mercy. Does that redeem me?

YOUNG WOMAN: Only in God's eyes, Mr. Wilkes. For me—you will still have to take me to mass Wednesday morning. *(turns again to leave)* I believe the expression is break a leg!

They smile at each other, she winks, exits.

***

Wednesday, January 6, 1864. The east end of Capital City.
Feast of the Epiphany. A light, half-frozen rain falls in the early morning. Some CARRIAGES and umbrella'd PEDESTRIANS approach a street corner where a small, steepled church stands firmly to the weather. Whitewashed wood outside, three sections of simple wooden pews inside. A few medium-sized stained-glass windows filter in beams of gray-clouded light. While a PRIEST performs the Eucharistic offering, the YOUNG WOMAN and THE ACTOR—she in a high, veiled fur cap and collared coat, he in a dark gray-striped suit and overcoat—kneel beside each other. She unwraps her hands long enough to entwine one of her arms through his before again folding them in prayer.

***

Mid-morning, same day. The rain has stopped. Still dressed in their church finery the YOUNG WOMAN, veil pulled up over her stylish hat, leads THE ACTOR through the Congressional

Graveyard to the crypt of her mother. As the rain begins again she offers to share her umbrella. He declines politely with a gesture to say his hat will suffice. Not to be outdone, she folds the umbrella and continues alongside him in the increasingly steady downpour. They laugh at each other.

THE ACTOR *(openly):* That is the third time in less than two weeks that I have been to church.

YOUNG WOMAN: And?

THE ACTOR: Nothing really. It is just that I can hardly believe it. *(laughing nervously)* I have not prayed this regularly in my entire life.

YOUNG WOMAN *(solemnly):* This is a very holy time of year.

THE ACTOR *(boldly):* I have no money, Miss Nash.

YOUNG WOMAN: What do I care?

THE ACTOR: I am sure I do not know. It is widely reported that I am very successful. I play all season, it is true. But I have no real means.

YOUNG WOMAN: Then what do you do with your earnings?

The Actor hesitates, looks away.

YOUNG WOMAN: No matter. I have enough money for all five of us.

THE ACTOR: Us? *(pauses, smiles)* Five?

YOUNG WOMAN: I would never leave my father. He must be a part of my household, whatever happens. And I will have twins, Mr. Wilkes. Nothing else will do.

***

It was at that moment that I can truly say I knew first of our fast but certain love. And when I say I miss that day I wonder if you will understand. I wish it had lasted forever, was lasting still, still with its cold wet winds and cloudy skies. I remember them as warm breaths, kissing breezes, gentler whisperings.

Was I so naïve to think it could be ever so—that I might retrieve and, with her help and guiding influence, perpetuate the time whose purity I had long abandoned for my ancient fear and doubt? I bless the day we met, curse the hour I fell in love.

We walked under spreading willows past the puddling, stone-marked and mounded rows. In two corners, I was introduced to her mother and, just to the side of a central crypt, three generations of her father's forebears.

***

Seeking shelter from a sudden downpour in the short eaves of a large monument inscribed "NASH" and with separate inscriptions below.

YOUNG WOMAN: My uncle told me you very nearly saved his life.

THE ACTOR: Your uncle?

YOUNG WOMAN: August last. Major Badeau?

THE ACTOR: I did not know the major was your uncle.

YOUNG WOMAN: My mother's half-brother.

THE ACTOR: It is because of his invitation we met. Why was he not at your house New Year's day?

YOUNG WOMAN: His place is no longer with the family. He is forever with his drunken commander, the general—General Grant, not Gillmore. I believe he was still with Gillmore last summer. Or was it Sherman? No, that has been some time, I believe. But how can I be sure? The war moves on, and whole alignments and loyalties with it. So my father says. Just so, Uncle Adam's present appointment has not yet been confirmed, but Grant has promised him the rank of lieutenant colonel on his staff. Of course, it may simply be the cigars and whisky talking.

THE ACTOR: May a man not be taken upon his word?

YOUNG WOMAN: What would I know of such things?

Father says you are sympathetic with the South. That cannot be true. A rebel would not have tended to my uncle.

THE ACTOR: Patriotism is not rebellion.

YOUNG WOMAN: A true patriot would love the North.

THE ACTOR: I believe a true patriot would see no North or South. Perhaps one day I could make you understand.

The Young Woman reflects for a moment, enters the crypt through an unlocked iron gate. Inside she kneels aside one of four marble tombs. Following her in, The Actor kneels beside her.

YOUNG WOMAN *(quietly after a time):* I wish you could have known my mother. She was very beautiful. Now you are as close to her as ever I can be again. *(thoughtfully, rising toward the gate)* When is your birthday?

THE ACTOR *(after her):* May. The tenth. Why?

YOUNG WOMAN *(mysteriously):* It's too bad it could not be four days later. Mine is next month. Valentine's Day.

THE ACTOR: That does not surprise me.

YOUNG WOMAN: It can be a horrible day for a birthday. Everyone gets presents, not just you. And I only ever get birthday greetings. Always birthday greetings. Just once I would like to receive a Valentine. To be asked to be someone's Valentine.

THE ACTOR: I find it difficult to believe that you never received one. Is that true?

YOUNG WOMAN: Of course, I am not the only one with a holiday for a birthday. My entire family, for example. My father's—but you know—is New Year's. My mother's was—this day. *(reading the inscription on the tomb)* Truth, honor, integrity.

The Actor looks at her searchingly.

YOUNG WOMAN *(cont'd):* Do you know the works of Machiavelli?

THE ACTOR: I know his name.

YOUNG WOMAN (with a schoolgirl's snobbery and perfect, if exaggerated accent): Not *Il Principe*, no, no; too much politics! *Il Mandragola*. This is where my mother found my name. Camilla, the beautiful heroine sought by all the handsome young men. *(posing distractedly)* Have you yet wondered what it would be like to kiss, Mr. Wilkes? If we were to kiss?

THE ACTOR: I have had little else on my mind since we met.

YOUNG WOMAN: And?

THE ACTOR: And I think we would be more than *[beat]* satisfied.

YOUNG WOMAN: That is a funny word for a kiss.

THE ACTOR: Kisses can be funny things.

YOUNG WOMAN: I hope your kisses wouldn't make me laugh.

THE ACTOR: Oh?

She turns to walk in the other direction.

YOUNG WOMAN: One day our children may be buried here.

THE ACTOR: And this is a funny speech for one who only talks of kissing.

***

She calmly slipped one shoulder, then another, of her now-soaked gown aside. Her fingers found their way along my lips and be-drizzled moustache while she rested her elbows between my arms and chest. Her eyes seemed locked with my own.

I wanted to kiss her but I could not. I was not sure at the time why. I am not sure still. How could I? She was so pure. So perfect. So unlike any of the women I had ever kissed before. She looked at me with the same confused understanding I felt inside.

And when I left her that day it was in my usual place of solace where I found my contentment. I knew well my nature then. Well enough not to allow a mote of it to intrude upon hers. That night I slept in the house of bolstered sateens and colored lampshades next to an empty bottle and another nameless woman.

Intermezzo
The Deed

The stage lights shone something amber upon an attentive house. A chandelier of fragile crystal hung suspended over the audience, supported by a cord whose bindings I controlled. This moment the counterweights held perfectly; the next, only I could say. The balance was mine. Not the idea, but its adequacy or lack. At any moment, I might decide, until the final line: "You sockdologizing old mantrap!"

My proclamation, the report of my pistol, my leap—my final exit.

Act III

The Mark of the Man

A REMARKABLE LECTURE!
JOHN H. SURRATT TELLS HIS STORY

A Vivid Narrative – History of the Abduction Plot – Surratt's Experiences with J. Wilkes Booth – Booth Hints at the Murder of Lincoln – The Other Conspirators Threaten to Withdraw – The Assassination – Surratt's Escape to Canada – He Implicates Weichmann in the Abduction Plot – He Denounces Weichmann, Judge Fisher, and Edwin M. Stanton – "John Harrison" – Surratt and the Confederate Government – Why Surratt Did Not Come to the Aid of His Mother

Evening Star, *Washington, D.C., December 7, 1870*

Scene I

Once I was pure as the snow—but I fell:
Fell, like the snowflakes, from heaven—to hell;
Fell, to be tramped as the filth of the street;
Fell, to be scoffed, to be spit on, and beat.

After two days, I decided what could be done in New York and Baltimore was done, at least for the time. The memory of that first visit with Edwin continued to occupy the better part of my thoughts, but I was not wholly convinced as to why. Something in our conversation that night continued to plague my recollection of the evening, but it would not make itself altogether clear.

Before leaving I stopped into a small walk-up photography studio near Tompkins Square and, feeling the excess of the monies given me by my brother, had my picture taken under the name of Jack Harvey. I specified the type of mounting desired and promised to return for delivery on Monday. But I doubted the photographer would be at all surprised when I did not return, despite my having already settled the account. He had eyed me suspiciously the entire time, as there could be no apparent reason for one such as I desiring a photograph. Only then could I be confirmed in my complete transformation. Not merely by matter of my disguise, but the masking years as well.

All the way to the rail station from my hotel the city seemed not more familiar for the past two days but stranger still, as the sounds of a Saturday *hazcarah* being performed in the Synagogue Shearith Israel rang in my ears.

This time my route was more direct and overwrought by the enormity of my task, I found the very climate of my surroundings now changed, it seemed, accordingly. Spending most of my time aboard the train in that kind of strange, half-sleep that attends not fatigue but utter desolation, I have only two incidents to report from the entire journey. Both took place within twenty-four hours of my departure.

The first of these incidents began in Philadelphia's Broad Street Station where the train arrived just after six-thirty in the evening. As I shook off my depression and rose to take some air, I noticed three white feathers on the floor of my passenger compartment. One of them was stained, the other two the purest white. It was an omen, I knew at once. But an omen of what?

Stepping onto the landing I at once remarked a kind of skirmish across the yard among the campfires of the dissolute. "Violence and bedlam!" someone shouted, and I quickly turned my collar up with a shiver and began in the opposite direction, sensing the indictment had been directed at me.

This may not seem like much, and of itself was not, as before long I found myself completely distracted by the stately environs of Independence Square. In the distance the Camden Ferry sounded along the Schuylkill and Delaware Rivers and I was pleasantly remembering my engagements at Wheatley's—where I made my professional debut for a single night the summer of my seventeenth year, playing Richmond in *Richard III* and returning the next year as a contract player for the entire season at Mrs. Drew's Arch Street Theater and the Walnut Street.

***

Time. Philadelphia.

The YOUNG WOMAN and THE ACTOR exit the stage door of the Walnut Street Theater.
"Take me for a stroll," she said shyly, "We can turn here on Sansom, may we not, and walk to Chestnut Street past Independence Hall? I would so like to see the birthplace of our nation. The government we were meant to have," she added as she took his arm. "You know, Mr. Wilkes, you are very beautiful. All the women say so. Not just the young ones like myself. All the women—even the ones whose positions

and marriages beg excuses for having said it."

They set out, but the Actor does not for an instant accept her ruse and uncharacteristic interest in matters either political or historic, lest she should have begged him take her to rather than past her alleged destination. But what was past it? Sansom Street, famous in all Philadelphia for its many diamond merchants, and known to all as Jewelers Row. Her flattery, on the other hand, was a different matter.

***

"Ledger?" asked the young churl who suddenly presented himself and his late-night editions in my path.

"Press?" asked another, one arm curled around a stack of newspapers, the other now poised around his companion.

"Perhaps the gent prefers the *North American?"* chimed a third from where he appeared out of the darkness. "It's the choice of the well-to-do, eh, Captain?" he winked at his friends as he turned to me.

"I haven't any money," I offered, unsteady to their purpose, particularly this third, who carried no papers at all.

"We can't very well pick the pocket of a corpse, can we mates?" cackled the leader of the three with a quick movement of his face toward mine.

Then, with a skip backward toward the darkness and a wave of his arms, he whistled to his two fellows, who followed him away into the night. I wasted no time in leaving off myself, resolved, however, that I must only walk—yet not at too brisk a pace, lest I confess my patent fear.

All the way back to the station, despite the well-lit avenues and occasional passersby, I expected to see the trio again but thankfully did not. Instead I boarded without further difficulty my next leg on the North Central.

By the time we arrived in Harrisburg I had nearly forgotten the Philadelphia incident, or relegated it to dreams at the very least. The sky was stormy here with flashes of lightning every several seconds followed dutifully by loud and rumbling strikes of thunder. That is all by way of depicting the scene, not as frightening but certainly foreboding, haunting to the extent that what I now report I cannot swear for truth any more than what I have just told.

Harrisburg was a short stop, with no time for a viewing of the capital or its grounds, but I found myself again in need of exercise and not the least tired, despite the unreasonable hour. So I determined to walk the length of the train, first in one direction as far as the club car, then in the other all the way to the caboose. This type of coursing was forever discouraged, inviting, in fact, the very sort of incident I had nearly suffered in the City of Brotherly Love, but I was determined that I should not allow my petty imaginings to dissuade the least part of my greater purpose. Feeling already somewhat satisfied with my regimen and fearless resolve, I felt I could perhaps sleep true.

On my deliberate way back to my seat, I was met between cars by a couple of passengers walking in the opposite direction and forced to stop in that windowless, if drafty part of the train where two cars are coupled together and sided with canvas. The grating rhythm of the rods and the smell of burnt oil confirms your movement when underway—if confirmation was needed. We exchanged cursory nods as the two fellows excused themselves past me. The door behind me closed, yet I distinctly heard the one say to the other, "I was exactly here when the news was learned of the death of Wilkes Booth."

It was more than coincidence struck me then. For, unless I am no judge of age at all, neither of these men was more than four and twenty, yet spoke of an event that would have taken place perhaps a year before their birth. But that was that, and nothing more the rest of the day and the next. Nor did I see again my two momentary companions.

Arriving finally in Chicago, I booked a room under the name of Harvey, continuing what I had already begun. The hotel was just down the street from McVicker's, where I had played so very many times and almost expected now to see one of my former company members. What would I have said? How now might I have addressed my cousin James, father of Edwin's late wife?

Hand had arranged to meet me the following morning, and wired that he had found for me the perfect disguise: two more traveling companions, in his description, "Blacker z'an my backside." They would accompany us to Oklahoma before heading on for hopes of western homesteading.

I cannot exactly explain what drove me to the theater that night—the same impulse that had caused me to have my picture taken perhaps. Some restless, reckless courage wanting to be recognized, acknowledged. It was not as if *The Corsican Brothers* was my favorite play, even for as many times as I had, myself, played either or both of the famed Francci twins.

*****

Time. Place.

"What is truth?" she asked with the searching candor of those days before we seemingly exchanged roles to my seeking her plain advice for everything, and the thought of spring was the only comfort of winter. Halcyon times.

"I'm sure I don't know," I tossed with scarcely a reflection. My nonchalance perceived not for the dullness it was, but for a deeper knowing. She hesitated to extract full meaning from the dark mystery of my flippancy.

"And what is villainy?" she continued, as if the one thought led naturally to the other.

"Now, that is easier," I mused, wondering myself where we would be led, and hoping, as ever, it would be to a final

165

intrigue soluble only with a kiss.

"Villainy is a refusal to act upon one's instinct," I sounded. "One has an impulse to do a thing, and it is right. Or one chooses to do another for fear or confusion? That is villainy."

"I don't understand. Are all our impulses then worthy?"

"All," I replied.

Strophe

Now I am an atheist, and there is no God—no justice. No plan, either—only compromise or disappointment. Neither is it the work of a demon, this earth. It is random chance and opportunity.

It is those who care too much and those who care too little. Those who want and scheme and plot, and those who think only of this day and the next. Nor will I be associated with any less than willful madmen, full of fury, full of gesture.

This is not new for Wilkes. As his name implies, this has always been suggested and ordained. I shall not think myself too little of a man while I may act in any manner whatsoever. Only when a sudden fit of conscience tricks and traps me again into believing there is truth—or God or love.

Antistrophe

A momentary lapse of concentration. Relaxation and an amnesiac's view of life. There was nothing before—no reason, no event, no consequence. A glimpse of eternity.

If I believe in God, profess faith in the ultimate, desire a universal truth and order, how will he not acknowledge me? Indulge me for an instant? Restore the memory whose chest does not pump or fit or tire to take a single breath?

I must look elsewhere. There is an ordered truth, but I have been so long outside its sketched frontiers that it is no longer concerned with me. I am abandoned. I have chosen my own patterned events as I dream and deem they should be. And now there is no ease, no trust, no comfort in the path.

What was begun must be continued. If I have chosen my course over that of my god, then I must complete the circuit, navigate the waters as one who has from the outset begged his commission as captain and may not later plead promotion's pre-maturity.

***

Time. Place.

"Uncle Adam calls me Cara. It means *dear one*. My father and I met with Uncle Adam in Rome the year after my mother had died. I shall never forget our meeting there. He would have been my favorite uncle even if he had not been the only one.

"Oh dear, that is not entirely true. He has a brother, you see, but one whose sympathies have made him both strange and stranger to the family. I daresay you may be able to understand that yourself. I think he is a spy.

"As to Uncle Adam, he was already in Europe at the time, and we had arranged that we should meet in Rome at the Spanish Steps. I saw him first from where we sat, as he stood in the piazza below—imagine, amid the throng—and he saw me, too. He never once took his eyes off of me, leaping the stairs three and four at a time until he was at our side.

"He took me up, kissed me quickly on the lips, on both cheeks, and on the lips once more, the way my mother had done, and exclaimed with the deepest joy and sadness all at once, 'Oh Cara!! There is nothing in the world I would not do for you!'

"Then he held me to his chest and I felt as if I had been borne upon the wings of angels and lay suspended in both

167

time and place. I wanted that moment to last forever, and in a way it did. I still hold him as dear as any man I could ever know.

"I want to tell you something right off. I'm not quiet or shy at all. Poppie likes to think so, though—and I'd rather do nearly anything than hurt him. I'm all he's got since Mama died. He had her for everything. Fix his supper, darn his socks, choose his collar, cravat and pin. He would even ask her advice on how he should view a particular issue during a campaign or referendum.

"Now he wants to ask me. He can't, you know. He needs to think all the decisions are his. Of course, they aren't. I let someone else do the cooking and sewing but I tend to the rest. Still, he doesn't remember a single conversation. As far as he's concerned I never say a word. Too timid. Disinterested in civic affairs. It keeps him happy."

"And now, I feel it only fair I should tell you something—right off."

"Yes?"

"Yes—well, you see—I am not the sort of man women take lightly."

"Oh, I know," she smiled wickedly. "I have seen them look at you!"

"What I mean is—I am scarcely prepared to fall in love."

"Oh, I shouldn't imagine you are. And if I were to fall in love with you—would you be terribly, terribly merciless?"

"What? Oh no. Or should I have told you all this?"

"No, I suppose not," she said with apparent disappointment. "I would be. I am. Without mercy completely."

She answered my startled gaze with a smile and a coy shrug as she trained her eyes evenly ahead. We continued walking together in silence, but I chuckled to myself and then wondered the more at her pert beauty and the possible evil that suddenly seemed to rest precariously upon her gently turned upper lip.

I found myself thinking there were three basic reasons Ella and I were ill-suited, and told her so.

One, age—to which she quickly rebutted that matches were daily made between girls her age and men twice mine.

"That may be so in your society, but not in mine," I contested, "where true love is the principle reason for marriage."

Two, the fact my profession would surely have a detrimental effect on her—and her father, and family.

"Then give it up," was her off-handed reply. "Talkers are no good-doers," she quoted from my own repertoire. "Go into some sort of business."

"I may have to," I admitted. "I am rapidly losing my voice."

I choked accidentally, if on cue.

"Then?"

"Three—and most importantly—we do not really belong together. Your society, as we have said, is very different from mine. It is evident. Look at your father. He knows. He can hardly wait for me to leave each time I have only arrived at your home."

She of course insisted that he liked me and was all the more adamant after my attempts to dissuade.

"Why, he nearly insisted that I host that horrible New Year's Eve party, and used your name to convince me, knowing how much I desired to meet you."

"I didn't know until that very day I even had an invitation."

"Nonsense. Poppie knew it the week before. Of course, he knows everything before it happens. Even Mama's death. He sensed it coming too. He had finally agreed to take her to Europe. Something she had long wished of him. She died on the last day of their visit. Very suddenly. He still hasn't gotten over it, or the fact that he very nearly wasn't able to give her the one thing she had ever truly desired of him. It is certainly why he spoils me as he does."

She paused.

"I have never been alone with a man before," she continued. "Oh, I have kissed a few. Most of them boys, really. Boys one day, dead the next any more. I guess this war has changed us all. But it is not the war, I think, that is changing me, Mr. Wilkes. It is you. Yes, I am quite sure, it is you."

Her eyes fixed deeply to mine.

Even before the melodious lyric of her voice took definite shape, the choirs of angels must have found harmonies in her breath.

It was the summer of 1858 when her father made good his promise to take her to Italy, a kind of posthumous bargain. It was a trip long-planned for the family, but with the passing of her mother the previous year it was much the assurance of a sacred memory. The senator had just won his third term, I was playing my first engagement in Richmond, and Boston Corbett was having his spiritual epiphany. Ella was barely 10 years old.

The trip across the ocean from all accounts had been uneventful if not uninspired. Young Ella dreamily weathered the occasionally restless seas singing renditions of *The Drunken Sailor*, with its choruses of "Hooray, and up! she rises." The sturdier passengers gathered, laughing at the less fortunate objects of the be-petticoated little girl's play, who were confined to regularly pot-changed staterooms. There was no daunting Ella's spirit, or the dreams and devotions she aimed dutifully to fulfil for her late mother's soul.

"If I pray hard enough," she reported herself saying to her father, "Mother's soul will be present when I kiss the hand of the Pope."

"Now, sweetheart, I told you, our audience is not guaranteed, and even so there will be hundreds of others to see him at the same time. There is no guarantee that we will be close enough to catch more than a glimpse of his robes, much less gain the touch of his hand."

"You are a United States senator. And I am a senator's daughter."

"Darling, Rome is in Italy, a different country altogether. That is why we must spend these weeks crossing the ocean. I have no authority in Rome. Less in the Vatican City."

"Then I will pray even harder. And if the Pope will not do it because my father is a senator, then he will do it because my mother was a saint. Surely he will respect that authority, even in his city."

I never asked her to explain her conviction, whether the product of her own invention or something she repeated after her father, uncle or another. But I was as sure then as I am now that her mother's canon and celestial nature is certified in her own.

"I thought Rome was in Italy," she said to her father that first afternoon.

"And so it is, my darling."

"Does this staircase lead to Spain?"

"No, dear," she said he chuckled.

"And why is nobody here speaking Spanish?"

"Those two gentlemen there," he pointed. "What is that? It most certainly is not Italian."

"It is Portuguese, Father. The funny lisping language of the sailors on our boat. It is not real Spanish, but only the kind of Spanish spoken by pirates and Moors and explorers."

"Maybe these steps were stolen at sea by those two pirates posing as gentlemen," was his playful suggestion. "Perhaps it is our duty to report them to our embassy."

"Shall we report them to the United States Embassy or the embassy of Italy? Or of Spain?"

How serious she must have found the matter that her father had to promise she might, at least, report the incident to the Holy Father.

And when she was admitted into St. Peter's court, and her father's persistence and her unfailing eyes found their way to the purple cordons, it was just in time to face the mitred robes. Having never been to the Vatican City, I am not sure I can do the scene even the cursory justice I feel—as a non-practitioner—its due. But perhaps you may imagine of your own the custom, the ceremony, the censered calm.

Nor am I in unpleasant company to have been the object of that same gaze that cast its early spell on the least corrupted flesh then made man. To hear her father explain it, as he did one afternoon almost unaware of my presence again, the sounds and forms of the multitude were suddenly vanished. All that remained was Ella's bewitching gaze and the extended hand of the pontiff.

As her face was held in the cushion of the Holy Father's blessed palm, her father swore he heard, in steady English as the Pope made the sign of the cross, a pleasure expressed at meeting the daughter of a true saint, affirmation her mother's soul was indeed at peace, and that Ella's girlhood prayers could now be saved for *the gypsies of the world.*

***

It was no coincidence I had long romanticized myself, in my youth, a gypsy prince. But on first encounter Ella recognized me for the truth of it, told me in so many words. She was kind, but I understood her meaning. I was a nomad, yes, but not of royal blood. Merely some scurvy pirate balanced between mutiny and shipwreck, marooning and the plank. What I had held as an alpine homeland was only a temporary perch upon some splitting mizzen.

Meanwhile, spring 1865 had not yet raised her head with the uplifting year. The naked limbs and knuckles of acacia were still wintry as they scratched at an overcast sky. And below that gray and just above the charcoal earth, six hundred thousand homeless spirits could be felt ghosting their way between the seasons.

Whatever certainty had been theirs, whatever confusion presided, their verging situation echoed of a deeper promise. Sorrow would not be forgotten. No, nor pain. Yet there was comfort even in these, to sense so near the balance of time.

***

"I've heard you are an engaged man, Mr. Wilkes."

"Am I? If that is the case, it is the furthest thing from my mind at the moment—or perhaps not."

"I'm flattered, sir. Whatever the case."

173

I imagine I was too. Though I wasn't thinking of that. I was still wondering whether I could believe what she had said about her father. And if it was true, how he knew of my invitation and acceptance sooner than I.

Each time my visits tarried later. Evenings began to linger into morning, mouths and hands into their favorite echoes and companions.

"Do you, are you, will you—John?" she asked.

She did not have to complete her questions.

I kissed her one last time on the back veranda of the senator's home. Long, two-story shadows cast by the well-lit porch reached toward the carriage house. Only the occasional murmur of stabled horses broke the silence. All was still, deep, certain.

Scene II

Pleading,
      Cursing,
            Dreading to die,
Selling my soul to whomever would buy,
Dealing in shame for a morsel of bread,
Hating the living and fearing the dead.

Ella's familial home outside Washington City was built in that
Italianate style that had, of late, invaded our evolving national
version of Greek and Gothic architecture. With its round-
arched windows, broad bracketed eaves and campaniles, it
looked very much like a Mediterranean villa—even amidst
the signature Columbian acreage. My mother, sister, and her
family had been expecting me this same evening, but Ella had
insisted we dine with her father and his friends. I do not think
she wanted to meet my family.

I hitched Cola beneath a row of cypress and found myself
upon the porch with a thought to rest the moment in an
unexpected bentwood rocker before knocking the
announcement of my arrival. This was not pure anxiety, I
assured myself uncertainly. An afternoon sun beamed past
the several squared and splintering columns, striping the
veranda against the grain of its bleached ash planks. I waited,
watched and wondered, some misfit pawn on a squeezed and
angled chessboard, until Ella appeared from around one
corner of the porch.

"Where have you been?" she said with some enthusiasm.
"My father has been awaiting your arrival and speaking only
of how much he wishes to talk with you and compliment your
work."

Flattered, I was yet disappointed it was not her enthusiasm
that was expressed. She opened the door and led me into a

roomful of essayingly eager and affectedly apologetic strangers, as regular and seemingly mutable or malleable as the green Venetian blinds decorating every window.

The senator was just another of those many legislators who truly merit the name politician, people whose pearly smiles along with a deeply sensed gentility and concern clothed or masked the deeper desire to meet their own ends. They would make of any discussion or issue what served them best, then skilfully award the populace with an amended rhetoric of pabulum to quell any hunger for reform. Virtues of which they knew nothing wrung from blotted platitudes and stretched parchment. Milk-and-water oaths, biscuit promises. Nothing of the fierce truth and vigor that had so characterized the first federal Congress. Republicanism was a political entity, not an honorable tenet. Democracy was a platform, not an ideal.

"I am familiar with your namesake, Wilkes," said the senator.

"Thank you," I responded with polity only.

"A fine actor like yourself."

"A what?"

"Like yourself."

"No more than yourself," I said wryly. "A politician."

"I was told—"

"And so was I," glancing sidelong toward Ella. "Excuse us," I added, gathering my senses as Ella followed me numbly apologetic into the next room.

"You said he was interested in talking to me. He knows nothing of me."

Her eyes fell low.

"Worse, that will not stop him from inventing compliments."

"He only means—"

Angrily, I turned to walk away. The senator stood in the doorway.

"Forgive me, son. I don't know what I was thinking. Of

course, everyone knows of the great John Wilkes, Mayor of London—champion of political rights and Liberty."

"Everyone except the senator," I answered his freshly-briefed self. "Lord Mayor."

Turning my eyes again toward Ella, I bowed and slipped quietly out of the house.

***

Spring 1864. Washington City.

"They are tickets," she said. "To see opera."

It was my birthday.

"Tomorrow night."

She looked pleased, yet I could see the opera meant nothing to her. A night at the opera, despite some identification with her maternal Italian heritage, was tantamount to an evening of whist. And she could not know that I had rather sit myself at a smoke-filled table of gambling strangers than subject myself to a single aria. Indeed, there were many times I suspected she was with the wrong brother, after all. But that all changed and I will never hear a single note of one without her voice too in my ear.

Of course I agreed most heartily that it should be a rare treat for us both, summoning my most convincing smile. By this time she was too pleased with herself to mark my charade. All I could think about was how Edwin would pant at this opportunity to mingle again with the cultural elite, nod at all of the foreign innuendo with which he could fill his pride for understanding, and share the approbative attitude of his fellow devotees when some unknowing audience member—perhaps myself—displayed a show of approval—through simple applause—in the middle of an orchestral movement. *Quel horreur!*

Such *faux pas*, certainly, though scarcely more than the manner in which the uninitiated can be remarked or improved, are the signs and tokens by which artlessly stone-

177

deaf ruffians secure and fortify their arbitrary stations, which no amount of wealth could readily guarantee. Hence the ritualized participation, the cultured *bravi*. Woe to the practitioner of spontaneous enthusiasm.

Having once arrived at the theater she retrieved the tickets held under the name Cara, while I watched remarkably on. These were no mean orchestra seats she had purchased for the occasion, but had us placed into a private box, house left. How we spent the better part of the opera occupied, curtains drawn, I need not tell you. For while we listened to every note, my hands still ache from the absence of her form and her scent lingers yet upon my lips.

***

If I tell you now I feel you thinking of me, will you deny it? Will you refuse the knowledge you know we share, which I more than guess? I know your silence like I know your breath. I feel your thoughts upon the nape of my neck. Taste your sweet and steady pulse. We can have no secrets, hide no desires, exclude each other never. When I hear anything it is you. When it is your music, I become you. I allow myself to want you until my heart can stand no more.

It would be as to have, in some future moment of retrieved gentility, an offered *salade au ris*, yet not think of you.

***

Fall 1864. Washington City.

By mid 1864, I had rented a second floor room in the pleasantly stylish if simple house of a certain Mrs. Fisk. From my front window I could see all the way up and down Pennsylvania Avenue. If one could ascribe a certain charm to this capital city of the North, it would be for its resemblance to the more deliberate urban centers of the South. There is little of the makeshift aspect of Boston or Providence, which some yet find so pleasant but can only be considered truly haphazard.

Late one evening, lying in bed and admiring the reckless rhythm of the October rain, I almost thought to hear a loud, long whistle in the night. Moments later, three distinct and unmistakable raps upon my windowpane interrupted my reverie at regular intervals to draw me to the sash. Standing on the macadamized street below with a dark overcoat and slouch hat, I could barely make out the concentrated gleam in the eyes of an otherwise expressionless face. The stranger held a fresh handful of stones in the right hand, a single other poised in the left, but once my attention was certain, dashed straight across the road to the side of the boarding house.

There was a playfulness about the quick scuffling up the trellis and across the short eaves below my window before the moustachioed face appeared in the blanching moonlight. I recognized the eyes, their deep sparkle and beckoning warmth. They were Ella's.

She smiled mischievously and somewhat out of breath as I opened the window for her to enter. She tossed off her hat and threw open her topcoat to reveal only a clinging wet gossamer nightshirt before falling atop me onto the bed in a deep embrace.

"Why you little monkey!" I laughed, getting soaked myself.

"I'm an ape. Apes don't have tails. You're the monkey!" she corrected with a laugh. "When I was a little girl, my father used to complain about my tree-climbing. I thought he was afraid I would fall. Now I realize it was simply premonition."

She drew her face to mine.

"Have you never kissed a woman with a moustache?"

"Never."

"Choice or habit?"

"Lack of occasion, I imagine."

"Shall I take it off? It's only applied with spirit gum."

I caught her hand on its way to her lip.

"That could hurt, but if it gets very wet it may come off of its own," I whispered with half a kiss.

She played her hand inside mine and our others followed into the sport.

"Your hands," she said. "Your pale white hands. I will never forget your hands," she continued, placing them upon her neck. "I'll have to leave before full daylight."

Then, with a slightly serious smile, "You have more spirit gum here, of course? I'll need to re-affect my disguise to find my way back without trouble."

***

Time. Washington City.

The YOUNG WOMAN and THE ACTOR stroll along the streets of the capital city. A theater marquis advertises Charlotte Cushman.

"Perhaps I'll be an actress some day. Like Charlotte Cushman. A great actress. Our children too will be great actors."

"I do not think to let my children devote their lives to the theater. It is too ruinous.

"As for you, you are far too beautiful to spend your talents upon some playhouse boards. Actresses are rarely as beautiful in real life as they appear, dressed and made-up upon the stage. Of course, with your moustache, you are edging on your Miss Cushman's tradition—to play the man's roles. But no, a truly beautiful woman belongs in the circles of society where people may view and judge her close and personal, not as some superficial character at a distance."

Strophe

She had what I had ever lacked—true will. It is a strange admission from a man, yet I know it to be true. Her control over me came within the confrontation of her willful nature and my desire to be under it. What she willed I performed, thought at the time, I truly believed. I was exercising some new-found, long-desired and well-deserved power. I see now

I only fell prey again to my own inadequacy and another's ability to control me. The one great deed I performed I cannot even claim as mine.

Why I was so, and why my argument will find such strong opposition from you I am not sure. Or am I trying merely for some desperate, hollow vindication? Believe me, babies, I would prefer you found me heinous than cowardly, disagreed with me entirely than found no opinion to contest. I am old, spent and in need of clarity—if only with, and for myself.

***

Given my opinions of that day and the certainty of this, I would hope I might now prove the power of my claims to do what demands the private hours of a man's desire, regardless of perception. After all, what guarantee can anyone give of this chaotic life? We struggle vainly, comically for order, sense and reason. Or can we truly lay claim to any?

***

I took Ella with me to St. Louis—still do not know what pretense of a cousin in need of a visit she made to her father, but the two of us were off and into each other's arms. My engagement at DeBar's was scheduled to begin the fourth. I called off the first week of my performances and spent it all with her. We learned a lot of each other that week.

It was her voice and laughter that ever ensnared me. Womanly enough to promise all, passably childlike to deny knowledge of any. Either one, or sometimes both together, bursting, gurgling forth from the clear, cool, sloping spring of her throat.

She knew of my father's love for the East, embodied partly in his naming my one sister Asia, as much after the continent as the wife of Prometheus in Shelley's *Prometheus Unbound*. She knew too of my shared fascination for the same. One afternoon in answer to her regimen of questions I had rattled off my favorite color, number, cuisine, author, stageplay,

181

children's names, and named the children of my father in their order, twice including my own in that order after first being questioned for omitting it altogether. I explained of all the destinations in the world I fancied, the East was where I would most like to visit, stay, live. That day when she introduced *nabobs* and *seraglios* into the conversation, I fooled myself for an instant into thinking she might share a conventional point of view.

***

Sunday, January 10, 1864. Hotel room, St. Louis.

Evening. THE ACTOR sits almost uncomfortably upon the high-backed wooden chair in one corner of the room. The YOUNG WOMAN lounges languorously upon the room's double bed. She wears a rust-colored dress with a simple bow. Next to the bed an open door gives to the adjacent room.

YOUNG WOMAN *(giggling):* Do they really believe I am your niece?

THE ACTOR: I am sure I do not know.

YOUNG WOMAN *(with disarming candour):* What do you think of harems, Johnnie?

Her playful nose angles delicately as she hugs one of several satin-covered throw cushions upon the bed.

YOUNG WOMAN *(cont'd):* I mean, what do you think of a man having more than one wife—several, ten times ten, or twelve times twelve—any or all of whom may be called to serve him or be discarded at any time. That's how the sultans of the East do it. Of course the Koran only allows them four true wives. The rest are concubines. But it is all the same thing. I suppose I need only go to Oneida—except their usage is far too practical. I have no wish to be too practical.

THE ACTOR *(hoping to please as he rises to look out the*

182

window): I do not think I like the idea of discarding anyone.

YOUNG WOMAN: No, nor do I. I would never be so callous. I would do my best to please and love each one. I think there would always be something for all of them to do. Of course, I think a hundred would be far too many.

THE ACTOR *(turning to her with half a laugh):* What? You?

YOUNG WOMAN *(frankly):* Why yes. Did you think I was talking about you? Really! That would not be like you at all. *(cataloguing on her fingers)* I could have one husband with whom I might talk about anything—the stars, the several varieties of birds, God. *(smiling)* And one who would be my lover—that would be you. How dashing you might look in a fez. And one to support me and make me very, very rich, and one with whom I could attend parties and the theater *(smiling broader)*—that might be you, too.

He does not notice whether she is still smiling.

YOUNG WOMAN *(cont'd):* And one who might be a little of all those things. *(pouting deliberately)* But that's only five. What do they do with the other one-hundred thirty-nine or so? Though I like the idea of having that many, I just wouldn't know what to do with them all.

THE ACTOR: They give them to their friends.

YOUNG WOMAN: Oh, yes! *(exaggeratedly)* But, I have none. Besides, I don't know if I could really do that—share like that.

Crossing to the bed and sitting next to her.

THE ACTOR *(whispering):* I think I would rather be the one who could be just a little bit of everything.

YOUNG WOMAN: Oh no! *(bubbling as she pulls herself close to him)* You must be my lover—my one true lover. *(kissing him as only she could, then biting his chin)* At least, most of the time. *(she inhales flirtatiously, then blurts suddenly)* No! Do not close your eyes! You must leave them open. Look at me!

183

She smiles as they kiss again, wide-eyed.

YOUNG WOMAN *(cont'd):* Do you think it is still snowing outside?

***

I could not be hurt or angry. Her laugh was so playful, her skin so fragrant, complete. Her kiss—how should I stop to tell you more?

Scene III

Merciful God! have I fallen so low?

I only ever wanted to be an artist. And ever thought of myself as such. Never an actor, Always, and only, an artist. Almost only. Actually, my first ambition was simpler, wilder, romantic. I wished to be a gypsy—but I have told you this.

I was under the impression I had but a few requisites to achieve this early goal: turban my head with a colorful silk—easy enough, a dive into any of my father's traveling trunks would readily yield the transforming tissue; pierce one ear—it was nearly a family tradition as my father, again, had long sported a jeweled ring both on and off his performance tours (in point of fact, I would here resemble his Richard as much as any Magyar prince); tattoo my skin—whether sailing ship, anchor, mermaid, leviathan or serpent, I would finally settle for my hastily crooked initials upon my wrist, of which you shall doubtless hear more.

All this attended soon enough there was then but one aspect unaccomplished. This alone some practiced months away—oh, to play the violin like Ritter or Paganini, and so serenade the loveliest of dark-eyed camp-dancers and crystal soothers, or fair-haired, tower-damsels whose dreams rolled over their stone-walled sleep into pin-wheeled wagons to the strains of my lullaby of Hungary or the pizzicato, bumped and bowed Caprice 24. Of course, in time I would learn the arts of tarot and palmistry—astrology too, but for now I understood the need for lessoned learning.

St. Timothy Hall at Catonsville had a fine enough orchestra. And its string section not so crude that the addition of true genius might even elevate it to remarkable heights. Or so I imagined. And armed with this knowledge I approached Maestro Halivas, the academy's music teacher and conductor.

"We don't need another violin," he politely indicated, his bobbed black mane combed straight back off his narrow,

Serbian forehead, and barely a glance at my steel-gray, artillery-cadet uniform. "But we are about to lose our second cellist this spring. Perhaps I could get you an early start in third chair come autumn? The cello and violin are essentially one and the same instrument."

Of course nothing could be further from the truth. But how could I explain the difference to him? The total absence of romance. I needed only visualize toting this cumbersome viol about before coming to rest in a squatting, leg-spread and knee-clamped position—romantic for a harlot at best—to know this was not my idea of destiny.

So I was to become only an actor, as my father. And I imagine that an ability to succeed in one form of creative expression may well predilect another. As the stifled desire for the violin yielded to the one—or that one, to the current undertaking of this manuscript?

If I am completely honest with myself, I am not sure how I feel about it. About any of it. But who could be? I only know how I view my very subjective self, replete with motive and rationale. And even that, I imagine, is only a half-true observation. Shall I pretend more objectivity than I readily decline?

Still, if I had chosen a different course, or, softly, a different art, what forces might have driven me yet to fulfill what must be met as destiny?

***

I never listened well. How many memories of unfinished conclusions crowd the conversations of my past? A point begun by a friend or confidante ending in my own words. How frustrated I would have been to talk with me.

When first advised of my faults I thought of them as nothing, nor could think of them at all. Could not see them. She saw them. I did not. They were then faults only to her. Thereby hers not mine. I did not doubt what she saw, only how. Denied the weight with which she had endowed them.

An unseemly habit, an ill-chosen moment or word, the repetition of a particular phrase, the half-echo of another for emphasis—very theatrical. But for emphasis. As such, what did it matter? But it mattered to her.

Slowly I began to note those very habits in myself. Became aware how often, indeed, they were performed. That bothered me. They were not merely habits. They were habitude.

Worse was when I began to take note of them in others. Nor could I be as impartial or forgiving of theirs as I had been of my own. Could not manufacture rationale so readily for another as myself.

How horribly they stammered, repeated, imbued with quasi-drama. How crude were their manners, customs. How shallow their very thoughts. Yet were all those negative attributes in fact only mine—re-examined and redirected.

There is nothing like the feeling of making someone happy. Even at the risk of being made unhappy in return. To risk and offer all for the chance of applause.

I would do anything to make her happy. Still, what would be right? What would be so easy, so perfect for me that performing it for her would be the same as for myself? Sharing it. If only such a thing existed. I would do anything for her.

And so I began to change my patterns, even knowing it annoyed me more. Was it for her or myself? Were there truths in her accounts, enough to warrant change? Was she the first, even my sister notwithstanding, to truly see and judge me for the needed change? What could I know for certain? What at all?

Here I had been so confused, by her, by myself, by there not being nor never having been anyone else, that I made my mind to do all and none. Prepare the change, yet not proceed. Acknowledge the faults, yet not amend. Determine the method, yet defer the means. Until somehow there was certainty.

I looked for certainty. Hoped for it. Prayed for it. Waited

for it.

All I got was complication. Confusion. Compounding of my desperate state. My love, my career, my country too rocked and teetered and looked to wreck. What could I do? What would I not do—for her? What ever had I denied?

Or was I not already victorious? Won by the plain devil and dissembling looks. For would not Satan be a woman if that woman would deign to share her throne of evil?

Or was she just the liquid in a pliant spoon of appeasement?

***

Tuesday, January 12, 1864. St. Louis.
Evening. The dressing rooms of Ben DeBar's Theater. The walls of the room are hung with mirrors and tapestried with newspaper pages of theatrical reviews. She wears a pale green dress with yellow trim.

He dons make-up as Richard III and asks Ella, "So, what do you think of St. Louis?"

"What can I think? We spent the first two days in the hotel room."

He smiles, then changes humor—of a sudden.

"Where is it?"

He paces from one side of the dressing room to the other, searching and re-searching every corner, every drawer, shelf and trunk.

"Where is my hump?"

She sits in his chair, back to the make-up mirror, arms folded into her lap with the innocent anticipation of an expectant mother. Rising, she says, "In fact, my darling, there is something I must tell you. And now may be as good the time as any other."

Turning side-to-side to admire herself in his dressing mirror, she has his character's shoulder-hump pad stuffed under the bodice of her dress.

"What do you think?" she smiles.

He smiles too. A nervousness pits his desires against abilities and needs.

"I wish you would not look at me like that."

"What do you mean?" she says with her eyes alone.

"So, we are in love. We are lovers. Of a sort. What of it? What more could we be? Do you think the two of us could live out of a single trunk? It would most certainly not work."

Those same importunate eyes fill half with tears.

"And that would be only the beginning. You mean to ask if I think you would be beautiful while carrying our child? Fine. After the child was born? And then, the rest?

"What of your brother?" she murmured finally, chin thrust forward.

"What of him? Would you serve him up for comparison? I am not my brother. His wife Mary could not live with his wealth alone. And what is now to become of little Edwina?

"Is that the life you want? Do you not believe the stories I told of my own youth? The father I never knew?

"Well, here is something I never did tell. Never told anyone. Not even Edwin knows. My father never married my mother. Not really. He could not. He was already married. Had a wife and a son in England when he came to this country as part of a theatrical tour.

"And never went back.

"Now, I am not saying I would do the same, only wonder how many other wives and children he might have had. He certainly did not spend all his time at Tudor Hall with us. And what time there was he spent snoring in between bottles."

My own affliction weighed heavily upon me and I thought to tell her then or never.

"It doesn't have to be like that!" she cried. "You're different. And I'm different."

"Am I?"

I wanted to weep a little, too, just to look at her.

"You are," I agree. "That much I know. I am afraid that is all I know for certain. Except—"

I could not continue. Only held her where she lay stretched uncomfortably along the divan.

***

"What will you do?" she taunted. "What is an actor without his voice?"

My throat was not sore but my mouth was dry and my voice nearly absent now for the better part of a week. I had called off the first week of my performances in St. Louis to spend time with her, giving as excuse my weak voice. Apparently the actor inside me had not realized it was a ruse and convinced my body I was indeed sick. The same thing had happened to me when playing the truant as a boy, each and every time I made excuses of not feeling well—the every time my excuse became prophesy.

"Perhaps I shall become a great playwright," I said with a rasping grate.

"Ah yes, as your father? And who has heard—may I ask—of a single one of his plays?"

"I produced *Ugolino* myself at the Boston Museum two years ago. But of course, you are right. Still, I think I can make a go at it. I must."

"You cannot write."

I stepped to the dressing table where I kept a decanter of cognac. It was my acceptable diversion, the one I openly indulged when she was about. This time it was not as accepted.

"Or just pour yourself another drink and forget all," she chided. "I'll have one too." Then added, "You will surely never match your brother's career. No matter how many times you criticize his skill as too academic. For all of your passion, his academic skill appears to have outlived yours."

"Perhaps you are with the wrong brother," I croaked, numbly.

190

"Ah yes, there!" she scoffed. "To hear you speak now I would have been better off with your younger brother Joseph. As profoundly dull as would be the life of a surgeon's wife, yet would there be some stability. And whatever insecurities and doubts he may have about himself, he surely would not trust less such a love as mine."

Scene IV

And yet I was once like this beautiful snow!

Ella stayed with me through the end of the St. Louis run and left for home as I went on, first to Louisville, then Nashville, finally Cleveland—the three-theater chain of a certain and successful Mr. Wood.

One night near the end of the Cleveland engagement I was met by a pair of friends in the black walnut lobby of the Neill House, where I had been staying as I started out onto the stone veranda for some air. The theater manager, John A. Ellsler, and Thomas Y. Mears, a gambler and former prizefighter, were if nothing else a very theatrical pair. They invited me to a local saloon for drinks, and though I understood I might be the one to pay, I chose to go.

"I have been thinking about going into business," I suggested shortly after our arrival, their boisterous laughter yielding suddenly to quiet astonishment.

"The theater is our business!" bellowed the elder Ellsler.

"And a very fine business, indeed!" rang in a supportive Mears as their brandy glasses toasted again to the repetition of the word "Indeed."

They laughed.

"What kind of 'business' did you have in mind?" continued Ellsler, with a less belligerent, almost reflective tone.

"I don't know," I answered bluntly. "But I have heard of great advantages being made in the Pennsylvania oil fields. Perhaps there is a way toward fortune there."

"Oil?" spat Mears. "How changed our companion has become since he has been seen in the company of a certain senator's daughter," and being sure he had my eye. "Yes, Lutz has told me about her. Do not forget that her father is one of the most trusted members in the government of that man upon whom you have continually vowed vengeance."

"I care no longer for such matters. Let politicians concern

192

themselves with politics and soldiers fight wars. We must needs concern ourselves with our own wellbeing. You both know I have had recently to cancel several engagements because of the worsening condition of my voice, last year alone rescheduling a dozen-and–a-half performances. And it is only getting worse."

"Is that your excuse for last month's absences?" poked Mears with a laugh and a jibe toward Ellsler.

"That is my business. What I am talking about is something else altogether. I am losing my instrument."

"It is only temporary," assured Ellsler.

"Possibly," I stared directly at him, avoiding Mears altogether. "Nonetheless, how long can I continue with the demands our profession makes? How long can any of us?"

"Oil?" he replied as if he heard it for the first time, had no idea of my insinuation, or simply did not care. "Not much to it is there, Johnnie? Not for one who has so much of the power that your brother Edwin lacks. You have the fire of your father, the dash, the touch of strangeness. I mean that as a compliment."

"And that is the way I will take it."

Mears nodded, then gestured grandly. "We could do with something a bit more lively; something with a deal of drama."

"Then let us call our venture the Dramatic Oil Company," said Ellsler with a raised glass and unmistakable support.

And it seemed done.

***

1863. New York City.
THE ACTOR visits the home of his successful OLDER BROTHER, single father of a two-year-old daughter. Their MOTHER has been living there since the death of the brother's wife the previous February.

"Is it impossible for you to favor any choice I make?" shouts the young man.

"It is impossible for me to understand why my own flesh should constantly speak out against our nation and its duly elected government. It is scandalous. I very nearly have to disavow your very existence."

"Only tell them that I have inherited our father's madness."

"I do."

"Yes, I am most assured of it. But this has nothing to do with politics. It is business. I thought you would be pleased that I might not much longer taint the family's reputation in theatrical circles."

"Should I be? Yes, I suppose so. Still, forgive me, *brother*, but I do not trust your motives—or your associates. I have not been able to do so since you donned Confederate gray to journey to Harper's Ferry for the hanging of a great man."

"On that, anyway, we can agree. Brown was surely that. A lunatic, but a great man—and one of conviction. I have more respect for him and his methods than for the rest of your Union and its government combined. Still, it seems rather odd the rest of you could one day condemn his murderous ways and the next hold him up as if his actions deserved papal canonization."

"I am sure it is no less distressing than finding you are one day incarcerated for damning the Union and the next day released upon the word of an oath of allegiance—only to hear continued rumors of your incessant tirades and treasonous speeches, as well as drunken midnight recitals of *Bonnie Blue Flag*. Even to the point that you have reportedly threatened the president with death."

"I only said that I can see no more appropriate an end for a tyrant. If he is such, let it be so!"

He storms out, leaving mother, brother and niece alone in the room.

"Why can't my sons be brothers?" opines the soft-spoken woman.

194

"Why, indeed?" cants the brother glancing at his daughter. "I love my brother, yet I fear for him. He is so impulsive, so passionate, too passionate—on and off the stage. I do not trust the friends he has, the reasons for his sudden decision—and I shall do my best to bring him back into the arms and care of his family."

The mother smiles. Pleased with this declaration, she is yet obviously worried.

***

Time. Place.

"Business?" remarks the actor to his love. "'How, but well, Signior? How, but well?'"

They both laugh as they sit amid a large haystack in the amber light of a lantern hanging from a high rafter.

"There is time enough to speak of such things. Not now, not now. For now, let lips do what hands do, my love—and hands do as they will." He grins, takes her strongly into his arms. "Soon you will be the wealthiest woman in Washington, and the envy of all its society."

"I shouldn't care if we had no money at all and slept for eternity on the threshing floor of a tobacco shed, that we could be together," she returns with a fire reflected in her auburn hair. She plays at the small ringlets behind his ear, quoting Sheridan, "'Throughout the world—I'll fasten to thy fate, I'll perish with thee; I stand upon the brink of destiny, and see the deep descent that gapes beneath. Oh, since I cannot save thee from the gulf, from the steep verge I'll leap with thee along, cling to thy heart and grasp thee with my ruin!'" Then, adding softly in her own words, "I'll be yours forever. For a universe, and more!"

They kiss.

We had so very much in common, she and I. So proud, so different from them all. Yet always trying, still, to have such prescriptions as were theirs. A haunting quality, initiated in dreams, and found ever-after patrolling the nights and idling days, an amity not easily won, the less easily lost once it had conquered, fragility of spirit that seemed to contradict the strength of heart that showed itself always first.

If we had not been destined to love, we were yet made to dream of being lovers, and anguish and question and suffer some part of that love until some miracle, some simple effect, which neither of us could devise nor providentially produce of accident, should bring us together or force us apart. Still, we had neither power nor faith to understand, only weakness to accept, if quietly and with denial.

***

In February 1864, during an engagement at Wood's Theater in Cincinnati, the real threat to my career made itself once again manifest. I was scheduled to play the part of Richard in Colley Cibber's acting version of *Richard III* opposite Mrs. Chanrau's Lady Anne, but convinced Mr. Wood to allow us to mount *Othello* instead. For this I took not the lead but the lesser if considerably more savory role of Iago, due to the condition in my throat. It was at its worst, to date. I knew the reason for its aggravation—knew it was not the malingering suspected by some, still could not act on my insight. As well, I thought, am I not better suited to play the role of the consummate villain?

Mr. Shewell was pleased with his promoted exchange to the title role, yet Mrs. Chanrau's Desdemona seemed to suffer when trying to convince her king she would not indeed rather have been the bride of his first minister. Nonetheless, the show was a success, and the season rolled on. I, the wild, instinctive colt, continued to plunge headlong and heedless. For all the time I had scolded my Cola for just such a blunder down a shale-strewn slope, I was no wiser when they were my four feet that longed to stretch their sinew and comprehended no reasoned rhyme that they should not.

The next stop at that year's circuit was the St. Charles Theater in New Orleans. On the Friday of the second week there we did an afternoon benefit in which I played Shylock in *The Merchant of Venice*, and that night began as Petruchio in *Katherine and Petruchio*, an adaptation by David Garrick of *The Taming of the Shrew*. Halfway through the second act, Mrs. C. F. Walters, as Katherine, asked, "Who knows not where a wasp doth wear his sting?" I had no answer. Petruchio had a ready retort, but I had none. My voice was gone.

I passed the next three nights in my room, the rain tracing its familiar pattern on the thin hotel windows. Ella cared for me as she could, the performances cancelled through Tuesday. I cannot begin to explain how she did not know or come to know of my dependence, only that she did not. It was, I imagine, one more aspect of her gentle naïveté, one more indication that indeed we were not suited to each other. Not if I could carry on in my own little world as if she did not exist. And there was certainly no room for her in the world of my addiction. Oh, there was room for her in my life, yet truly not in my world.

I suppose if I had then been a smoker or a needle user, there would have been less chance, if any, to conceal my preference, even from her. Ingestion through the nose was relatively traceless, however, and she only once or twice questioned my habit of walking away into a hidden corner or other room for a moment before returning outwardly unchanged, if completely refreshed.

And did I not use her ignorance as insidious confirmation that I was yet alone? That, while we professed our love for each other time and again, we were strangers at the heart? How might I have supposed she should have noticed it galloping away with my soul, when I was myself too familiar, too expert with the ride?

Even with the change in my situation, the completeness I felt when with her, the total loss of the feeling of spiritual and emotional desolation, which those months before, had led me into my situation.

***

Time. Place.

The street. THE ACTOR and the YOUNG WOMAN walk along at half an arm's length. She wears a silk pelisse over a white watered-silk dress, short kid gloves and a broad-brimmed bonnet set with pearl flowers and velvet streamers tied to one side of her chin. Thin pink stockings disappear into narrow ivory shoes.

The crowd courses by, a parade of silks and satins, ribbons and tassels, parasols and canes, gaudy hooded and lined cloaks. The couple nod respectfully to those who pass. It is obvious they wish they could be closer.

YOUNG WOMAN (quietly, privately): I have missed you. I need to be in your arms.

A woman holding a parasol passes by, her nurse pushes a perambulator alongside her. She and the Young Woman exchange courteous nods.

YOUNG WOMAN (cont'd): Naked. Now.
THE ACTOR (coughing as he says facetiously): In my hotel room, with the windows wide open, a fire glowing brightly, rows of candles along the mantle and at the bedside?
YOUNG WOMAN (perfectly serious): Yes!

***

Time. The actor's apartments.

198

Evening. Candles lit upon the mantel. A freshly lit log burns in the fireplace. A red tinted oil lamp on a nightstand. The bed sheets are turned down and a single rose rests atop the foot of the bed. THE ACTOR sits in one corner of the room smoking a small cigar in calm anticipation. A knock at the door on the far side of the room.

THE ACTOR (choking): Isn't it open?

The latch turns and the door opens. The outside hallway is dark. The rustle of a crinoline petticoat as a female silhouette walks toward The Actor and the fire's glow. She is a PROSTITUTE.

PROSTITUTE (meaningfully): Is it?

Sidling up to him, pushes her dress against his legs, lifts it.

***

I never knew a woman could drive a horse as she. Not that there might not have been such an Hippolyte. Euripides' claim was plain to that effect, if only meant to humor. But I had never known her before, neither to my eyes nor ears.

And, while she spurred and whipped with that certain brutality to which alone a strange beast will answer, Cola needed only to feel me on his back to know my mind and obey. Still, there was a kindness in her way, and that same courtesy led her to hire, each time we rode, the half-blind and discouraged dapple gray, as if he were the only choice, though the stable was full, and its master willed her choose another.

"A horse more suitable to the grace and needs of a true lady, I should warrant."

Yet she and the gray held a dignity when bridled together that none could deny. And I fancied the beast even forgot his affliction, only pretending to stumble, of occasion, that none would suspect the vision her mounting restored. And so, when given circumstance to hire for myself, there was no choice which one I would have. If ill-fate would find me stumbling or caught, it would be on her horse and for her sake, and I would as soon be blinded myself as forget the vision of perfect form she had held those many mornings, as we drove our obliging friends into forgetting both cares and duties of the day.

***

"Do you remember the ride we took that night to the woods at the point?"

"It was only this past summer. The moon was extraordinary."

"You brought that flask of cognac, and I swore I could talk with the horses in a language only they and I understood—and you believed me."

"I did not!"

"You should have. I can."

"What?"

"It's true."

Scene V

Once I was fair as the beautiful snow,
With an eye like its crystals, a heart like its glow;
Once I was loved for my innocent grace,
Flattered and sought for the charm of my face.

That summer at Franklin, Pennsylvania, they called us the two Jacks—with all due deference to Samuel Hart. Harrison and Wilkes. Hector and Lancelot, and both of us tolling Ogiers. The brothers Edwin's cholera had ever prevented us from being. Poor Edwin. Too much red meat.

The crickets awakened the morning along with the carriage wheels as we rode out to the Franklin fields. The four of us mounted our newly purchased company horses just at the edge of one small field dominated by a silent derrick. It was already costing me quite a lot of money to become rich.

Ella did not wait for my help to the saddle, but shot me a look while Surratt guided Anna's right foot into her stirrup.

"This is the way we will get rich," he said. "And let them fight a war."

"If all you want to do is get rich, there are many easier ways," chirped Anna, "than the Dramatic Oil Company."

"This one allows me to wear the face of a gentleman," he replied stone-faced.

"To be a man of property?" asked Ella, high to her horn.

"We are men of property," I said.

He looked at me, then back at her with great intention.

"Exactly."

"And Ellsler, and his henchman Mears?" she questioned next.

"Ellsler is already a prosperous theater manager. Mears is retired—and was a successful prizefighter."

"I want more than that," I interrupted, spurring past them all.

Ella followed me straightaway. That was the last we saw of the others that day. Ella seemed relieved.

We crossed as deeply into the fields as the horses cared to go, each taking turns leading the way first north then east. The sun gained height. We spread our luncheon of stewed chicken with smeared case and cream upon a blanket made of our two bedrolls. The horses' hooves were silent as that first derrick now. Their panting promised mechanics to come.

"It will take a lot more than property to make Mr. John Harrison Surratt into a gentleman," she said as I leaned to kiss her. "I almost wonder if that could make him truly merciless."

She edged slyly. My kiss fell short. A host of cicada offered their applause, prompting me to try again. But here, instead, she kissed me. A quick first on the lips, a second on the right cheek, third on the left, and final fourth on the lips again.

Then she just looked at me and smiled for an instant.

"This is the way my mother's family always kisses."

***

August 1864. The same night. Place.

The YOUNG WOMAN reads the final page of a small manuscript while THE ACTOR hovers expectantly over her.

THE ACTOR: Of course, it is only a start, but what do you think? Will you like it when it is done?

YOUNG WOMAN: I don't know, Johnnie. I just don't. Of course, I like that I'm in it. *(coyly)* Although you fancy me much more—manipulative—than I am. *(she smiles)* Well, perhaps not very much, but more. Certainly more.

THE ACTOR: It is the story of great events. Great people. Of course, I had to put you in it. But it is not our story; it's about a world beyond this. Where adventure and glory and fame are possible. Always possible. That is why I have given it this name.

YOUNG WOMAN: Yes, the name. I don't understand it. *The*

Avenger?

Saturday, October 24, 1864. Corby's Hall, Montreal, Canada.

Evening. A cold, clear and windy night. THE ACTOR performs to a moderate house. Solo readings from The Merchant of Venice *(as Shylock, trial scene),* Julius Caesar *(as Mark Antony, forum scene),* Hamlet *(selections),* The Charge of the Light Brigade, *and* Remorse of the Fallen One *or* Beautiful Snow.

Much of the audience leaves before the end of the recital and only two or three PATRONS venture backstage to ask for an autographed carte-de-visite. *The last of these admirers leaves, and The Actor, alone, puzzles over his tired features in a large, ornately framed, but worn mirror.*

Another figure JACK appears at the door. The Actor speaks, but does not turn.

THE ACTOR: If it were not for this girl I could feel easy. Think of it, Jack, that at my time of life—just starting out, as it were—I should be in love.

The same night. The St. Lawrence Hotel, Montreal.

THE ACTOR and his companion JACK swagger up the stairs and down the hall to their rooms. They speak naturally as they stand at adjacent doors and fumble absently to fit their room keys into the locks. They have been drinking.

THE ACTOR: I can hardly bear to think of it. Once I could fill a theater within a moment's notice of my engagement. What can I do now? Not even keep those who attend, and impress few of those who politely stay throughout. Am I so old?

JACK: No, nor hopeless, John. This is the North. Why, it is more than North. Besides, that is not the reason we are here. I knew this was a mistake.

THE ACTOR *(opening his door):* Perhaps it is a mistake to be here at all.

JACK: Oh? And will it be absurd to collect one hundred twenty thousand dollars? *(these last words are spaced for effect)* That is more than you could make in five seasons of full houses. More than your brother could make as well.

THE ACTOR *(glowering):* Do not mention my brother. *(hands raised in the air)* What do I care of him? What do I care of money? This is not about money.

JACK: No. I am sorry. It is about the South. *(dramatically)* The beautiful South! Our mother soil. Our—

THE ACTOR: To hell with you!

THE ACTOR enters his room and slams the door behind him. JACK shrugs with a smirk and struggles a moment longer with his own door before successfully opening it, going in and shutting his door, if less dramatically, behind him. Further down the hall the sound of yet another door being closed is heard. But there is no one else to be seen.

***

Why do I laugh to think of my choices? What was it about J. W. Watson's *Beautiful Snow* that so captured my imagination?

> *Oh! the snow, the beautiful snow,*
> *Filling the sky and the earth below;*
> *Over the house tops, over the street,*
> *Over the heads of the people you meet;*
> > *Dancing,*
> > > *Flirting,*
> > > > *Skimming along,*
> *Beautiful snow! it can do nothing wrong.*
> *Flying to kiss a fair lady's cheek,*

Clinging to lips in a frolicsome freak;
Beautiful snow, from the heavens above,
Pure as an angel and fickle as love!

Oh! the snow, the beautiful snow!
How the flakes gather and laugh as they go!
Whirling about in its maddening fun,
It plays in its glee with everyone.
     Chasing,
        Laughing,
            Hurrying by,
It lights up the face and sparkles the eye;
And even the dogs, with a bark and a bound,
Snap at the crystals that eddy around.
The town is alive, and its heart in a glow,
To welcome the coming of beautiful snow.

How the wild crowd go swaying along,
Hailing each other with humor and song!
How the gay sledges like meteors flash by—
Bright for a moment, then lost to the eye!
     Ringing,
        Swinging,
            Dashing as they go
Over the crest of the beautiful snow:
Snow so pure when it falls from the sky,
To be trampled in mud by the crowd rushing by;
To be trampled and tracked by the thousands of feet
Till it blends with the horrible filth in the street.

Once I was pure as the snow—but I fell:
Fell, like the snowflakes, from heaven—to hell;
Fell, to be tramped as the filth of the street;
Fell, to be scoffed, to be spit on, and beat.
     Pleading,
        Cursing,

Dreading to die,
Selling my soul to whomever would buy,
Dealing in shame for a morsel of bread,
Hating the living and fearing the dead.
Merciful God! have I fallen so low?
And yet I was once like this beautiful snow!

Once I was fair as the beautiful snow,
With an eye like its crystals, a heart like its glow;
Once I was loved for my innocent grace,
Flattered and sought for the charm of my face.

But how did it end?

***

Friday, November 25, 1864. The Winter Garden, New York City.

The day after Thanksgiving. (This is only the second year—1863 being the first, by declaration of Lincoln—of the national observance of the holiday on the last Thursday of November.) It is snowing. The brothers prepare to perform Julius Caesar *for the Shakespeare monument fund. THE ACTOR as Mark Antony. JUNIUS plays Cassius. EDWIN plays Brutus.*

THE ACTOR (to Edwin): We do not have to be friends. We are brothers. That must suffice. Especially tonight, of all nights.

JUNIUS: You sound as though we will never be together again.

EDWIN: Our little brother has plans, June. And they do not include anyone, save himself.

THE ACTOR: There is a patent absurdity in such an insult from you.

EDWIN: If you have something to say—

JUNIUS: Quiet! Both of you!!

Friday, January 27, 1865. Grover's Theater, Washington City.

Late afternoon. THE ACTOR is dressed for his evening's role as Romeo, in Romeo and Juliet. *He paces and mouths his lines. The YOUNG WOMAN sits at his dressing table.*

YOUNG WOMAN: Jack has asked me to marry him.

THE ACTOR: Has he?

YOUNG WOMAN: He says we will spend our honeymoon in Italy. Are you surprised?

THE ACTOR: Not at all.

YOUNG WOMAN *(coyly):* You look surprised. You should be.

THE ACTOR: I am not. Just curious.

YOUNG WOMAN: Why shouldn't he ask me? Do you think you are the only man who finds me desirable?

THE ACTOR *(casting an incisive look):* Certainly not.

YOUNG WOMAN: You're not being very fair. How dare you question me! You know that you're the only—

THE ACTOR: And yet, as often as Jack calls on you at home in the mornings and afternoons, he can not be mistaken that your evenings are ever mine alone.

YOUNG WOMAN: When you are not engaged in New York or Montreal or—

THE ACTOR: Exactly. Perhaps you are the business often keeping him from joining me. Is there something you want to tell me, then?

YOUNG WOMAN: You're not being fair! No!

THE ACTOR: It seems there is—

YOUNG WOMAN: You were the first man I ever really kissed!

THE ACTOR: Clearly, not the last.

YOUNG WOMAN: What is a kiss, anyway? Nothing! It holds no passion in and of itself—no promise, no deep truth.

THE ACTOR: I imagine that would depend on who was

doing the kissing. It might even be comical. Presently, I imagine your kisses only ridiculous.

YOUNG WOMAN: Why should you care if I marry another? You would still be my first love. *(deliberately)* And my favorite!

THE ACTOR: Would I?

YOUNG WOMAN (laughing somewhat nervously): Of course! *(haughtily)* And I will always be yours.

THE ACTOR: What makes you so sure?

YOUNG WOMAN: If I want you, what choice will you have?

THE ACTOR: There are choices. You seem to know about them.

YOUNG WOMAN: Alright. I kissed him. Twice. I kissed Starrett, too. And I'll probably kiss a handful more before I reserve my mouth for only one man. What of it? Did you really expect me to begin and end with you? It's too pleasant, too easy. And the looks on their faces are far too agreeable not to advantage myself—on occasion. You've sampled life, but you want me to satisfy myself with borrowed accounts and testimonies of something *purer*?

THE ACTOR (confused): Did you think I was lying when I told you that?

YOUNG WOMAN (defiant): No. I believed you. I believe you still. That's you, not me.

THE ACTOR (angry): I thought we had some things in common!

YOUNG WOMAN: We do! Don't you see? *(laughing)* Those are exactly the things you would deny me. I've told Sothern of my plans to go on the stage and he thinks it's a great idea.

THE ACTOR: He doesn't know anything about it. All he understands are his father's business interests. If that.

YOUNG WOMAN: You talk as if he's the only man who received help from his father, or entered the family trade.

THE ACTOR: If that is supposed to be a pointed remark, you can save it for Edwin and June. They're the ones who went on tour with my father while "little Johnnie" was expected to be content with a military boarding school.

YOUNG WOMAN (*mocking*): And was that very, very, difficult?

THE ACTOR: No. But it wasn't very, very easy. And it wasn't what I wanted. I had to get that on my own.

YOUNG WOMAN: So you say! The one thing I ask of you, you can't do—even with your family name.

THE ACTOR: What? What have I ever denied you? What have you ever asked of me that I did not give?

YOUNG WOMAN: Success! To succeed! At anything!

THE ACTOR: You told me you would love me regardless of that.

YOUNG WOMAN: I was a girl then. I am a woman now. You seem to be having troubles with that too. Today I just want what should be mine. What I deserve. All I ask of you is to follow through—with anything. You don't see that do you? That, at the least, is something Surratt knows to do!

THE ACTOR: Then marry him!

YOUNG WOMAN: I don't want to! I don't love him.

THE ACTOR: Whom do you love, really?

YOUNG WOMAN: Really? I don't know. (*pause*) Maybe—you?

***

Enid, Oklahoma, is not the kind of place a national hero would be imagined to live out his days, especially one who had been born in London and spent his youth in the great cities of the eastern seaboard. The trail there was miles only of uninterrupted monotony, filled with the kind of dust imaginable only as part of some desperate dream of reconciliation, some vision of frontier revival. Still, when Hand and I arrived I felt a strange sense of relief. Corbett's crime against me had brought no reward at all. His existence was equally dismal as my own, and according to Hand's accounting of it, possibly worse.

Hand was still grinning as we stepped out of the coach, and I was still confused. He waited until our companions—another cousin, bound for California with his grown son—occupied with our brief luggage, would not hear our dialogue, to reveal his plan. Then did I recount what he had told me.

"Let me understand, after the war Corbett returned to his milliner's trade, and even obtained a post as a Methodist lay preacher, but soon went onto the lecture circuit, milking his part in my 'death' to its fullest."

Hand nodded.

"He then removed to Kansas, trying his hand at farming and continuing to deliver an occasional address to whatever congregation might listen. Thereafter he received a mysterious appointment as doorkeeper to the Kansas State Legislature and even more mysteriously broke into the chambers one day screaming 'Glory to God' with his pistols blazing!

"Miraculously," I returned Hand's constant smile for effect only, "no one is hurt. But Corbett is incarcerated in the Topeka asylum for the insane and remains there for more than a year, after which time he makes a daring escape and, as far as the authorities are concerned, has disappeared. And now he is here."

"Z'at is rh'ight."

"I will not ask how you discovered he came to be here, and can be so sure it is indeed him. I trust you have some undeniable proof. But how did you think to trace him to the Kansas frontier in the first place?"

"Does h'eet not make sense?"

"How so?"

"Oh! my frh'iend, must h'I explain h'everhyz'ing?"

But he did not.

***

It is difficult for me to detail the entire life of this man whom I

210

never knew, yet of whom I feel so much—what? Not kinship. Not amity. Certainly not amity. Yet perhaps some peculiar familiarity. How can one not feel some sort of familiarity to one's own assassin? Then let me do my best to tell you what little I knew of him from the occasional journal and odd report of a mutual—mutual what?

Thomas P. Corbett was born in London, England, of simple stock in 1832 and moved to Boston, Massachusetts, about the same time John Brown was making headlines and I was myself first playing in a scene of a different, if more honestly dramatic sort. There, after losing his young wife to childbirth, Corbett became involved with a church of Methodist Episcopalians. This particular congregation was fundamental revivalist. Such were the times.

Corbett's revelation in that city caused him to adopt the name Boston as his own, and thenceforth would answer to no other—any sooner than Boucicault might have answered to any name other than Dionysius. Corbett was of "small stature, slight form, mild countenance and quiet deportment," or so said the *New York Times* the day after my "death."

In the spring of 1858, Corbett found himself engaged in a bar-room debate over morality and the will of God. This was not the result of having had too much to drink. He had for some time forgone such earthly pleasures and entered the saloon for the express purpose of confronting its less reverent patrons. So outspoken was he in his opinions and condemnatory of those about him that trouble, it is said, could be seen mounting in the bay. Corbett, first scorned and ridiculed only, was invited to leave the establishment, which by his own oaths he doomed to brimstone and perdition. Still, he continued on his path of self-righteousness. Some men know not their limits, nor those of their god.

Several of his opponents, sincerely assailed by continued and relentless insult, finally felt the strains of vengeance tugging at their sleeves. While two of them arose from their seats and prepared to battle the short but capable Corbett, a third approached from behind, breaking his mug upon the bantam's skull.

When Corbett awoke he found himself only beginning to receive the revenge of his accursed opponents. In a small chamber above the inn's tap room Corbett came to his senses, finding himself lashed to a bed, completely stripped of his clothes and with two gaily painted and highly expert prostitutes teasing and probing his now-protesting body. The roars of approval from onlookers and his obvious arousal indicated that, though senseless, he had not been altogether reluctant. The unconscious spirit was as weak as the flesh.

Corbett fought the continued advances of his perfumed assailants, but modesty and chastity were completely sacrificed before he was released from his bonds and left alone in a low-wailing misery.

Not thirty minutes later, and without another sound heard from the upper room, Corbett descended the stairs with a look of grim resolution in his eyes and a bloodied knife in his left hand. The entire saloon began jeering and whistling until, on an instant, they all fell quite silent. Corbett held something in his right hand that he proffered palm up to them as a tribute to their cruelty. His pants were all stained in their middle and deep blood oozed from between his curled fingers. One of the whores fainted sick at the sight.

"Oh dear God," the barkeep might have whispered. "He's castrated himself!"

***

"You're a friend of his?" she winked habitually and cocked her head.

"He gave me your name."

She sipped a drink the color of whisky and stuffed the bills I handed her into the black lace ruffles of her low-necked dress. Its yellow taffeta rustled encouragingly.

"You're lying," she said with another wink. "He doesn't know my name, and I don't know his." Then, half-relenting,

"Although he might've learned it from another." A semi-colon pause. "Not a very good friend, I hope," she winked yet again.

"We still keep secrets from another," I replied, hinting at an unknown meaning.

"I hope you are better at keeping things than he," she said with a strange, seductive smile—secretive and somehow hopeful but sullenly resigned, in the manner of all saloon girls. "Yes. I suppose he is a customer. But a very different kind of customer."

She leaned to me in a whisper and I could smell the spiritless odor of sugar from her glass and on her breath.

"He pays me to let him watch. Just me, by myself. Oh! one time he asked me to let him watch another. From the closet. Begged me to allow it. I said no," she sat upright with self-satisfaction. "Then he offered me such a handy sum that, well—I told him if he so much as breathed, I would have whatever was left of him to have." She paused, sipped at her glass with years of practice that even made her seem to wince, and checked the room. "He has no genitals. None!" she began to roar raspily, then brought her voice back down. "He has the barrel, but no powder, not a single bullet. Not even grapeshot!"

She sipped again and handed her glass over the bar to be refilled. The keep reached under the ledge to oblige when her fingers ran to cover the glass. She looked at him and shook her head slightly, then held the glass straight out. He grabbed the bottle of brandy behind him and filled the glass to its very rim without hesitation, so she had to go to it.

"Dismembered hisself," she continued with mixed shock and perverse pleasure as she sat back down. "I suppose it takes a real man to remove his own manhood. But we'll never know for sure—no!"

That was what she said and I knew there were two things Corbett had abundantly: courage and conviction, if not discretion.

She sniggered softly, the perfect rows of front teeth yielding to the silver-traced truth of those behind. For all her powdered saloon features still, there was something attractive about her. She squeezed her breasts together with her arms as she pressed against my side.

"You, on the other hand," she cooed, "seem more than equipped. What do you say?"

She arched one stenciled eyebrow toward the second floor landing.

"Who was that man? The one my friend paid to see?"

She smiled, then shrugged with those same years of resignation and resolve.

"I should have known. I will not—good day," she said, rising, a single tip of her head emptying her glass.

"I only wish to know his name," I said as harmlessly as I could manage.

"I should not have told you at all. It was just a story. You have no proof."

I offered her another wad of folded bills.

"Will this pay for the story's ending?"

She took the money quickly, pleased at its minting, and snapped, "He no longer comes here. I never knew his name either. Your friend seemed to know him, however. He seemed to know him well. Now go."

Strophe

What part of me did you kill that night? Or should I ask what part of me did you leave alive? What is there left of me? This is not a life I lead. This is but the shadow of some former self I knew. Some half-surviving shape or shade, left to wander unfamiliar roads and unmanageable situations. Less capable than that already beaten form that had sought sanctuary from the truth in the hope of some proposed falsehood.

All for which I had dreamed was an extended moment of luxuriance in your mother's arms, those eyes and that heart that once held me close and dear. For half an instant it had seemed enough to close my eyes and breathe one final breath. And I would trade this moment's promise of a longer life for the security of any of those uncertain others. As I lived them, so they were. Unmistakable, unforgivable. Now I should simply let them pass.

***

We found Corbett there. As conspicuous as I tell you he is, or was, or should be, or must have been, I never would have known him. Not until I heard someone call him, this man who killed me, by his new name, the one Hand had confided to me. Another thing he seemed to have learned so easily. And if I had doubts I had fewer still when I remarked his strangely crippled gait and the pallid wonderment of his upturned gaze.

"Thatcher!" came the shout again. "Tom Thatcher! Give a hand, the legislature's almost in."

What is there so unmistakable in a man that can be recognized with a glance, though he should change his look and his name, his humor, his wealth or poverty, his self-worth? More than the eyes, could it be his very soul? That part of his spirit that must inform his corporeal strength, and in Corbett's instance dictate its ruthless passions that his body would never again deign to utter its own?

From the moment I saw him limp across the avenue I knew not only that all those wild stories were true, but also that there might yet be truth to one still untold, by me only imagined. For why else should our paths have crossed so neatly? Providence was finally moving her hand in my behalf, if this time I would only listen to her and not another's voice.

He had all the attributes of a zealot. The glazed hollow glare, infected voice and affected vernacular that peeled like a sermon for the Society of Friends, or commended itself to address a camp meeting. To compound these, he wore his hair past his shoulders because it was *so the manner of the Christ.*

What had made Corbett mad? Who can say? I can only guess. What could I know of such things? They touch me only somewhat—and, after all, what does it matter? Surely he is. Whatever madness led to his emasculating revelation was heightened tenfold therein. Perhaps, it can be said, he makes even Wilkes seem mild and moderate-minded.

Corbett was not merely mad. He was a fool, but exactly whose fool, I was not yet sure.

Antistrophe

The sins I have committed—unlike some young boy's methodical execution of neighborhood cats—I will not dare to guess if they have been against God or man or nature. They have given me power. Out of darkness is born light. Out of much darkness there can be, but little light—but it is light. And out of more light, when the power of that light is raised and occupied, compassion.

If I fasted for the entire month I spent at the monastery it was still two weeks less than a holy man. A man must confront all his demons if he is to achieve clarity, and in thirty days I confronted only myself. Still, this was a positive confrontation; that when next met, those demons, those sons of darkness would be wholly battled. Then, as now, my heart ripped and tore for Ella and our children more than any. Less for myself than I should have ever thought.

***

I could not have scripted a more effective drama. Nor could Mr. Taylor a more engaging comedy, I am sure.

"Booth isn't dead."

He looked at me deadpan, brushed past and continued walking, his companion too neither acknowledging my claim nor my presence.

I ran to confront him again.

"Booth lives," I repeated.

He stared numbly as he loosed a plug of chewing tobacco

into the roadway.

"Then, brother, you have no claim to what is mine. At any rate, $1,653.84 is not a sum worthy of further quartering and distribution. Perhaps you might seek out Mr. Conger or Lieutenant Doherty. They at least have an amount capable of division."

He spat again.

"He is not dead."

"So you would retrieve my money entirely? Well, it is spent. I have nothing. Nothing! Or, if this is another of those wild rumors, let me ease your mind. He is dead. I shot him. He is dead and he is gone. He was only a man."

"The man lives, and he may be looking for you."

He stopped now. This had taken him by surprise.

"Why?"

"Perhaps he thinks you know something," I intrigued.

"I only know my duty," he spoke quickly and defensively, his wad transferred from one cheek to the next. "I was hired to do a job, and I did it."

"To kill him."

"Yes—to kill him." He stopped chewing. "Who are you?"

"I believe that is what he would like to know."

"Who are you?"

"Just a friend."

"Not mine, brother."

"I am hoping I might be."

"I have no friends. Nor need of one. This world is not long as it is."

"If you would speak to me—"

"Speak to you?" marvelled the man with the kind of wild ferocity I had known in my father's madness. "I should sooner spit!"

He did so yet again, though less at me than, distractedly, dribbling on himself.

"Why? What would you have of me, my life?"

Here he hocked what was left of his tobacco and railed into

a single howl—the purest lunacy imaginable—from his aspirate throat and widely gapped teeth.

"Don't you know why I was picked to be your executioner, Mr. Booth?" he addressed me by name without hesitation, suddenly affecting a mock reverence for one so gladly dead. "There can be no temptation held to me, neither good nor evil, that could persuade me to perform what I will not. There am I surely unlike your understanding, who have inherited the unfortunate custom of assuming a posture for the promise of a portion of the house receipts."

He turned about with a slight hobble, continued across the avenue and into the State House, leaving me to wonder and wait. When finally at half-past-eight Corbett exited with his companion, he did not see me, and I imagined he might have thought the entire incident some twisted vision of penitence. From the shadows I followed the two of them at a distance. Tarrying before the doorway of the saloon, his eyes had not fought to avoid a lingering at every darkened passage, before they entered a meeting hall at the other end of the street.

***

"I, grand cyclops of the den, with the aid and assistance of my two night hawks, under the laws and statutes of the Order, and with due regard for the imperial wizard and his genii, his most grand dragon and attendant hydra, the dominion's grand titan and his furies, and with direct consent of the provincial grand giant and his four goblins, do hereby convene this body of ghouls for the purposes of sacred initiation.

"Bring the candidate forward."

A shuffling of feet, the sound of chains and armor.

"Do you believe in the supremacy of your race and the inalienable right of self-preservation of the people against the exercise of arbitrary and unlicensed power?"

"I do."

"Will you devote your intelligence, energy and influence to

218

the furtherance and propagation of the principles of our Order?"

"I will."

"Will you, under all circumstances, defend and protect persons of the white race in their lives, rights and property against all encroachments or invasions from any inferior race, and especially the African?"

"Yes."

"Are you willing to take an oath forever to cherish these grand principles and to unite yourself with others who, like you, believing in their truth, have firmly bound themselves to stand by and defend them against all?"

"I am."

"So swear."

He was handed a bible and began.

"I do solemnly swear, in the presence of these witnesses, never to reveal, without authority, the existence of this Order, its objects, its acts and signs of recognition. Never to reveal or publish, in any manner whatsoever, what I shall see or hear in this council. Never to divulge the names of the members of the Order or their acts done in connection therewith. I swear to maintain and defend the social and political superiority of the white race on this continent, always and in all places to observe a marked distinction between the white and African races, to vote for none but white men for any office of honor, profit, or trust. To devote my intelligence, energy, and influence to instill these principles in the minds and hearts of others. And to protect and defend persons of the white race in their lives, rights, and property against the encroachments and aggressions of an inferior race.

"I swear, moreover, to unite myself in heart, soul and body with those who compose this Order. To aid, protect and defend them in all places. To obey the orders of those who, by our statutes, will have the right of giving those orders. To respond at the peril of my life to a call, sign or cry coming from a fellow member whose rights are violated. And to do everything in my power to assist him through life. And to the faithful performance of this oath, I pledge my life and sacred honor."

Then spoke the leader again.

"Brothers, you have been initiated into one of the most important Orders that have ever been established on this continent, an Order which, if its principles are faithfully observed and its objects diligently implemented, is destined to regenerate our unfortunate nation and to relieve the white race from the humiliating condition to which it has lately been reduced in this republic. It is necessary, therefore, that before taking part in the labors of this association, you should understand fully its principles and objects and the duties that devolve upon you as one of its members.

"As you may have gathered from the questions that were posed to you, and which you have answered satisfactorily, and from the clauses of the oath that you have taken, our main and fundamental object is the maintenance of the supremacy of the white race in this republic. History and physiology teach us that we belong to a race that nature has endowed with an evident superiority over all other races, and that the Maker, in thus elevating us above the common standard of human creation, has intended to give us dominion over inferior races from which no human laws can properly deviate.

"We know, besides, that the government of our republic was established by white men, for white men alone, and that it never was in the contemplation of its founders that it should fall into the hands of an inferior and degraded race. We hold, therefore, that any attempt to wrest from the white race the management of its affairs in order to transfer it to control of a black population is an invasion of the sacred prerogatives vouchsafed to us by the Constitution, and a violation of the laws established by the Deity.

"It then, becomes our solemn duty, as white men, to resist strenuously and persistently those attempts against our natural and constitutional rights, and to do everything in our power in order to maintain in the republic the supremacy of the Caucasian race. This is the object for which our Order was instituted, and in carrying it out we intend to infringe no laws, to violate no rights or to resort to no forcible means, except for purposes of legitimate and necessary defense."

***

Most of the procedure was familiar to me in a strange, unknown manner. What was it? What seemed so familiar about these rites? Why were their imprecations and general systems so within my grasp? I knew the answer.

Until then it had only been a rumor, like the alleged collaboration of one Shakespearean play or the contended sole authorship of another. But to the player, he who reads again and again, memorizes and performs those lines night after night, there could be no mistake. One man's voice is as distinguishable in the written word as his vocal pattern or phrenologic profile. The words themselves demand it. There is a quality in their syntax which, when pronounced, sings differently, uniquely from any other.

Albert Pike. The Scottish Rite's Sovereign Grand Commander, North America's leader of the world's largest fraternal organization. The frontier lawyer who rose to fame and position within the fraternity of Freemasons and then cast his lot with the Southern cause at the beginning of our Civil War, questioning the motives and methods of the pretended movement toward union.

The author of state constitutions, tracts on state's rights, translator of ancient Indo-European, Greek and Hebrew texts. His knowledge of the American Indians and fluency in numerous of their dialects predisposed him to write treaties enlisting the red man's sympathies and aid to the Confederacy. His entreated brotherhood bound the tribes of the Cherokee, Muskoki, Seminole, Choctaw, and Chickasaw nations to do all in their power to take and return any

221

Negroes, horses, or other property stolen from white men.

The greatest compiler of Masonic arcana, his knowledge of man's philosophical depths, led him to self-imposed exile before the war was ended. Quitting his commission in the armies of the South under circumstances echoing a breach of power and purpose, Pike fled to Canada before he was to have been tried in a martial court for outrages committed by the frontier soldiers and Indians under his authority. Whether or not he had sanctioned the cruel methods of his command would never be known. Shortly after Andrew Johnson succeeded the presidency, a pardon was issued to all outstanding war criminals in an effort *to extend the healing arm of the war's end*—as it was said Lincoln would have done.

Outcast it would seem, by both North and South, stripped of his lands, titles and honor, Pike was yet the presiding officer of an entire and ever-united continent of brothers. What he willed had three million fraternal ways toward assistance, even from across the Canadian frontier. What he should command would be done and with honour, by any of Masonry's adherents, regardless of flag or apparent political bias. And, as with Pharaoh in times of old, the chain of command was as immense and incalculable as the Great Pyramid itself. Obvious for its might, sublime in the uniform secrecy of every stone.

While Pike ably moved well outside the bounds of general scrutiny, the rumours of his involvement with the Klan were not unknown. In a way they were natural. Having had more than a hand in the development of the current form of the Freemasonic ritual, the association was understandable. And not just for the comparative ranks and titles and jurisdictions that were so common to the two organizations, but in a strange way its aims as well.

To aid the white man, in a republic established by white men, for white men alone.

I had heard this before, but only now, after witnessing the rite itself, did I know it to be true. I have heard his voice within the utterance of the words, seen his thin lips part the wiry gray mass of his long beard to give them shape. I felt his ominous presence behind each participant this night, but mostly I saw his power and influence in the eyes of Boston Corbett, now known as James Thatcher, the man whose life revelation had appropriately been in the city of Pike's birth.

***

I caught him unawares as he exited the building, now alone.

"Tell me! Tell me who paid you!"

"Or what? Wouldst thou kill thy fellow man?"

He howled again, his lunatic howl. The crippled wolf ensnared by steel, daring pure destruction. In flight he had been urged for survival, in captivity he knew only rage.

"Thou couldst not suffer me to endure more than I have already," he glowered. "And at mine own hand, brother. At mine own hand!"

It was true, though I had scarcely envisioned his crippled gait for the truth of which it spoke; knew what it represented but not wholly. Behind the glint of the mad eyes and flashing smile was the madness of a mind so tormented it had long since led its victim to an act of self-abasement so absolute, even exile was no punishment for him.

I pitied him and feared even having him in my grip, but he could not be at my mercy. He was right. He had already fallen prey to his own mercilessness, his fanatic view of a heavenly promise's required duty, and bore easily what I could never—lovelessness and worldly exile.

***

There were dozens of secret fraternities, each with dozens upon dozens of chapters. The Knights of the White Camellia, the Golden Circle, even that group to which my father and my brother Edwin belonged and from which Hand had finally to explain my signet ring and much of his frequent intelligence had come, the Freemasons. The Know-Nothings, too—my

223

political party of choice, though short-lived, were of this type and boasted formidable social and political power. But none, even the Royal Arch of the Masonic brotherhood, held as much sway over the minds and spirits of its members as the Circle Society, the Ku Klux Klan.

As with the other organizations, Klan membership was confidential and bestowed only upon those whose trusts and loyalties had been tested. They were then sworn under oath. This oath, or solemn vow as it was styled, carried with it a series of penalties so grievous and gruesome that even if one were not to take them literally the mere gravity of their pronouncement would be enough to impart a binding nature. And there was no shortage of stories about the impious or treacherous brother who disappeared entirely, leaving others only to guess at his true fate.

Divine law was invoked, but man's justice, too, would intercede wherever the former might fail. The stories of vanished brethren were ever absent of details, but these could be inferred by even the dullest of imaginations, perhaps all the more readily.

***

"Gift and call. Everything is gift and call," explained Corbett. "What He gives freely to us, bless His name, and that which He would call upon us to freely do. He gave you a kind of talent, I suppose. You squandered it, and He called on me to end your prodigal path."

"He did not call on you. Surely you know your God is mightier than this. What you heard was the calling of a man."

"He called on me through this man."

"Yes, but which man? Which man?"

"It does not matter. He was but another tool. Like myself. Like you."

"It matters to me. It matters now. Who is this man?"

"A messenger. One of the Elohim."

"An angel? Really? Is this another grandiose ceremonial

title borrowed by your Klansmen?"

"He has no form. He takes only that which he needs. Why should I help you? What we are doing now is not His work. It may be. But it is not. It is more like yours, Wilkes Booth. But hatred and murder are a kind of purging. Atonement for what has gone before. Contrition. A sacrifice for the inevitable good to come. You hate the niggers. They hate the niggers and immigrants. I only hate myself. We must trust to God's love and find the way of His will. Yes, some good may come when a man sees his own reflection in the burning of a cross. The shadows are elusive but they are long and they are there. Even in the light of morning, their scorched shadows are there."

"Was he there tonight?"

"He is always here."

"Was he there tonight?"

***

The three of us feasted on cracklins. If such a feast is possible with the gristle of pork fried until it is brittle and not the least tender. And yet it seemed enough for me then, despite the breaking of my fast from red meat. I felt at last close to the end of my search. What had been a kind of frustration with Corbett was yet a victory. For meeting him at all, for the glimpse within his soul our meeting had provided.

The major was due back at camp any moment, having chosen again to nurture his natural aspect rather than eat with the likes of our two companions. He never hesitated to call them by the same name as every decent white man. And while the major had never held any formal education, he had learned the sciolist tact of the carnival and prided himself that, even for his accent, he never spoke with the 'dese 'n datss' so common to his race.

Then this young buck, who with his father had accompanied us all the way from Chicago, presumed nothing of the kind. He spoke right out with his cant as comfortably as he might address the English queen. And something of his style allowed that thought more acceptable of him than ever it would be of the otherwise articulated major.

"Blame my buttons! D'em e'nt d'a same men ez you'ns wuz aksin' fer t'day," his skin glimmered in the dark and his eyes shone like moons in their sockets as he was the first to sight the intruders.

"How can you be sure?" I questioned, remarking their masks and robes.

"Cuz," he flashed with perfect teeth, "E'nt none ob d'ese w'at walks on a limp, nor none w'at owns d'em fancy polished boots as d'ose I seen t'day. I sho' 'mired d'em boots. 'N t'ot how'n d'ey wud perdy near inbite o'r follin' wi'd all d'a moonlight be bouncin' off!"

By this time I had joined his smiling humor, but could not help then wonder, "Who are they then?" And, "Where are the others?"

"I gots a feelin' we's gonna finds out," he tendered with sudden gravity before again falling silent and watchful.

"Demon," I heard him whisper, and laughed to think it was only my freakish friend. "Pa!" he called again as he ran toward the flaming timber.

Hand's small, sharp features poked up just above the rise of the other side of the ridge. They seemed frozen with a strange kind of fervor as he furiously whipped his horse. He looked toward me with the blank expression of fear that I had known in him but once. Reflexively I continued to stifle a laugh, yet unaware of the horrible truth.

"Who's scaring whom?" I wondered as I looked at my fellows. But they did not look at me, and they were not laughing.

No fewer than twenty horsemen followed Hand's mount. I started instinctively toward them when the younger of my companions tackled me from behind while his father threw off his coat to squelch our campfire.

"Dis ain't no place fo' da likes of us," breathed my subduer half atop me and with his huge hand tight around my mouth. "Nor dem wha's wid us!" he nodded as much to himself and the others as to me.

As Hand's captors maneuvered him into position under a great live oak, one man and his horse solemnly oversaw the action from atop a commanding knoll, high hoods and long, dark capes lending a phantom evil to their aspect. I saw myself hurling my body at this man and grabbing him about the neck. I could feel the veins swell and the face pale as I screamed out my anger, then realized I was still pinned and silent on the ground, a helpless spectator.

The short legged and bootless body writhed helplessly among the ropes atop its equally nervous mount. Without warning, a switch cracked on the spine of the animal, the reflections of a dozen torches in its glassy eyes, causing it to rear halfway and charge ahead, riderless. Hand bounced up for a moment before falling back to one side, straightening with the tension of the rope. His body jerked a single, mighty spasm and quickly relaxed, bobbing slightly before it twisted lifelessly in one direction, then the other. His right foot seemed pointed deliberately toward the ground, while the other rested in a natural position.

The task complete, the other horses and their riders rode solemnly and quickly away. A hunter's moon began its slow descent on the heels of the dog star as a nearly audible fog settled in the valley. In the distance, hoofbeats of an unknown breed could now be heard making their way north-north-east through the night. Only then did my companions stand up to remark the scene, one of them drawing an experienced knife as he walked numbly toward the tree. I sat up but was otherwise unable to move.

The dwarf, my true and only friend, was dead.

Entr'acte
The Diary

The flags draped low over the balustrade of the presidential box, so much that, from the seats below, we might have felt a certain connection with the loge occupants. But there could be no such thing. The flags would sooner drag upon the boards of the stage. The forward position of the proscenium boxes made that doubly true. And it was so.

All seemed quiet and complete overhead. Even the rumored and probable snoring of the president was as soon the echo of jubilant fireworks as the rumbling of some distant and persistent cannon. For though Johnston's rebels were still afield, and one might wonder if there would ever be a peace, tonight it had arrived.

The theater was dotted with soldiers—blue uniforms trimmed with gold, newly pressed. No sooner the attire of war than the suits and gowns amid which they beamed of their victory. But then, the Capital had scarcely been the litmus of truth those several years. More like some deep forest pool's reflection of a windy and over-clouded day. Swim in it and create the ripples; drink from it and taste its chill; look deeply into it and see only your own face. This night, the images were everywhere. Frozen grins and postured profiles, ready for the photographer's art or any else. Who could guess at the collective dream?

From the moment the curtain was raised for the opening act there seemed a business in the air beyond expectation. There was a low murmur adrift like the waxing utility of bees. Taylor's phrases seemed wholly different. The words were no longer his: their expressions those of the actors; the actors' movements the notions of the stage manager. Nothing was its own. The very scenery belonged to a different play, yet to be written, the perspectives to a different world, where atmosphere and oxygen did not exist, except in some cherished memory.

And up there, somewhere just to the right of the stage and its dreamlike production, there sat the man who controlled all, whose mind had given rise to that slumbering absence, whose stirring would then signal the time for all to awake and view again the day that had been postponed. That hand that held the folded program might have been his. The leg crossed comfortably at the knee, his leg. The figure that leaned toward him, a minister of his wishes with eyes that looked into his eyes to find them looking back. Or was it he?

My wife and I only dreamed he would be there that night—My husband first learned of it as we entered the lobby—My parents had forced my attendance with the promise of his presence.

If I had known I might have prepared myself. I might have dressed differently. Perhaps not. But, surely he would have. She looked fine. We might have been dressed for church. It was Good Friday, after all. But those seats were forty times more comfortable than some stiff, wooden pews in a stuffily incensed church.

Mrs. Mountchessington exited in a flurry and a single player stood upon the stage. He had only just delivered his lines with a certain, unexpected enthusiasm when a shot rang out. The phantom ruffian shouted, jumped, glared and ran. The house around me stared and shook before it rose. That was all I knew.

Act IV

Contrition

"Useless!—Useless!—Blood! Blood!!"

Reported last words, "John Wilkes Booth"

Scene I

Father,
  Mother,
    Sisters all,
God, and myself, I have lost by my fall.

I had never thought of him only as a dwarf. An oddity. A thing. But there limp in the moonlight it was all that was left for him to be. And it was important for me to view him exactly that way. Not as the mock military officer. Certainly not as a friend. Not as anyone who had ever been close to me. Who had, himself, been responsible for our both being—at that moment, one dead, one barely alive—in the fracturing moonlight.

He could not be any of that. He could only be dead. Gone. Useless. Useless!

The mere thought of that word suddenly worked the magic upon me that I had escaped so many times before. How absurd that it should come to me at this moment—and like this. And, while I was not entirely convinced of the integrity of my revelation, I felt uncannily sure I was finally glimpsing the bitter truth.

Corbett found me the next morning as I was leaving the hotel. My two companions, who I had come to learn were Hand's own brother and nephew, had continued west on horseback at first light.

He startled me as he approached cautiously and distractedly from one side of the hotel porch. "You are not the only man willing to kill for his convictions," he started. "A black man of any stature does not belong with a white woman of even the lowest order. He was a gambler."

I looked at him somewhat surprised, but saw in his eyes that he knew what had happened the night before, perhaps even participated.

"You mean prize-fighter."

Pulling a small soiled bag from his shirt pocket, he opened it with stained, unsteady fingers and stuffed a plug between his gums.

"Both, yes. I knew it was not you—but not before I fired. The man I killed held no Union banknotes on his person. I was told there would be many. Thirty thousand dollars."

"How did you know? How would you remember this amount?"

"How could I forget, one thousand dollars for every piece of silver? I know more than I have been told, that I was given this appointment to get me out of the way, for example. Not that anyone would ever listen to me. No difficulty proving my lunacy."

"But why? Whose orders?"

"This I do not know. My information came from the surgeon who had treated me—when I was—"

"A surgeon? Did you know his name? Do you remember?"

"Of course," he spit again. "As I told you, he had treated me—in Massachusetts General those years before. Never did tell me what he was doing down in the capital. Seemed a little odd at the time, what with the war and the field hospitals some distance away. A good surgeon like himself."

"What was his name?"

"Bickley."

"Bickley? Lieutenant Bickley?"

"I don't think he was an officer. But he shared the information. Told me this might be a chance to do glory to my god and my country —and myself. It was quite a lot of money, would still be. No, he was no officer. Just a doctor, and a friend—or so I thought."

"He was an officer. Just not in the Union army."

***

I presume you have seen Mr. A. Gardner's photograph of Lincoln's second inauguration. If you look carefully you will see me in the upper balcony. What a splendid chance I had

234

that day to kill Lincoln then and there, but that was not the plan—nor would I have risked it with Ella in my company. We had made plans to meet at the affair, she having come in her father's carriage, which attended her return. But when we made our way back to the waiting coachman, and after assisting her into the cabriolet, I took hold of the reins, pulling at them so that the driver descended to discharge them from me. As soon as he lit I pretended to hand them to him, but instead flipped them up from the terret and mounted the carriage myself with a whistle and a whip and we were gone.

Ella was so surprised she was almost giddy—especially to see the elastic look on her father's high-hatted driver, as she called it. Nor was it easy to contain her enthusiasm as I urged our mount to muscle its way past a train of gentility.

"My wife," I variously called ahead to them as we impatiently approached, grabbing the blanket from beneath our bench, "is about to have our first child," and rubbing at the bumpish lump of woven woolen with a broad smile.

"Shall we name him Abraham?" I ribbed sideways to her alone

Ella both enjoyed our little game and dared not contradict my pretense, but scowled at me to suggest she might look parturient, blushing all along so that I almost imagined she looked as though she was.

And every encounter received smiles and shouts until we nearly thought the day was ours, and all had come simply to extend their blessings and share our joy. It was the fourth of March, 1865.

***

Saturday, March 4, 1865. The capital grounds, Washington City.

Afternoon. Abraham Lincoln's second inauguration.

A clear, breezy day with scattered high clouds and a bright blue sky. Wearing a high silk top hat, THE ACTOR stands on the balcony above the stand from which LINCOLN is speaking. On his left is the YOUNG WOMAN. Theater-owner JOHN T. FORD approaches through the crowd from the right and the two men exchange greetings. They appear surprised to see each other. On the lower level, far off to one side. THREE MEN of average height, ANOTHER MAN, rather short and swarthy and still ANOTHER MAN, very tall and large, exchange covert looks throughout the ceremony. A middle-aged WOMAN too seems to share their anticipation. Their names as yet unimportant, they all have somewhat familiar looks upon their faces.

***

The idea was simple. Thousands of Confederate brothers lay wounded, half-starved, and untended in Northern interment camps. Without them it was certain the South could not hope to launch a meaningful offensive or do much more than merely linger on, the fighting continue indefinitely. With them certain victory could be ours.

What ransom would bring the Union machine to the bargaining table if not the life of their leader, their president? It was not merely some pipe-dreamed notion. It would work, would it not? It must!

I have heard the stories of the plans to introduce malaria or other such infectious disease into the cities of New York and Boston, contaminated clothing and blankets into the White House itself. I know not truly if it is Northern propaganda or if the individuals who prompted me to perform my duty had tried other even more desperate measures.

I cannot swear even such gross inhumanity to be beyond them—even as it was not beyond their fathers, nor hope to convince you it would be far beyond me. You will believe, as I, what you must believe. Yet, listen, still.

The Union president marched out regularly, and rarely with more than one or two troops in attendance. It would surely not be difficult for a well-briefed raiding party to abduct and secrete him, and hold him hostage to demands of prisoner release, it was thought. We had borrowed the very stratagem from the North, which had planned a similar raid on our Richmond capital but met with disastrous ruin. Such was the folly of the North that thought for a moment it might match our Southern abilities. Even manufactured a story that such a plan had been devised as early as February, but the intelligence of the otherwise inept agent Pinkerton and his men foiled it.

When the idea was first brought to me it seemed a simple task to find a small party of trustworthy men to aid me. There were two men, Samuel Arnold and Michael O'Laughlin, recommended by Lutz to me as being perfect for the mission. Ultimately, thick-lipped Arnold, some four years my senior, would keep well his endorsed trust throughout the six served years of his life sentence, while gentle O'Laughlin's silence, likewise kept, was sealed by an untimely death two years before his term could be similarly commuted. I was wanting only two or three more to complete what was described the "perfect number" for such a duty.

Lewis Payne and George Atzerodt were men of little mental ability. Still, the one had the marvelous habit of asserting his natural size and the other a desire to do so based upon his lack of it. How could I ever think to blame the manifold fears that prevented foolish little Atzerodt from performing his role, fingers nervously working holes through each of his empty trouser pockets while he paced the floor of #26 Kirkwood House, the room above Vice President Johnson's? Or the bumblings of the large and loyal Payne, whose puppy instincts delivered him, after his errand was at least attempted, into the hands of an executing master, not his supposed and remembered strokes and pettings. The gallows forced a sure and steady, if simple, conclusion to each.

David E. Herold and John Harrison Surratt were not complete opposites either, and Herold seemed particularly useful for a time. Though his working as clerk in a Mr. William S. Thompson's apothecary store, at the corner of Fifteenth and Pennsylvania Avenues, where the Northern president habitually had his prescriptions compounded gave rise to an intricate if unfounded story of our early attempt to dispose of our target by the cup. And Surratt's tavern on Northwest H. Street, managed by his unfortunate if repentant mother, seemed both convenient and inconspicuous until the end. Herold's refusal to die with honor at Garrett's and the treacherous Surratt, whose betrayal of my trust extended not only to a desired usurpation of my only love but even to a kind of silent and complacent matricide, I will not lightly excuse. He has blamed Weichmann for his perfidy. I swear both have an equal if dissimilar share.

Spangler too I must mention, whose incidental and unrehearsed part yet sentenced him to the Dry Tortugas for six years—where he might easily have died along with O'Laughlin in 1867. And Mudd, sentenced to life along with Arnold and O'Laughlin, whose medical skill during the malaria outbreak helped win the freedom for all—Arnold, Spangler, and himself, in 1869.

All were engaged for the plan with only a minimum of expense money but the promise of enormous rewards when the operation was completed, as well, of course, as the laurels for having truly benefited the South. There were many moments when it was felt this was all we would ever receive for our trouble. For all our dedication to a Southern cause it seemed scarcely enough. And though I had always been uneasy about our proposed success still, at the time, we were ready.

There is no South. There never was. There is only the direction I have chosen and the source of every manner of illumination—the East.

Here I mention, as historical footnote, the progress of my role in the deliverance of the Union president. The claims of my insanity and desperation are legion, even seeming to grow with the years. Ever fewer, by comparison, are those who understand my purpose. All are confused by the compilation of the facts. But who knows better than I my story?

Sometime in February 1861, as it has lately surfaced, the Union president was warned by several sources of a plot to abduct his person. The veracity of the scheme is borne out of its several corroborations, not the least reliable of which was the account of Mr. Allan Pinkerton of the National Detective Agency. The execution of the plan was reputedly scheduled for Baltimore, my home. As a result of its exposure and thwarting the plan in its very formation, there being neither success nor apprehension of any of the villains, I have since been made to bear the stain of its design and failure. This is but one of two great debacles that have conveniently and circumstantially found their way into the camp of my detractors for the purpose of furthering my ignominy, the government's claimed effectiveness, and the final defeat of a longstanding conspiracy. I can, however, claim credit for neither, whatever their effect on my reputation and person.

The second of my alleged involvements is readily refutable. The story suggests a plot to poison poor Abe in August 1864. Evidence is commended in two pieces of what *The Herald* terms disguised writing. The first, that I engraved a Meadville, Pennsylvania, hotel-room window with a declaration of the completed deed, and in Washington, the president's usual prescription being filled by an accomplice pharmacist's clerk. A second writing sample is the somewhat cryptic and obviously forged letter, openly incriminating its recipient, Lewis Payne, in a manner unbefitting even the most amateurish assassin. The closing signature of Charles Selby, is an alias that I would never have thought to use while still openly naming the addressee, his wife, and at least two other agent-contacts. Surely the transparency of this hoax to further vilify Payne during the conspiracy trial of May 1865 is obvious.

And, if one accepts for truth—and this is—the story of my attempt to abduct the Union president in March before the final deliverance, how might one also suppose I had been ready to kill such a worthy hostage nearly one year earlier?

Then, to the facts.

By October 1864 I was actively seeking to fulfill the errand for which I now tell you I was hired. I would tell you the name of my employer, but I still know it not. Only the aliases, or counter-names of his several agents, and only one of these can I say for certain I met on more than one occasion.

The first time we tried our hand at the plan was mid-afternoon of March 15th, 1865. Not, coincidentally, the historic ides. My group and I had for some several months scouted the territories between the capital and the underground route to Richmond, that series of backwoods roads used by Confederate agents for the transportation of goods and information through the Union lines—and by certain Unionists for the transportation of a different sort of good. It was from Surratt that I had first learned even that such a route existed, and it was while scouring the same that I first met the feeble-minded Atzerodt.

We carefully confirmed a series of checkpoints where we could be sure of aid and assistance in our errand—the home of this surgeon and that sympathizer, where hot meals and fresh horses would await us in our proposed flight. All of this Surratt easily arranged as per his previous usage on missions for the Secret Service of the Confederacy. Had this not, after all, been the reason for his introduction to me in December 1865 by Dr. Samuel Mudd, who had the previous season been introduced to me by Senator Nash?

***

Wednesday, March 15, 1865. Surratt's Hotel, Washington City.

Morning. Kidnap attempt.

By noon on the fifteenth we were all met at Surratt's, talking nervously of everything else except the impending task. Pacing frantically about, pretending we were only storm and sinew. How funny to see Herold and Atzerodt adopt their postures of might and resolve, even at the time. Surratt and I escaped for a moment to a back room where he joined me in a pipe of my now-favorite mixture. This was not the first such time he accepted my invitation. We returned to join the rest in the salon and two or three shots of brandy later I felt ready for anything.

By two o'clock that afternoon of the ides we left for the Seventh Street Road where it was reported that the Northern president would pass that evening on his way to a review at the Seventh Street Hospital, or Soldier's Home. He was to be, as usual, in an unguarded carriage, with only his driver for protection—easy prey for even those less cunning and desperate than us. The only difficulty in the execution of the plan was in crossing the Navy Yard Bridge, but that was arranged, and all that remained was the deed itself.

The Union president did not travel to the home that day as planned, whatever the reason. Secretary Chase went in his stead and we, disgruntled and disappointed after our months of preparation, disbanded for our several homes. That was our first and only time as a complete group, our only attempt at kidnapping. Completely disgusted, Arnold and O'Laughlin went their ways, unable and unwilling to remain for further promises of reward or lucre. I knew something more had to be done.

With an even eye on my options and Lutz's confirming recommendation, I began to formulate the second, lasting plan.

Strophe

What was my dream? Not of an independent South, only of that South's right to independence. Not separation of the races, only acknowledgement of racial difference. Not the death of a president and leader, but the end of a tyrant with eyes too stony to see the stains of squandered youth and

241

vigour he washed absently, guiltlessly from his hands.

I awoke from a tossed and fevered night. Shaken with sweat and fear, I remembered my midnight choice. This time I could not try to forget. Every simple action, thought or word recalled the same. And as with any dream decided—envisioned past the dawn—the separate plots and parts become more certain with every contemplation, each meditation a staged rehearsal for the approval of prospective players.

When first I sought my cast, my quiet madness only seemed to script my play. The voice and eyes of schooled declamation advantaged for my aim. Yet soon the contagion ran its course. The heralded dream became the completely embraced vision.

Who could withstand the passion of the plan? Not Payne, of hands that daily dreamed of power and purpose. Not Atzerodt, of quivering lips that longed to grind a steady, mindful beat. Not Surratt, of heart and courage closest to my own. Not Herold, the eyes deeply searching for exchange of some forbidden urge, approval and acceptance of his misguided soul.

And all then for their reasons ready. Arnold and O'Laughlin too. With their fury and speed. The several limbs and attributes primed for performance, posed for the couturier's first fitting.

Why? If you have not asked—truly asked, you truly will. You must.

But how can I answer? For when I tell you I was commanded, you shall rightly ask, "By whom?" And how can I explain? Divine inspiration? It will not begin to elucidate the matter. Yet I tell you now—I swear—it was his voice I heard. It could have been no other.

They said the South had lost the war. They were wrong. That the ruthless Sherman's burning of Atlanta—the proud and beautiful "jewel of the glorious Southern diadem," said Senator Nash—had wrecked the Southern spirit, broken the spine of our resistance. They were wrong.

To resist tyranny is not a task to which one's back is yoked. It is a burden of the soul. Immutable, unyielding—it exists in the soft marrow, where souls are deep and true.

As for General Lee's surrender—let him rot along with his forgotten oaths. Proud General Johnston will not yield in the East. Steadfast Major Quantrell will not yield in the West. The South lives! Its sons are still willing. This Booth will not forget his honor, cannot yield to oppression.

Who are these people whose emancipation has engendered the enthusiasm of the unwitting? How is it believed their treatment is unjust?

Looking upon African slavery from the same standpoint held by the noble framers of the constitution, I have ever considered it one of the greatest blessings—both for themselves and us—that God ever bestowed upon a favored nation.

Where are the voices of the Northern factories and shops where people—white people—bear their children in attics and sweat in windowless closets the very days of their deaths? Their children never learn to sing but pray only for deliverance, anticipate cataclysm, that a next world would be of necessity kinder.

Oh gentle South. Your seasons are long, your days over-languorous and balmy beyond nature, nor bitten with winded frost. Yet do your sons and daughters dream through their nights, rejoice at the sun-blessed days or even thank the storms of autumn and spring for the kindness of their torrents, the fury of their lightning strokes. A million firebugs rejoicing in the damp aftermath as their wings reclaim a day of flight.

That some men are more favored we know. That all will find salvation is scarcely wondered. Let us teach our children, black or white, to know the several blessings of our God. Only let us not give arms to babes, skilled instruments to the

243

ignorant, powers to the inept. Free the niggers? Sooner set loose a herd of wild beasts upon a planted field. Franchise them too? Lay your first born in the fresh-turned furrows, all the same.

***

How had the metropolis of my youth changed? Not very. I felt familiar with it all. Every brick, every lamp to light a brand new street, still had the mark of a kinsman. And walking past the Merchants' Exchange—where I ever remember seeing my father pose for a moment's parlay with some vest-thumbed cheroot chewer, to dream of a more genteel life than that of some circus vagabond—my footsteps felt so planted, so sure, I nearly crossed toward the Holliday Street Theater, but settled for the quick deposition of two cents for a look at the *Sun*, that somehow should have mention of my latest triumph or my next challenge.

But when the capital city was spread around and below me, as engines scrawled their final course of tracks, it was no Tyrian carpet, even to my musings, no fabled kingdom promising wisdom to all who entered. And the silver piece that found its way unknowingly into my nervous hand, as the station pulled itself ever closer, managed to show only its tail-side through thirty random flips. This, though I promised I should replace it in my pocket as soon as it had blessed my mission with the propitious showing of its face. Then flip a coin, yourself at any time you wish to have it land face up in your palm—it is always the tail.

If I have seemed preoccupied with the detailing of my recollections of this or that theater in any other city, it is nothing compared to my feelings in Washington. The memories of Grover's, the Washington, Ford's, of course, overswept me all at once, that I could smell the spirit gum and cold cream, blinked to clear them from my clouded eyes. Though I still held Saturday's half-read Baltimore paper in my valise, I could not wait to purchase the *Sunday Morning*

Chronicle, to see what fare was being offered this week.

Still, how should I think of this fixation? How can I not but wonder at the remarkably unreal aspects of the occupier of my fancies, the catalyst of this fact. Somewhere I had been absorbed by a world of fantasy—yes, and soaked through the skin. Yet still was I lost in my attempt to reconcile its nature, to give it substance where my instincts knew there was none, that my shaded self might gain form and stature in its company.

***

Time. Place.

"Just think of it," she said with her head upon my chest and her right hand massaging my shoulder.

The reflections of the lantern were lost in the auburn weaves of her hair.

"You will be the hero of Richmond."

"Richmond has fallen. The South has surrendered."

"Those are the reports of the Federal newspapers. You believe them?"

"They are all that is left to believe."

"This is not the man I love. Where is your spirit? Where is your strength? What of the immortality of which you spoke? *The ambitious youth who set fire to the Ephesian dome—*"

"*Outlives in fame the fool who built it*? That was brandy talking. If you remember, I could not recall that youth's name. I cannot now."

"Wilkes!" she returned with a start.

"What, I? There can be no purpose now. No troops to exchange for the hostage president. The man you love is here. Who else would have had the courage to smuggle drugs under the watchful eyes of Grant's army? And wave his own pass coolly, defiantly in their faces?"

Something caught the corner of my eye and without pausing to think I felt myself avoiding some strange shadow playing ominously at one side of the room. There it seemed to dance, or at least declaim with mighty strokes in a manner befitting some skilled tragedian, bent with age or hapless station. That vision of my death bravely interrupted, presented unrehearsed by my one true, if unmet friend.

"No. You have tried to kidnap him on two occasions. Tried and failed. Now, kill him."

"What?"

"You said—"

"That was the brandy, too."

"Perhaps it was the brandy, also, that spoke of your love for me."

"Never question that."

"I am not the only one—"

"You are my only love."

"Then?"

"To what end?"

"Revenge. It is your destiny!"

The words of both the gypsy and John Brown raced helter skelter through my mind, seeking some balance, some form, some artful cohesion.

"You confuse me with another."

"Perhaps I do. Ah, yes. I remember, now. You are the one whom Edwin Booth assured would *not startle the world.*"

"I will not have you repeat that again. That information was not even mine to give you, but told me by my brother June in a moment of confidence. Edwin often fills his letters with casual observations. He is not one to long contemplate his thoughts before expressing them."

A silence matched in depth only by her hazel eyes ensued. I swallowed hard and felt the ancient wound in my throat.

"And if I fail?"

"You will not. Or I will follow you in infamy in a free South."

***

Late afternoon. A stately home.

A drawing room furnished with overstuffed chairs and divans, dark, low tables with spindly legs and high, narrow sideboards lined regularly with bric-a-brac. An oriental carpet in the middle of the floor. Two large, planted vases flank curtained French doors.

YOUNG WOMAN: I cannot love you, Johnnie. I cannot. You know I want to—only I cannot let myself.

THE ACTOR: And you can stop it just like that?

YOUNG WOMAN: No, no; but my father can.

THE ACTOR: Your father? He has always despised me. Damn his duplicity. He despises me and he does not even know why. *(gesturing)* Because I am an actor.

YOUNG WOMAN: That isn't true. Poppie isn't like that. It would be different if—

THE ACTOR: If what?

YOUNG WOMAN: If you were famous—really famous—like your brother. Poppie thinks Edwin hung the moon.

The Actor begins to show signs of anger.

YOUNG WOMAN: Poppie likes you. You're just—well, he's done everything he could, spent his whole life to see that I had every advantage. Oh Johnnie! If you were rich I should marry you tomorrow. Today. This instant!

THE ACTOR: If I were president I would only have made three thousand dollars more last year. Did you know that?

247

The difference between my income and the president's? Three thousand dollars!

YOUNG WOMAN: And if you could make that money in an instant? Thirty thousand dollars! That would be enough money to pay for our wedding. Did you know that?

Her eyes show of desire. The desire they had once held unremittingly for him. The desire they would ever stir within him. The desire he felt that instant that she should be his or not at all.

He looked one more time into those passionate, flaming eyes and drove the dagger deep into her breast.

***

Saturday, March 18, 1865. Ford's Theatre, Washington City.

Evening. A dressing room. WILKES prepares for his role as Pescara in Richard Lalor Sheil's The Apostate. *His sister, ASIA, writing letters in one corner of the room begins to speak without looking at him.*

ASIA: Your wish is to be famous? By killing the president? The conflict is over. Jeff Davis is the one who continues and will not stop. Lee has surrendered his sword and pledged himself to the Union. Lincoln is for peace. You still think the issue is saving the South? That would be wonderful. But save yourself first. Let your bullet find Jeff Davis in his sleep. Quiet him. Then you will be famous, and you and your Ella can live in peace.

WILKES: You do not care much for her, do you?

ASIA: You have changed since you met her.

WILKES: As have you—since your marriage to Sleepy.

ASIA: I despise that name for him.

WILKES: And yet it is so appropriate. Besides, it is Edwin's invention not mine. And it is true. He is lazy, too lazy to make a career for himself. You know that is why he married you.

248

ASIA: So you tell me.

WILKES: You cannot accuse her of the same. If anything she is risking an otherwise certain future by her involvement with me.

ASIA: Perhaps. But she will remind you of it ever. I do not like her for you. But I shall be honest. I do not know if I would approve of anyone for my brother Johnnie.

WILKES: I sensed as much, and I love you for that. And I thank you for coming to see me. Do you remember that gypsy curse? It seems now so absurd, so far behind us. They have confirmed my commission as colonel in the army of the Confederacy.

ASIA: But? You are not enlisted.

WILKES: What does it matter? Can you think of any man who would look more handsome in a uniform than Mr. J. Wilkes Booth?

***

Same night. The dressing room.

THE ACTOR removes his costume while the YOUNG WOMAN vies for a place in front of the dressing mirror to adjust the bodice of her dress. The Actor defers his needs for self-reflection to hers.

Who is Gessler?

A villain. A horrible villain and tyrant. It was he who persecuted the noble Tell and bade him shoot an apple from atop his own son's head. Where did you hear this name?

And what happened to him?

That same arrow next found his own blackened heart. What is this about?

Poppie says it will never work. Your plan.

He what?

Of course, he doesn't know that it's your plan. But all Washington knows it is a plan. Don't sound so surprised. He was speaking with some gentlemen friends after you took me home the other evening. I heard them through the parlor doors. They were smoking the most dreadful cigars and I kept hearing the clanking of glasses. And who is Tinkerton?

Who?

Tinkerton. Poppie didn't actually say it wouldn't work, just that Tinkerton might get in the way. "He interfered once, and could again."

Did he say interfere or prevent?

I don't know. Does it matter? It's the same thing, really. Who is he?

You're right. It doesn't really matter, because I have been assured he won't interfere.

By whom?

Ella, you haven't ever spoken of this to anyone else, have you?

No! I can't believe—

No one?

No one.

Only with me?

Only with you. Only you, darling. Oh, Johnnie. You are so very—

**

I would say I took her then, but I am not sure how it happened, only that we kissed.

Scene II

The veriest wretch that goes shivering by
Will take a wide sweep, lest I wander too nigh;
For all that is on or about me, I know
There is nothing that's pure, but the beautiful snow.

Cara,
    You will not be completely surprised, my darling, when you read this rather than meet me tomorrow morning.
    How could I take you at your word? You are too fine, deserve so much.
    I will be lucky now to find sanctuary in the meekest and stalest of your tobacco barns.

    Remember me,
    John.

***

John,
    How could you leave without farewell?

***

I am older than you are. What of it? Should I apologize for my past, my experience? As well to make excuses for my manhood, and that would I never.

You have often accused me of relying upon my form instead of character, yet you insist that no one will ever be able to share in one part of what we are, now were. This will change with time, and the memory of us will lose its substance, its reality, its form. Dissipate into nothingness.

What I will not believe is that you can name our children with me one day and forget our dreaming the next. How will you ever call your children by those long favored names without seeing at least my eyes, or mouth, or "too-small ears?"

251

Oh! Pet,
  Why haven't you written?

I continue to shave the moustache you long attempted to persuade me to abandon. I do not believe I look as ridiculous as I feared I would, though you might disagree.

My deepest regret is that only once we could have been together, fully, completely, recklessly. Will you so easily find new loves? How will you forget my scent for theirs? What names will they call you and you them? Any pet will never sound the same unless it sounds too much my name.

What lips will kiss your ankles in dark theaters, whose hands—I cannot continue. Is it not enough to know you hold my heart, or must you also see the spell that binds the deepest secrets of our love to painful memory?

Did you ever know my love? You said you did. I wonder if you knew your own. Or if you had, if you quite understood how knowing it would forbid you from ever truly knowing the love of another.

I know that I have not always been fair. You are far more, I think sometimes, than I deserve.

No one will ever be able to replace what we have. It will remain forever. You are too deeply a part of me.

But I must continue. I can not keep the schoolgirl fantasies. It seems knowing you kept my womanhood at bay. I must become the woman, wife, mother, I have always been.

How I will miss your dark curls and too-small ears.

Cara,
  What could have been —

***

April 14, 1865. Washington City.
Good Friday. Afternoon.

    A handbill in the showcase window of Ford's tenth street theater announces a "Benefit! and Last Night" performance of Miss Laura Keene in Tom Taylor's comedy Our American Cousin, *with Mr. John Dyott and Mr. Harry Hawk, orchestra conducted by Mr. William Withers, to be followed the next night by Miss Jennie Gourlay in Dion Boucicault's* The Octoroon.

***

And did you know? That night Stanton's own strongman Eckert was asked to go as guard for Lincoln, but Stanton refused him leave. General Grant was supposed to accompany the Lincolns but excused himself at the last minute for the reason of returning home with his wife to visit their children. It was at this point Lincoln invited Major Henry Rathbone and his fiancée Clara Harris.

***

Cara,
    I am afraid to say you were right. Afraid to think the passions of my heart were always wrong, never one with the passions of my soul. Simply, I am afraid. Of life and love without you, and of what—yes—I have done to us. Mostly to you.
    It will not change anything, make any of this better or easier to deal with, but if I think of you crying, hear your tears as I did this morning and know that I have been the cause, I am only miserable.
    I wonder how I ever thought I could deserve you, how I could have taken you down with me. How I was so foolish, selfish, callous, blind. It will not help to know I loved you, even at those most ruthless moments.

Strophe

What little I have left of integrity, honor, truth—there is some—could never be enough for you. From that, as many other things, I am far beyond hope. I question and wonder only what is left for me. The final pain cannot be worse than this.

I have been a coward before. Yet through some unearned miracle have acted with occasional courage. It is not brave still, to do what is right. It is only just. It is brave to face it, perhaps, when it has always been simpler to turn away, shake one's head and smile as if everything is fine.

What are you thinking? What must you feel inside? What success could you have in suppressing our love?

***

I cannot truly be alone, or all those days and nights have never been. If somehow a curtain were to fall on all this play, still would I be lost in my character—be he lover, fool, hero, coward, or all of these. But walk away, simply and without memory, I cannot.

I was there. To feel your warm breath on my neck. Have your hands clutch at my shoulders and sides. And remember the playful toes nibbling swollen calves, plucking at the coarse, unruly hairs that mark the legs of a man for your jests and taunts.

Can you have no memory? Of the laughter, the sighing aftermath, the blessed afternoons of companioned strolls. How foolish I would be to recollect some other's disapproval, a jealous instant borne of love, your teethmarks on my wrist.

What would I do to have back your love? If I continue, you will hate me more. Hate me for the tears that I will shed. The tears that you found more onerous than the verses I sent you out of love. Tears that were forgivable only as a part in some drama or the offspring of another drunken fit. Why was that our purest moment? What was there locked in both our souls that escaped only as we drank? Where was manhood in the cache of fears and tears and sober feelings?

Yours, ever,
John.

***

That afternoon I had taken Cola to run through the streets and whoop as loud as any man might. My object was clear, my mind made up. Still, how could I be sure of what I had to do, and then of how I could explain it to myself, to my god—to her.

Approximately 2 P.M., long after I had received word that the Northern president and his wife were sure to attend the theater, I received a strange message via my old friend whom I had met by accident outside Smitty's tavern. There was no name attached to the message, merely a place and time, and the code name I had begun to know so well and accept as the signature of a true friend, *H. A. B.*

As I began to steer my horse toward the Adams Hotel where I had been summoned, I observed an unshaken figure in the middle of the street. It was a dark stranger of medium build with a long moustache visible beneath the shadow of a wide-brimmed hat. Black patent boots shone nearly new under pin-striped pant legs. If the day had been a moment further along, and were it not for the stylishness of the clothes, I may have mistaken it for Herold. The eyes sparkled. It was Ella.

She looked at me with that particularly serious sense of playfulness she shared so readily with a young child. And, as the children of any age, which she so reluctantly yielded, if only in the face of mature reason and tame logic. It had been less than ten hours since I had kissed her goodbye for what I thought would be the last time.

"I am ready," she said in a low voice without meeting my gaze.

"You are going home," I insisted. "Before your dilettante stagecraft alerts all of Washington City to my plan."

Producing a dark cheroot, she remained non-plussed as she

255

proceeded to light it with a long, deep gasp and answered gruffly. "The tobacconist did not even flinch when I ordered his finest belvedere."

"He may not have well seen your face, but even a fool could not mistake those hands for those of so much as a young boy. What is your enduring interest in this expedition? How must you find insufficient the fortune your father has surely promised?"

"Not for me, John. These are not things I want for me. What do I care of me? You. I want them for you. I want them because you want them. Because they are a part of you. You deserve them. They are you. You are fame and success."

"And you are a little fool!" I snapped. But I did not believe it, even then. Even as I could see my world collapse about me. Even as she turned away.

***

When the first snow fell in the city to dot and dash only the tops of so many pugnacious hedges and upstart shrubs, I felt I too could not be completely enveloped in its annual ritual. This year, this season, an unquestionable pair of eyes would continue to stare ever into my own and reign defiant spring.

No one ever looked at me like that. It was always my eyes that had been avoided, my stare refused with denial's laughter or nervous appraisal. Mine, which unconsciously canted the same spell that must have been my father's mysterious hold upon an audience. Mine, whether studied or innate, gifted or practiced, was only theatrical. Hers was pure. No words, no favorite or familiar phrases, no scripted eloquence, no goading passages demanding certain and glib reply. Just sure and silent confrontation, confirmation of a deeper litany and an entreaty to recognize its seasonless rite.

How could I walk alone again or imagine icy images of doubt or death or dormant expectation, but be held by their power, their private prayer. And behind each frosted window, each wreathed alcove and huddled street corner conversation, I saw their hearthside sparkle, felt their gracious welcome from the chilled day, heard too the voice that sweetly accompanied their soft-piercing stare.

Each wrapped and mufflered traveler approaching even from the direction opposite where my mind knew I had only just kissed her blushed and tender cheeks goodbye, my heart shaped into her. And any bustled tread behind my own I dreamed as being their pursuit of one more eyeful embrace. I could not leave her wholly or simply as I had done a hundred others.

***

It was the last night and it was our first night—for we had kissed and held and slept never more. I eased my body cautiously on top of hers and met her mouth first slowly, then complete; watched her eyes recede, their silver whites gleaming from under half-lifted lids. She fluttered beneath me. Her body heaved forward and my hands scooped up her shoulders and the small of her back to match her swaying with my own.

I kissed her lips and chin and jaw, the hollow of her neck. Her skin's own perfume filled my head like some remembered yet unknown scent—the incense of an ancient mystery, ceremonies we had performed in five-thousand flaming dreams until this night forgotten.

She hurt and I could not hold her close enough. The rocking of our bodies shed in our minds the clothing we still wore. My hands traced their way along her back and sides to her soft, full contours.

"Don't make me wait," she whispered while she grabbed at the back of my shirt.

Or was it just a sigh?

We were swept into a wordless poem. No words. No words. No words. Lips, mouths, tongues, but no words. Cheeks, noses, chins, but no faces. Arms without memories, genius hands, legs and feet that sprang suddenly forth from where bodies once were. And her life and my seed, mixed silently in the faint glimmer of eyes, open in the dark. The truth of the one, the thought of the other, tangled in mutual curls. Hers light, mine dark.

I felt my seed push, stir surely, subside to purer passion and stir once more. We danced again, our murmurs mingling in thick, curtained memories of moonlight.

"Make love to me," she said.

No tone, no tinge of this or that.

"Make love to me."

Again. And sure.

"Please," she murmured.

If there had been some doubt—hers, mine, that of another, many could have come to mind—it was not heard. All was sounded in a moment, and only one word returned, remained amid the deepest channels of the lyric that had been and whose passing ghost would rise again and be eternal.

"Now."

One shadow, one reminder of the unspoken. One truth, one feeling above the erst-summoned censures. One echo, one simple susurration—absolutely silent to any else. We heard it. Felt it reverberate. Knew its peal. Now!

Again the urge exacted, the promise of progeny, painted fields with harvest claims. The now was then.

And when the dance was finished, the panting musk changed to a whisper, tomorrow pressed between our flesh, the amber light—invisible and bright, I lay broken. As a horse, a heart, an arm or leg, a chair—a cornered sack of murphies. Broken and spent, but whole for what seemed the first time. I felt her next to me and let go one last breath.

Scene III

How strange it should be that his beautiful snow
Should fall on a sinner with nowhere to go!

Do not try to follow. I would not want you now, as it is.

***

The morning before we arrived at Garrett's Farm, Herold and I lounged on the doorstep of a deserted house that lay hidden deep within the security of the short pines and thickets which lace the Southern banks of the Rappahannock. We had spent the past week-and-a-half traveling the underground route, being well-received by nearly all—the one exception being a certain Dr. Richard Stuart, may he rot along with General Lee—and only just left the warmth and comfort of Office Hall, the home of Mr. William McDaniell. Well-fed and rested we were startled when two low, whooping whistles, followed after a short interval by a third, interrupted the silence. The sign of a friend. Still did we grab for our guns as two figures approached through the dense undergrowth.

I soon recognized my own former slave and friend Henry Johnson, with a man he introduced as Badin accompanying him, both looking as if they had spent a fortnight walking the distance from New York to Richmond. That explained the condition of the man shot by Corbett. For Herold and I, as explained, experienced nothing in the way of palpable hardships—save my twisted ankle—since beginning our flight. Badin's clothes were torn rags and his face thin, all of which led only to encourage my belief in him.

"Who and what do you know?" I inquired.

"What do you?" he correctly responded.

"I know nothing. You?"

"Nothing," offering his hand simply.

He claimed to be a former prize-fighter and officer in the Virginia militia, having only just resumed his residency in

Washington. At the news of his prize-fighting I customarily asked if he knew of my former associate Thomas Mears. He said he did not. I was almost relieved, having never very much liked nor trusted Mears, though it was he who convinced me to carry a derringer, bidding me never fire it from a distance greater than my arm's length.

Badin said he had knowledge of the approach of Baker's command. He would not tell how he had come by this information, but I trusted it for truth and asked him what I might do about it.

"Escape," said the ragman bluntly, licking his sparse moustache as if he had just finished the dream of a large and gravied dinner. Clearly he had not.

I looked at my hobbled leg and asked how he thought that might be done, my movements inhibited to such an extent that I could in no manner keep pace with my ever-nearing pursuers.

"Do not worry, we shall lead them on a chase such as they could not expect."

"We?"

"I shall continue on with Herold. I am weary from the road, but can still travel quickly. We will lead them inland while you lay in hiding."

"What? Just wait? Henry and I?"

"Just you. Johnson will travel on down the river. The current is swift here and will soon take him to the one who can lead you to safety. You shall be out of danger by the morning and home again by the end of the week."

"Surely the Union troops will not be so easily fooled," I worried.

"I shall lead them due south. That is the direction they expect you to take, after all. There will be no reason for them to suppose you have found any help. We will exchange clothes you and I. You must give me all your effects, everything you have on your person—in case they have brought dogs with them."

I hesitated at the thought of giving up my small brocade medicine kit.

"Even that is not a complete guarantee," Badin continued. "You must promise me you will not move. It is the only way to be sure. They expect you to continue in your flight and Johnson must be sure where you will be in order to leave perfect instructions for his friend."

"Will he not be with his friend?"

"No. He is being missed this very moment back in Baltimore. Surely you can imagine where they must think he is. No, he has much to do. He must leave yet another false trail, in the event he is discovered. His friend will be back for you. You will recognize him by his signal—just as you recognized mine."

"I do not know," I protested. "I do not think myself well enough to travel alone. One more night. That is all I want. One more night in my fellows' company."

"Yessir!" agreed young Herold enthusiastically as ever. "One more night. He is not well enough. Yessir, our rendezvous tonight is set and he will need a good meal and rest before slogging off alone—if that is what he must do."

"Very well," conceded Badin. "One more night. I will learn what I may about the movements of your pursuers and meet you—"

"Yessir! At Garrett's Farm," volunteered Herold.

"At Garrett's Farm," he repeated. "At midnight."

And so Herold and I continued to our rendezvous and were well-met by the Garretts. I do not believe the children knew anything of my identity, nor had they yet heard any news, but they understood their father's sympathies and that I was his *very special guest*.

"And handsome," said the eldest daughter, too forwardly for her mother's approval. Garrett just laughed.

The boys took Herold and me to the tobacco shed where we were outfitted with crude but adequate beddings and presently brought a hot meal with freshly baked cornbread. I picked about my stew while the nervous Herold only paced and fretted.

It was nearly midnight when Badin re-appeared, true to his word. With his return, we discovered the door had been locked with a small but sturdy padlock. One of the Garrett boys acting on orders from his father to ensure our safety from intruders, we reasoned. Fine thinking. Badin came around the rear and easily slipped through a rather large break in an already scarcely slatted backside.

With Badin's accounting of the surrounding area, Herold's drooping spirits were immediately lifted, anticipating the near and fortunate conclusion of our days in flight. But I was nervous. After having exchanged clothes per our agreement and rescuing over some objections the several pages from my diary on which I had begun to write a sort of stage play, I watched the others settle in for the night, silently grabbed my brocade kit and leather satchel and stole out through the same gap at the back of the shed. I needed to find a place in the thick grove beyond where I could ease my pain with a little morphine.

That was all. Almost as quickly as I found myself under the moonlight I heard the approach of horsemen. At first I thought it only the effect of the drug, but even so, hid among the vines of a small ravine and, crouching, cursed the ragged shoes of Badin.

There was a long, baying commotion at the Garrett home. I heard Richard Garrett's voice trying to calm the sobbings of his wife and family. A young girl's scream and the barking of orders were interrupted by the higher pitched shouts of the youngest boy. The frenzy seemed to continue for a long time.

Some moments later everything went quiet and still. I started to make my way back, still low in the brush a hundred yards or less away when I heard another burst of voices. More commands sounded and I recognized Herold's voice calling out. Still more commands, followed by Badin, in theatrical tones, confidently addressing the officer-in-charge.

Then, I saw it. At first just a small glow in the dark, it grew brighter and larger until I began to realize what was happening. They had set fire to the shed. There would be little defense now. A single shot rang out.

With that, I rose and turned and began to run. And I did not stop for a moment to look behind me for half-an-hour, an hour more, another. My foot was still swollen, but I felt nothing of it until I was far into the woods and the sun began to rise over my right shoulder. Realizing my exhaustion for the first time I collapsed at once into a tuft of tall, dewy grass and felt the separate pains of my lungs, my foot, my fears.

I was truly alone.

***

The first three days after fleeing Garrett's Farm I scarcely moved a muscle. Concealed in the bed of underbrush my stalked scrambling had found, and never truly sure of my security or seclusion, I tried to sleep. The tiny quantity of morphine left from that final night with Herold and Badin I carefully rationed to encourage a rest otherwise hard fought.

And every day-lit hour or two I would awaken again, some winged pest lighting now in my nose, now in my ear. And every portioned sleep would send patrols of hapless images: columns of mounted, blue-coated pursuers, red-faced Herold and a featureless ragman; a theater full of somewhat familiar figures, mostly topped with hats or veils of mourning, among them Dr. Mudd and poor, devoted Henry Johnson. From the rear lobby, one hand beckoning to the crowd, eyes lifted to heaven, the tyrant's tall, gray, lanthorn visage. At one side his portly wife, held fast to him by a silk-and-gold braided tether, the start or end of which seemed indistinguishable, at the other, my beloved horse, Cola.

Exiting all at once, the audience became a processional, my own ghostly heartbeat drumming the rhythm of what I certainly knew to be a dirge. Under an enormous shadow cast by a stovepipe hat, six hooded figures palled an ebony casket trimmed in swirls of tooled silver. The lid propped open several inches, a thick red lining was revealed. Inside it now, the celebrated form.

Three full days I lay in still and quiet hiding, watched the shadows of three suns and moons rise and fall across my unfamiliar homeland yet dare not move, nor barely breathe at all. And each new dawn was another threat of hounds or men, and every night escape into a world of dark where alone I could rest until my dreams were filled with as many threats as my fevered head could hold, my dreaming having increased each day in clarity and effect upon my waking. Barking, baying dogs, uniformed and walking upright through open fields or scattered woods. Howling signals of intent to each other, their grinning teeth dripped streams of brandy, gathered into awaiting snifters throughout the field.

By the morning of the fourth day my fever had broken, my ankle was healing. My leg had never been as bad as the newspaper accounts, but nonetheless caused me to limp. I feared I would never fully ride again. Nor play Richard to be sure. But I could walk and, my only hope of promised haven somewhere to the west, knew I must. Only at the end of an entire day on my feet was my gait strained and the old wound noticeable. This was a small price to pay for my liberation I thought, in moments when that liberation did not seem wholly accursed.

Despite my meager ration, aimless wandering and withal, I began to feel better. I had no knowledge of the exact fate of Herold and Badin but sensed the one had more than saved my life. I had felt a kind of silent debt from the dawn of my first day alone, an unrepayable favor done by an unknown friend, a spectral devotee's wordless prayer said for the sake of an unknowable God. My flight renewed, his fearless faith became my own. As it had been my strength for those three nights, it became my hope for asylum where he had given his own.

Of course there could be no thought of finding sanctuary

with my family. Even had they wished it, they were, every one, closely watched by the secret police. Later I would learn Edwin and Joseph had indeed been arrested, though released after only a brief time. But I already intuited this, knew the pain of even a moment in a cell and wept for them. None of this was for their suspected part certainly, though for the pleasure of those who hoped I might still arrive as some dim-witted Lewis at a guarded and impassibly sentried door.

And there were others. Relations whose ties held no familiarity yet still enough blood to command, I should think—if only temporary—relief. In the Carolinas, Tennessee, and far away Mississippi. But what good was that? Eventually they too would be summoned. If not by some local magistrate perhaps by the greed within their own bond-refuting souls.

Of all my kin and cousins, even friends, whom could I trust? That man only, still unmet. Small, swarthy, and blacker-skinned than the newest arrival from Africa's interior. He alone was competent with my person and secret. He alone had reason to exchange my confidence. Still, his skin, dark as it was, paled to his trustworthy soul.

So for the time I took my chances along the winding rivers and hillsides, ever traveling westward at night. By day I burrowed like some creature of the fields into thick underbrush to rest. On the eve of the third of these days I awoke from my bed of grass and leaves to discover myself in a wooded glen at the base of a low hillock. Surmounting it was a deserted ore mill, the kind for which these hills are famous. Or so it first appeared.

The brook, from which I had artlessly washed and drank that morning, sprang wonderfully from the greening crags atop the hill. Across its mouth spanned a rough-hewn tower forged of the kind of ancient stones that dressed the tiny valley where I had passed my latest night of perspiring dreams. It was not an abandoned arrastra after all, but the newly consecrated monastery of St Alban.

I cannot explain my feeling of relief or the soothing effect of the plain white cross of which I had been told, marking the foot of the small winding path. With hardly more than an iron-ringed knock upon its simple oaken door, the man in tatters—and I looked more like Badin this moment than any member of my true family—was taken in for supper, a necessary bath and my first real night's sleep in more than a week.

So, for three fortnights I lived the life of a Camaldolese monk. My rags were exchanged routinely upon my arrival for coarse but clean muslin trousers and a rope-belted frock. Neither was I questioned, nor was I engaged in idle conversation. The order, being devoted to a contemplative life, our days were spent in silence and prayer—and work.

During the day I helped the brothers complete construction of individual shelters—the second of which became my own for the time I was there, the first having become that of the Abbot. They had spent most of their initial time building the hermitage's place of worship, a central hall for washing, cooking and eating, and the adjoining dormitory where I spent my first week with all of the others. After sunset only group prayer was considered before retiring for the night. The vow of silence certainly worked in my favor, and because of the past several anxious months, I welcomed the change toward workmanlike monotony, enthusiastically joining the brothers in their otherwise humdrum society.

From morning vigils and lauds to evening vespers, we labored together, with only an hour's repose for Eucharistic prayer and meditation. Two small suppers, each granted a quarter hour, were shared during the day. The simple meals of wheat biscuit and chicken fixings, or corn bread and common doings, were eaten in silence and alone when possible.

This was a brand of Catholicism I had known nothing about but which aimed at a spiritual and physical purity I could not but help admire. Whether it was the fact I continued to keep my face clean-shaven and hair shorn, or the unlikely rags in which I had first appeared, or the disassociation from all things material and the news of the day, I never felt suspect—not for a moment, though this complete lack of distinction had a rather strange side-effect for me.

Strophe

I am dead. In a Benedictine monastery of the Camaldolese order in the Lost River wilds of Rockingham County. Sworn to work, silence and prayer. My secrets are my secrets, my sins are mankind's. But who is my God? Where is He? Will He only show Himself when I no longer seek His face; be mine when I no longer hunger and thirst for His presence, comfort me when I am finally ready and able to console myself but need no consolation?

***

It was not Henry Johnson who came at last one evening with a signal whistle throughout the coomb below my hermit's cell, as the thrush opened their throats for a last sunlit song upon the deepening world. What trail I might have left for any to follow I cannot imagine but when I heard it first, still was there no doubt as to its purpose or intent.

"Whooo-whit," came the first of the three partridge trills up through the gathering mists. "Whooo-whit," again, then finally, "whooo-whit-whit."

I gratefully awaited the last of the series before responding with three of my own. Shuttering my window with a deep sigh I then gathered my journal pages and folded them back into the small leather satchel, reflexively tightening the belt of my frock. My ankle was newly wrapped, and I was ready.

Henry's cousin startled me as much by his looks as by his appearance at the door to my cell, carrying an overstuffed valise as if he meant to join me for the week. Brother Pascal stood just behind him with a strange though trusting look upon his sun-freckled brow. Then, with a solemn almost knowing look he retreated wordlessly to the other side of the flagstone courtyard where he finished helping Brother Arnaud light the several torchieres around its perimeter, always left burning at night.

"Who and what do you know?" I asked simply.

"Everyz'ing," came the hushed and throaty shrill of my visitor. "What do you know—Booz'?"

His skin was very black, much more so than Henry's, and his accent was Creole. I must have turned quite white with surprise as I nodded assent to his one-word question.

"H'eet eez no wondair you find my rhace so strange, as cou'zahn *Henri* 'as told to me. We share z'e same eyes, but mine h'are zhust z'e reflexion of my skeen. I wondair what h'eet eez z'at yours do mirroir?"

I looked at him quizzically, first to be sure I had understood what he said and meant to say, and then doubly when his constant gaze confirmed I had. I wondered if he had the answer, as he seemed to, for his own question.

At his silent beckoning, I accompanied his waddling form through the courtyard and out into another unknowable if somehow less uncertain night. I waited for a moment at the monastery door for some sign of farewell from Pascal or Arnaud—or any of the others, but soon realized there would be none. I caught a glimpse of the two of them as they continued their silent rounds without a glance in my direction, and I closed the door behind me.

***

"Marechal Antaeus Philippe de Mercure et Le Main," he said with a thick accent, deep flourish and a courteous pride as he led the way down the path, and past the break where the small cross marked where I had first caught sight of the monastery after stumbling up from the river.

"You must call me Ma'zhor 'And, h'as do my coo'zahn."

The major, Major Hand—Henry Johnson's cousin—the man to whom I was now entrusting my safety, was perhaps three feet tall. Black as pitch and three feet tall! Stopping for a moment only he quickly addressed my unspoken if obvious concern.

"Do not worry, *Monsieur* Booz', I h'am steel enough z'e man to 'elp you to h'escape. I h'am a dwarf, not a mizh'ette, which means my 'art beats h'as strong h'and eez h'every beet h'as big h'as yours. Yes, and oz'er z'ings, h'as well," he smiled strangely. "I h'am certainly more z'e man z'an *Monsieur* Boston Coh'rbett!"

He let out a quiet shrill that I soon realized was intended to be a laugh.

"Who?"

"Oh, z'at eez true, eez eet not? I h'am sorry. I forget. You 'ave not been but 'ere z'ese several weeks. You 'ave not 'eard z'ee news? You h'ar dead, *Monsieur* Booz'! Yes, quite dead, indeed. And z'e man w'at keel you eez *Monsieur* Boston Coh'rbett."

As we entered the twilight wood he let out his shrill laugh, pleased with himself. Laughing all the while he intermittently turned in stride in a quick circle and using his bag as counterweight, as if he were dancing at some fairy cotillion, before continuing on. Curious, I followed him into the deepening night, often noting how his winding steps ahead of me appeared influenced by the phantom music of an elfin jig. Or was it just his size and aspect?

I had spent six weeks at the monastery. It was June 14th. By sunrise the hermitage would be nothing more than a memory. There was a kind of irony in this, though I was not altogether sure of exactly what. And three weeks later Hand would lead me at last from the woods and up the gentle rise for the first time to the rustic cabin where I would spend the next twenty-five years in seclusion and effective hibernation.

***

The road west. Two travelers with a looming storm behind them.

A DWARF: Would h'eet be to z'e advantage of a master to

269

wheep h'or maim 'is properhty beyond value?

THE ACTOR: The old argument. No, nor any man's advantage to murder his brother. The hand of justice will surely deal with all.

A DWARF: Ah! H'out of z'e mouz's of sinners?

THE ACTOR: Yet, penitence is possible.

A DWARF: Not for me!

Scene IV

How strange it would be, when the night comes again,
If the snow and the ice struck my desperate brain!

Was Cain justified in his brother's murder? I have often puzzled over the story. Found reason behind this *first crime* to pity the hapless Cain, and with him despise the brother whom God had favored for no particular reason.

It is not that I was irreligious. I was, if anything, perhaps too devout for my own well-being. I accepted religion not as an answer but as a series of questions demanding inquiry. The more I inquired, however, the more dissatisfied I became with the replies. Forgetting for the moment, of course, they were my own responses.

It began with Cain and Abel. I moved past Adam and Eve with the kind of resolution that sees necessity to beginning the story of earthly man, not the creatures of Paradise. Resigned that somehow man had fallen from grace and it might as well have happened at the hand of a woman. Had to, in some ways. Still, no one ever seemed to take that part of the story too seriously—except Corbett—although women, I expect, must feel a general brunt of the guilt, if only implicitly.

But Cain and Abel. That story bothered me. Confused me. Tried my faith until the point where perhaps I have found understanding in the unskeined moments of true reflection.

Why was Abel favored for his sacrifice? Both had worked with equal faith. Both had made their offerings with equal piety. Why wouldn't God accept those of Cain?

Why shouldn't Cain be angry—with his God, with his brother? I would have been.

That is where it started to unravel, for me.

I imagined how a father might treat a favorite son. Harder and more severely than the rest. Expect more of him. Test him at every turn.

Perhaps God was merely testing the favored Cain. Pushing

him to see how far he would go. How much he could endure—as with Noah, Abraham, Moses. But Cain gave in. He failed. God's favor was misspent.

God tests me. How much may I endure? Surely I have been favored. In many ways been blessed, and now given a second chance. What must I do to prove my devotion?

I would retrieve that purer time, before the fall of Adam and his Eve. Forget the manifold errors of our choices to relive those first moments when love seemed the only issue.

***

Time. Place.

"You're funny," she laughed deeply. "You're really funny!"

The ACTOR simply smiles.

"Why do you never think to do comedy?"

"The truly great comedians are those individuals whose lives are filled with sorrow and tragedy."

"Are the lives of the great tragedians then—is your life—so very comic?"

"This moment—yes. I have never been happier. I should think my next performance may grant my best reception yet, by critics and public alike. Yes, even if I were to play to the audiences of the North."

"Your brother is always successful with the New York crowd."

Angrily.

"I am not my brother. I would never be my brother! Not my brother Edwin, at any rate."

The ACTOR smiles again.

"And all true comedy ends with a marriage, you know."
"But I would never marry you. Surely, you know that."

***

My hand was ready to meet her face. Feeling its imminence she pushed at me with all her might, but I was frozen. And then rather than fly at her in any manner and without yet thinking of what I was about to do, though certainly with less fervor than I might have easily managed, I still insulted her—and myself—in a way I find it hard to now recount. Directly into her eyes, I looked hard—and spit.

It was not she who insulted me by holding some vain and superficial affection for my brother or some inconsequent suitor before my eyes as bait, to set my juices to roil. It was some instrument of feminine wile thinking only of any way to change my course.

Yet it was I who knelt and wept to take her up and blot her face with my kerchief. I who sought only to protect her from the beast that seemingly devoured us both, one slow fanged mouthful after another.

I cannot return nor undo what I have done. Nor think yet to remain here in the shadow of so many ills. And this considered, then move on. And if I cannot change the baser aspect of my soul, then will I dream her out. One murder have I plotted and performed, and so another shall I accept.

Strophe

I am lonely. Yet, I cannot name the single thing to make me whole. In a crowd of people I would crave adulation and applause. With a woman, she would be just a woman, and I her man. I lack love.

My solitude is scarcely bearable. Where, upon a time, I had longed for the peculiar perfection of an evening alone, unoccupied in times when every night came to a crescendo of ovations and dressing room attentions, now a single furtive gaze or sympathetic voice would calm my anxious heart.

How could I have needed so to impress or impel? If I thought, had really thought I was so deserving, why did I ever entertain a moment's doubt or despair?

And now, to hear this?

"What about Aunt Julia?" I asked myself, the tread of my heels clapping down the street behind, the capital city strangely quiet. She had been living in Boston since 1863, but visited mother at Tudor Hall in March, not one month before the fatal shot. I too was down from Baltimore at the time and something in her manner intimated a strange knowledge of my work. But how could she have known?

She who gave the most glorious of verses, her *Battle Hymn of the Republic*. She who had also written my condemnation in her *Parricide*, the day of the Union president's funeral, but eight days afterward eulogized me with *Pardon*, when she read of the incident at Garrett's farm.

> *"Death brings atonement; he did that whereof ye accuse*
> > *him, —*
> > > *Murder accurst;*
> *But, from the crisis of crime in which Satan did lose*
> > *him,*
> > > *Suffered the worst.*
>
> *So the soft purples that quiet the heavens with*
> > *mourning,*
> > > *Willing to fall,*
> *Lend him one fold, his illustrious victim adorning*
> > > *With wider pall.*
>
> *Back to the cross, where the savior, uplifted in dying,*
> > *Bade all souls to live,*

> Turns the reft bosom of nature, his mother, low
> > sighing,
> > > Greatest, forgive!"

She knew all of them. I remember being surprised that New Year's to see her in Washington. Yet not so surprised. She had after all distinguished herself in all circles. Still, what might she know? What cipher might lay hidden in her verse?

Surely, I was reeling, desperate to catch hold of some final truth. Any truth at all. But truth was, I could scarcely expect more from Julia Howe than I had received from John Surratt. I had to search elsewhere.

***

There is an arbor between Pennsylvania and I believe it is West Third Street, at the edge of a tiny park. In late autumn one may there find perfect refuge from sudden bursts of rain. The perennial boughs allowing infrequent droplets to fall through and soothe. Shelter and sanctuary without complete cloister.

In the middle of this park is a bust of some forgotten hero of a more glorious war and time. He may have been an expatriate volunteer of a sympathetic foreign power. Or a frontier farmer forgetting pastoral pleasures for high ideals and moral calls. Perhaps he was a wealthy landowner who pledged his sacred honor by hiring the blood of lesser men. He is silent, cold, nameless in my memory, the mere sentinel of an occasionally occupied garden.

As I walked past what seemed a newly planted row of trees, a fresh easterly raced about my collar with portents of a possible Atlantic storm. How many times I had prayed with her for the same. Now it only brought shivers to my heart. Shivers and the thought of once-spent tears. Still, the city was sweet with the scent of lilac. Not as sweet as Richmond's magnolias but sweet nonetheless.

From the Symphony Hall I could hear a movement from

Rossini's *Tell* straining through the air. Or was it Verdi's *Rigoletto*? She unknowingly introduced me to opera, that theater of her maternal homeland, and likewise my love for both developed simultaneously. It is for that I can scarcely bear sometimes to hear a single note, or less, a phrase of music and its foreign verse.

Wandering west on Cherry Street toward my rented apartments, I watched my shadow dance and bob pale gray under the moonlight. And though this was not new to me, to watch my own reflection, it was perhaps the first I noticed the inability, nay refusal, of my knees to so much as pretend to meet where my legs pivoted past each other.

Tomorrow I would head south again.

Strophe

How hopeless seemed the weight of that crippled cross. How hapless he who dared consider it a burden at all. The years still pass and it is scarcely remembered. But weights and tasks I have aplenty. And so reality mirrors strangely its own call from afar.

***

I trotted past a shop on Baltimore's principle street. Not an expensive shop, though one the likes of which was far away and wholly forgotten of the Kentucky woods.

There was in the window on this particular day a mannequin upon which was draped a wedding dress. Again, it was not of the latest style, brought late of Vienna or Paris, but it was long the most fashionable dress I had seen in some time. And though I could almost hear Ella's complaint for its want of train and lace, yet I could not hope but see her in it.

***

Time. Place.

"My father has promised me a great wedding," she said

abruptly that first full night together. "And a rich trousseau—when I have found the man I wish to marry."

And wishes to ask you, I thought to myself, confused.

"All Washington will be invited. Perhaps the president himself."

"Yes?" I said disparagingly. "As if he might add some grace or splendor?"

"Why, o' course. Whatever do you mean? His wife owns the most beautiful closet in the nation."

"In the North, perhaps."

"Why must you always be so bitter?"

"The bitterness is only the scent of squandered blood from men too young to die."

"And gruesome," she turned her face away from me.

"I have seen it more than once and tasted it ever since. Each laced collar, each pleat, each ruffle on her sleeve was once a platoon, a column, an entire regiment crippled, blinded or unceremoniously buried in some field or pasture. Soon to be forgotten, turned and ploughed under by a future generation with no memory of the countless names that once were men. No recollection of the reasons that brought them to arms. Only the propaganda of the reigning politics, whose scribes are empowered to tell the story.

"So were spun the glorious tales of Pericles, Alexander, Augustus," I continued. "So always will be the conqueror, the tyrant, the *favorite in His eye*. So shall the vanquished be ever silent, but for the few who know the truth and dare remember."

"Must we always speak of war? You would have yourself be one of these few?" she taunted. "It is you who would seem the tyrannical poet who fancies himself some divine mouthpiece. Or were the muse's words whispered to you alone that I could not hear? For tragic Melpomene could just as easily be masked Thalia, having her way at your expense. Mine too, if I might allow it."

Antistrophe

I must have loved her. Loved her only. For I had never before felt the complete emptiness that her reasoned wit and occasioned rebuke easily engendered in my chest, the hunger of my body and soul for those kind or sensible words to remedy my pain. Just thinking of her finds me vacant and longing again.

***

The perfume of timothy and clover permeated the glaucous mossed and misty air. Spring drank deeply of its muted colors and aromas, lending through her mild enjoyment what vibrancy an April, though heartily, pretends. Everywhere shadows of gum and dogwood heaved thawing sighs of appreciation for the feasting scene as I approached.

Sweet-scented myrtle hedged a six-foot coppice along the edge of the property's lane. An intoxicating barrier, it guided one's path with the faint threat of loss. Evergreens, reeds, brambles, brush, tulip trees and oaks abounded and seemed to breathe only of truth and life. In the distance marsh hens called a lonely tune that echoed past the rotting planks of old slave quarters. Ahead in the middle of this 1,200-acre plantation stood the colonnaded home, unchanged, uncannily serene—especially considering the havoc indiscriminately visited everywhere else within calling distance.

Casually tying my hired mount to a carriage post, I thought to walk around the back, to certify the strangely proposed calm, but felt it could be trusted despite my intuition. Besides, what would change, and might I not gain less suspicion by merely continuing my way straight up the front steps?

Perhaps I had been spied by chance through the *oiel de boeuf* in the narrow passage leading from the entry to the great hall by one of the maids who scurried through the corridors upon my entrance, or perhaps it was the hesitant sounds of my newly heeled boots upon the hollow porch before I had summoned the courage to knock. The door immediately opened, and I was invited in without question by a comely and handsomely dressed black whose smile was curiously hung from small but protruding ears like a pair of spectacles.

I was taken into the main parlor as he left to announce me. Without my name, I wondered, as what?

***

"Pale sherry for our guest, Johnnie," he commanded without hesitation and was likewise obeyed by the young white manservant appearing in the doorway.

Should I have been startled by the coincidence? It was just a name.

"How is your brother?"

His tone was both as frank and removed as ever.

"Of course you have been to see him before coming here. Do not look so surprised. Or was I neither to expect nor recognize you? I daresay, I know many more things than you would care for me to know. Though many of them are well-within my province. Now, what exactly is it you want?"

"What do you mean?"

"Come, sir. Must we have secrets? I was her father. That makes me," he hesitated, "grandfather of her children."

Senator Nash said this in a manner totally unlike anything I could remember, then stopped long enough to receive our drinks and dismiss his manservant before continuing. Of course he made certain the serving carafe was left upon the small silver-wrapped tea wagon and was neither upset nor surprised when I declined the offered crystal pony glass.

"It cannot be money," he started, putting down the one glass. "You must still have plenty of that. Am I right?"

"There was very little to spend it on—until now," I said frankly but distractedly with a glance toward a young housekeeper who dusted about the secretary desk at the far end of the large and sumptuously decorated office.

"Still, I may be sure that you managed. It is, after all, well within your ruinous nature."

279

He eyed me with a suspicion whose source I could scarcely deny. I fidgeted with my cap, as if to examine its lining.

"I can see by your nervous dissipation you are your same covert and insecure self, afraid to know the mind you might then speak, lest you chance disappointment. Allow me to ease your curiosity, regarding your family."

The senator hesitated momentarily, now only long enough to dismiss the young maid who had begun again to enter the room but apologetically took hold of the double pocket doors and slid them shut with a silent nod.

"Pardon me but the household is surely curious about my ragged visitor. They are used to expecting political figures and foreign dignitaries. President Harrison was here not one month ago," he recalled with a glint before continuing. "They probably think you a spy—and would not be far from right, do you say?

"If I thought any good could come of it they would all be here with me," he continued in a confidential tone, resuming the prior topic with his usual callousness. "But, Mr. Booth, that is impossible. The scandal would undo my family name. Everything I would like to give them would just as surely be taken away."

"Not to mention your political career."

"This is not outside consideration, but makes little matter today. At my age you must see it is rather the least of my concerns. What I care for is my daughter's wellbeing."

"Which makes little matter today."

Nash finished his glass in a single sip and turned his back on me to look out through the high oriel.

"As you say, Mr. Booth."

"Is this why you had arranged for her to meet me? For her wellbeing?"

"What she chose to do was her own affair. Obviously. Or, perhaps you believe it was my desire she should bring bastards into an otherwise genteel world!"

"But you went to so much trouble."

"Oh, you mean when I introduced myself as if I thought you were your brother? Mistaking performances, and all that? That was really nothing. Just a little assurance that you would strive all the more fervently to distinguish yourself. Your relationship with your brother was not unknown—nor that unusual, after all."

This was more of a declaration than I had imagined and the senator seemed suddenly aware he had told me more than I had ever guessed, his manner changing at once.

"I am afraid you need see no more of me. It is my brother-in-law, Badeau, you seek. But I will make you swear to keep your identity—and paternity—secret from the children—or understand, I will track you until you are a certain corpse. The past is past, gone. Dead as the man you once were. It is not some idea of principle, Mr. Booth. Nor has it ever been. But business only, as everything. Purely business."

The senator's frame had been compromised with the years but not so his intent.

"The same as when we discovered it was not your body in the barn. What to do? Your little conspirator friends had failed, as I suppose we ever knew they would.

"But you know I trusted you, Mr. Booth. Damned if I know why. Even argued that you were our man indeed. And I suppose you were. It was not easy to convince my associates. Or, at times, myself, I admit. Of course, I knew as soon as Ella reported our lack of confidence you would again work all the more diligently. You are so predictable in your dramatic choices, Mr. Booth. Then that is why it was so simple to know you would be here."

The senator refilled his glass until it almost began to overflow, took a large mouthful and filled it again, nearly as full.

"But those others. We had to hang the ones who knew about the money. It took us three days to be sure Mudd and those others did not. Poor Mrs. Surratt could not stop talking about it. How she knew it was not you at Garrett's Farm on account of the money not being found with the body. Thought that would save her. Did quite the opposite, you know.

"Of course, we would have liked to pay you the rest of it—although I imagine you had more than enough where you were.

"Where were you, anyway? Oh, never you mind, it does not matter. You are here now. Aren't you Mr. Booth?"

He motioned as to put his glass down but kept it in his hand, raising it to eye level and absently viewing its vague prisms as he turned it first in one direction then the other.

"Still, I owed you something. A chance to live. You had not failed us. I knew that. But, of course, the initial fear was that you would be captured and tell all you knew. You understand that now, don't you? Why we had no choice? Rather ironic, isn't it? Assassinate the assassin?

"Then when it was discovered Corbett had killed the wrong man, we had another choice. We could have come after you, nearly did. But I knew you would see it as your chance to escape. That you knew the plot had ultimately failed. Your plot, Mr. Booth. Not ours. Never ours. You were always very clear about that.

"How could you return knowing there would be no bows, no applause, no bouquets tossed up from the pit? And no woman ready to become your wife?

"That was the one thing I had to certify. Because, you know, by then, Ella would have gone anywhere with you. Despite everything. Unless—she thought, you had left—with another woman."

His eyes looked straight into mine for the first time since I had arrived. Maybe the first time ever.

"Do not look so shocked, Mr. Booth. You know as well as I, it was a very easy thing to imagine. Almost as easy to prove, but quite unnecessary."

He laughed his hollow, vacant laugh.

"An amazing coincidence, the pocket full of photographs. Your double could not have done you a greater disservice, even in his greatest of sacrifices. Ella at once believed and disbelieved it was you for this very reason—other women, not one, but many—finally convincing herself she was too trusting."

"Are you finished?"

"Ah, you mean—shall I recount the tale of your sweetest Ella? So pure and so divine? She was mine too remember? Before she failed her desired vocation, like generations of others who preceded her and have yet to come. Still, she made her living, at the theater—in the theater district, after all. In the shadows of the stage doors and the alleyways for a time. Her mask positioned, her part well-rehearsed, Mr. Booth, as only you might know. As you had certified. *Sic semper coitus!* Thus ever to harlots!"

I suddenly stopped thinking about his having described my new suit of clothes as ragged, though clearly it was not of the quality to which he was accustomed, his lightweight gabardine jacket draping perfectly over a crisp linen shirt. The blood he had kept subdued at the first now rose to his cheeks as he continued.

"You know my Ella had always been the devoted one. To me. To the memory of her mother. Then to her children. Unfortunately also to you, Mr. Booth. Always to you.

"If she had received a single word from you she would have been by your side in an instant. For this alone I can take the credit. I knew as much as you would want to write as many letters as you might start you would never send a single one. You had to feel she would be better off without you. Am I right, Mr. Booth? That you could not take her with you into a world of infamy or obscurity? And that has not changed. It would ever be the same situation, the same dreaded outcome.

"Now, as to the matter about which you have come here. What matters is not the life of some frail has-been senator who might have gotten what he thought he desired, nor any more of some once-famous family and its heirs. The future. The only thing more precious than time and life itself. The promise of tomorrow.

"Swear you will honor this, Mr. Booth. Only then may you see my brother-in-law—and your children. Johnnie has Badeau's calling card and address for you at the door. And swear one other thing, that you will do what is right and put an end to the past. Then leave me alone. I have a bottle to finish."

He may have owed me something from back then, but I owed him nothing, less than nothing, and he knew it. As for his threat, I held little fear, for as Corbett had made me see I was already a corpse. Still, what he said about the future made me think. Though I wondered about this oath and the past to which he referred, I would understand what he meant, if anything, soon enough. Without another word or glance, I took my leave.

***

At Badeau's I was received anonymously but with great affection. There, unlike at the senator's, I was but another of the busy home's many unannounced guests. Time had treated the old bachelor as well as he could have hoped, and somehow he credited me with much of his happiness. Strange, how in a world full of loathing and self-hatred there could yet be held high opinion of such as I. His career, his adopted family, his wealth, it was all due to the man he introduced to his foster son as, "a very dear old friend, who once saved my life—would he have been there when my brother was killed," turning a strange smile toward me.

"So you see, we both owe him a great deal," he added and winked at me with a kind of friendship I had never known, not even from Hand. "It is too bad your sister could not be here to meet him as well. I am sure he would be surprised to see her resemblance to her late mother," he added with pointed deference, before leaving the two of us to get acquainted while he attended to some important paperwork.

***

I listened to him speak calmly of all things. Of his plans to start a family, of a career in politics like his sponsor-uncle, of the great inventions and opportunities of the future, of the great and precious mystery of life—a mystery that had claimed his uncle's brother just after the close of the great civil war, of the horrors of all war. Calmly and never else. And never one mention of his father, neither good nor evil.

And I thought, where is the turmoil of which his sister wrote? But when he mentioned her and the position she held as an attendant in the house of a great politician I began to remember the young maid's eyes that caught harried glimpses of me as she shuffled past on some pretended errand. Current circumstances were certainly very different for her.

Still, if he had purged himself of his hatred and his hated past, why could I not do the same? And it struck me. Did he know full-well who his uncle's mysterious visitor was? Had she known who had been her employer's quick if graciously received guest? Or did it even matter? What difference, after all, would it make upon the face of the future? This was the oath the senator wished for me to honor, and I now found worthy of consideration.

And by the time the truth became apparent, I was too far past shock to register it openly. Their mother had not been dead, after all. Not until that very week, while I was at my brother's. The Sunday before my visit to the senator. He had only received the news himself that very day, else he would not have spoken of her as he did—drink in hand throughout.

The real reason for the senator's attempted candor and intended stupor was that Ella had died a stranger to him. He had indeed disowned her, but she responded by refusing him also. After the birth of the children she took the maiden name of her mother and moved to Chicago where she raised them on her own. She accepted the senator's regular offerings of money and seasonal gifts, but never allowed him to re-enter their lives. And kept her distance even after she accepted on behalf of Viola the position he had offered in his household.

It was not that they did not simply know the identity of their ignominious father, they neither knew the identity of their illustrious grandfather or the truth behind the senator's continued benefaction. It was his identity, not mine, he wished to keep secret.

Their mother had died of a sudden. She had not been dead, as Hand had believed. And she had not been ill, as their letters had described. Why, then? Closure. They had thought to deny me the only reason I might have had to return, without understanding the knowledge of my paternity would have been enough. The ultimate in self-denial and humility.

"Very Caz'olic, h'indeed," Hand would have said.

And now Ella would never be mine again. Her father's wish, fate's hand, and my own actions, all satisfied in a moment of absurd and horrible irony. Especially since I had been twice to Chicago in the past weeks while she still lived. She had been so close the entire time. Whatever had I accomplished or resolved at which I could now point with pride?

Strophe

And when they dragged his bleeding body from the burning barn, his dying breaths provided a message to the successful hunters. He thought it surefire, unmistakable. Like Mary Surratt, however, what he hoped would be his passport to freedom may have instead decreed his death—had it been understood. Yet I, as those whose glowering faces surrounded him in that fire-lit dawn, choked what air he could suffer to strain from the smoking dark, misread a thousand times the epitaph he styled for himself as he raised his arms to heaven.

For it was not futility he uttered in that momen—save it was with Laocoön's knowledge of his word's unheeded portent, it was the name of he who had sent him to raid, along with the rest, the life and soul of one whose only sin was to

286

believe in his own patriotism and trust those who professed the same belief. I know now what horrid syllables repeatedly poured forth from the dying dupe. Was it the name of the man who betrayed us all, yet on whom the fates had seen, until his death, to smile?

"Ulysses, Ulysses!"

***

In order to have the indictment lifted from his head, and in order to exact a certain vengeance upon the North as well, Pike ordered—from his position as Masonic Grand Master—the execution of the president. From Pike to Stanton, of Steubenville #45; from Stanton to Grant, of St John's of Galena; from Grant to Dougherty, Conger, Jett and the rest. Now were they all dead except the one—and the senator of course. So let the past be past?

Still atop the pyramid, Pike was safe from any scrutiny. Like Pharaoh himself bidding the super-vizier to perform his duty, and that vizier passing the word down to another underling until finally—yes, to me! Was it not the more fitting that the engineer of the most visible machinations, the man whose identity was whispered in the dying breath of my proxy, was named Hiram?

Hiram, Tyrian, Widow's Son, Sendeth to King Solomon. It was Hand who finally solved the riddle of these letters, told me the meaning of the cipher. Laughed at my ignorance. Did I not even know I was a Lewis?

"What's a Lewis?" I had asked.

"Z'e son h'of a mason—and, *Monsieur* Booz', z'e broz'er h'of one, too. *Et les exigences d'un frère doivent être fournis par ses frères.* What one bro'zer requires, z'e o'zers must supply."

I always knew my father and brother were Freemasons. To me, it was simply one more private bond between them. One more thing they shared without me. No surprise, no special mystery. Many men of fashion and influence belonged.

Who did not know Washington himself was one? And

287

Madison, Monroe, Jackson.

But you cannot understand the political machinations that pervaded the government at the time of the war and its conclusion. Whigs, Republicans, Know-Nothings like myself. Let me remind you of a simple truth. Prepare your slates and ready your sticks of chalk.

At the time of our nation's birth there were two great factions of power—that of the Massachusetts delegation centered at Boston and that of the Virginia delegation centered at Richmond. The first site of the national capital was New York, closest to Boston; the second Philadelphia, somewhat equidistant. The decision was arrived to build the capital at the new city of Washington—unmistakably closer to Richmond. Where was the true power?

During the war between the states, the government of the Union continued to function at Washington, though the government of the South was maintained only a day's ride away. Richmond was still the focal point of the South.

At this same time the order of the Scottish Rite, the predominant Masonic Society of our young nation—and not forsworn to only a Christian God, was delineated into northern and southern jurisdictions. The northern jurisdiction was predictably headquartered at Boston—and ever is. The southern jurisdiction, established in 1801, was headquartered at Charleston, South Carolina. South Carolina, the first state to secede—and in which place, at Fort Sumter, the first shots of the war were fired. But Charleston was nearly razed during the war—we need not imagine why it had become the particular target of certain union soldiers, and at the close of hostilities the Fraternity's headquarters were moved—not to Richmond but to Washington City. The nation's capital.

What would that say to any Northern brother who makes his home at Boston?

Born in Boston, Pike, the modern Masonic father, brother to a king and fellow to a prince, the master builder and great high priest of earthly architects, dreamed beyond the bounds of geography with aims of universal liberty. Though somehow he found purity only within the race of white men. The black men and red men would have their place, but it would be beneath those whose Aryan heritage had long prepared them to rule.

As Pike's involvement and ideals crystallized, so did my own impressions of their fanatic effect. Upon him, of course, but also upon that part of me, which had once thought to preserve and promote what I was also so sure had been divine. What else could it be called when Pike's wife Mary Ann died of a sudden fever April 14, 1876—ten plus one years after the event he had orchestrated.

How close I was now to final accomplishment, to what must have been, all along, my divine errand. How many times had I lately slept and dreamed more frequently of my ever-clearer quarry? Each time the vision of my dream was remarkably familiar. Each time, my path was chosen, my performance seemingly complete. Through veiled and shadowed mists of sleep, my way was ever clear.

***

At six foot two inches tall, over 250 pounds, and with long silvery hair and beard, Pike was not very difficult to locate—even in the bustling capital. Not surprisingly he was living at the Supreme House of the Temple at the northern end of the city. Here he had been housed *by the Order* since shortly after his return from Canada, when Masonic brother Andrew Johnson succeeded the presidency and pardoned Pike and others of their accused war crimes, the scalpings by Confederate troops and their Indian-nation allies at the Massacre of Pea Ridge. The needs of the supreme brother were met by his myriad brethren.

As I would soon discover, Atzerodt had not actually lost his nerve but fled before accomplishing his role in our mission, having already received the balance of the funds originally promised me. As Nash confirmed, everyone who knew anything about the money was doomed to be tried, without a chance to testify, and ultimately hanged.

From the Temple Pike wrote the volumes of scholarly matter, which had both aggrandized his name and made his style so recognizable for its sheer erudition. No other man in our country could boast a working knowledge of ancient Greek, Latin, Farsi, and Hindu. All of these he studiously added to a dozen or more dialects of native American tongues, as well as his abilities in the four principle languages of Europe.

But think not that this man, albeit inflicted with gout and an unquenchable thirst for bookish knowledge held no outside interests. Though I could hardly believe myself the happenstance of his biding passion. Nor could I refuse the obvious opportunity this affection presented. I chuckle even now at the thematic uniformity with which all seemed to unfold.

***

Needing a post from which the aging general's movements could be monitored without attracting too much attention or suspicion, I rented rooms nearby, again under the name Jack Harvey. This nearly took the balance of what remained of my small fortune, having given the lion's share to Badeau, to be anonymously split between the children—with certain provisions—the primary being that he should wait until their twenty-fifth birthdays, just a few months away. With little enough to spare, especially without knowing exactly how long my surveillance might take, I decided to seek work.

Not two blocks away from the far corner of Sixteenth Street Northwest, there stood still the small pharmacy where once David Herold had worked unconsciously to foil my first and simplest plan. How much would have changed had that lad been of any other than the dimmest disposition. What a fool was I for thinking him capable of carrying out the thoughts of another when he was incapable of producing a single one of his own. Still, what was done—or, more correctly, was not done—was past, as palpably proven throughout the modern city with three of five metropolitan train lines operating electric streetcars.

It was not my first attempt of the day, I introduced myself to the aged pharmacist as a Marylander returning to the region of his birth after many years on the frontier. With ironic honesty I admitted I had been loathe to return in the aftermath of our late Civil War, only recently feeling any sense of security or desire to do so.

When I gave him my name as Harold, it pleased me to watch him start for just the instant with a concerned wince before I completed my breath with the name Springer, confirming the former as my given not family name, and subduing the old gent's heart after only a single, nervous palpitation.

"Well met, Harry," he addressed me straightaway as much, I am sure, to override his own associations as from any gracious sense of familiarity. "Who sent you? But never you mind, we just so happen to need an extra hand about," he phrased in the local style, then squinted, "But I'm afre'd we can't pay you very much."

"Hal," I corrected, then confirmed, "The work, I want to work."

"And that's what you'll do!" he snapped. "Startin' tomorrow. Te'k it or leave it," he smiled genuinely, extending his hand.

The next day Mr. Phipps began showing me how to stock the shelves, how to feed him the prescriptions, and even let me watch as he went about filling them. He kept the list of names of those for whom he weekly worked, and on it was old graybeard himself, Albert Pike. Already 80 years old I imagined he might not be well, but I could scarcely have hoped for such fortune. And I began to recognize that it was not fortune at all but fate that should have woven our lives so closely together.

291

I had only to wait until the day—Thursday, I quickly learned—for Phipps to fill Pike's prescription and make a note of the medication and dosage. With access to the entire stock I was certain it would be of little difficulty to find an appropriately shaped and concentrated dosage of some very effective poison. With hardly an effort the next week, or any week after, it would be delivered, taken and received for its fatal effect.

But that was almost too easy. As Pike's daughters Lillian and Yvon were currently sharing his lodgings in the Temple House, I felt anxious. Could I be sure of his taking all of the medication and not leaving any part of either of them or anyone else? Would another accidental death or two, intentioned or no, be too much for even my vengeful soul to bear?

Phipps had also told me in passing that, while the name of the prescription patient is always carefully written upon the dosage package, along with the date by which the medication must be taken so spoilage can be certainly avoided, both of those indications were regularly ignored.

There was something else bothering me too. The thing that had haunted my dreams. Pike had to know I was the cause of his death. He had to know why his life's thread was being cut short. He had also to stare his last stare into my eyes. This was vengeance. Poison on its own was too silent, too gentle, too forgiving, too anonymous.

My revenge would have to be more. And to bring it to its finest point of dramatic fervor, nothing could have been more perfect than Pike's own passion. Theater!

It must not be thought surprising that he too embraced the favorite recreation of every other Washington notable. The theater was where they all went to see and be seen. They did not have to love it or even understand it. Half of them slept the entertainment away as it was. But still they went, and with them Pike.

Here would I write the final scene of the drama that had

begun to unfold long before I understood the theatrical nature of life itself. No coda could have been more conveniently devised, more appropriately applied, more perfectly executed.

At this same time there came into the service of the Supreme House of the Temple a somewhat withered mason from an outlying lodge and whose arrival coincided with the strange and sudden disappearance of a local druggist's clerk, only recently hired. To look upon him he might have been an aging suitor of Bianca, or the venerable didact of the Danish prince's court. But he was silent, steady of purpose, and his intentions were neither amorous nor necessarily instructive.

Because of the new man's duties to care for an even more aged mother, he could only volunteer his time in the evening after she had gone to sleep. Yet this was the time most desired by the principle occupant of the Temple apartments, for he worked there from dawn to dusk on his translations of ancient Aryan texts, and could not suffer interruptions during daylight hours. His mania for labor had driven him to secure, within the Temple walls, the remarkable and conspicuous absence of a single chair that rocked.

Come the night there were tapers to light, fires to stoke and doors to secure—nor could the sovereign grand commander or his daughters be expected to caretake also for the various chambers of the shrine. No, nor cook their own meals. Had he not devoted his life's energies to the craft, was he not currently lending credence to its heritage and scholarship? Were they not his beloved daughters? And were they all not also particularly fond of my beer-baked pork?

Everything was in readiness. And then it came to me. Nash had wished for this very thing. Indeed, had orchestrated it, pulled my strings again as he had before. Baited me with taunts of hope and goads of the children that would never be mine. Why else would he have begged my visit to Badeau? Been so cool in his admissions? What other oath could he have hoped so certainly I would keep?

How or why I did not know. But it was sure. Sure that

293

somehow Pike himself had come into disfavor with the other inner circle. Was even now upsetting some next series of political plans? It did not matter how, only that it surely happened.

But, no. They did not need me to perform the deed, only needed me to try. Must not the senator himself have reveled at the dramatic possibility? The would-be two-fold assassin. A final vengeance visited upon the man who had stolen his most-cherished prize.

And I had come so close. So close to repeating again the folly of my past. And for what? It is not my decision who should live or die or worship as he will. I can only answer for myself, and this alone I must ever do.

Strophe

I

I am a man. It seems so simple. It is so simple. I am glad of it. Rejoice in it. The life I nearly surrendered. The soul I have retrieved. The miracle, the blessing of it. Still, I know that it has not always been so. And I wonder what was I before I was a man?

II

Squirrels make their daytime nests in the crooks of trees from which they watch me like so many fur-tailed Pinkertons, guessing at the conspiracy of my admissions. The beauty, life and quiet of these woods, returned now with their nameless hermit. And that hermit, at last, happy to leave his fate and that of others to the God whose love he now understands.

I see my reflection in nature. The family of possums that has lately taken to play at night upon my newly-shingled roof mirrors strangely my situation. The one I've come to call Dicky Crookback or just Dicky appeared this evening with a wounded hindquarter. Irony that he should embrace his role? Though not seemingly fresh, I have not noticed it before and wonder at its source. I never felt his subtle kinship so strongly, and he came much closer to me than before to where I sat upon my crude porch as if to see what I could do for him. For want of a nail?

Seen closely his leg has the look of being crushed by the wheel of a cart, though I can scarcely imagine how it might have happened, or again, when? How should he have journeyed so close to a driven road, so far from his score of habited trees.

On seeing this, I felt a strange compunction and found myself talking to him, and he seemed to listen. I bade him stay while I fetched some dried grains from my pantry, offering them to him in a wooden bowl at the foot of the stoop and returning to my seat. He did not move for some moments, then scurried away—his crippled limb conspicuous, without venturing any closer to the offered meal. But I let it stand and hoped he would soon feel safe and sure of my intent. Perhaps he will come back tonight with others.

Scene V

Fainting,
    Freezing,
        Dying alone,
Too wicked for prayer, too weak for my moan
To be heard in the crash of the crazy town,
Gone mad in its joy at the snow's coming down;
To lie and to die in my terrible woe,
With a bed and a shroud of the beautiful snow!

Strophe

I

Instruct your sons and daughters to know the difference. Between leadership and tyranny. Between principle and loyalty. Question not that they succeed nor withstand. Teach them no, but teach them yes. Yes, I am. Yes, I can. Yes, I will. Yes, by God and man!

II

That man for whom my vision of the heavens hungered—for even in my hatred and contempt or all their certainty, who knows better than I that judgment is an earthly bond alone? Who knows as well the perpetual torment of a topsy-turvy world? Yesterday I would have hanged his heels beside my own tomorrow, forgive, forget all to celestial strains.

I have in Cymmerian lands been living as in some dream. Far across the rivers and woods of even the western wilderness, without sun-bleached refuge of island balm or beach.

And I have cursed his name a hundred thousand times without knowing it, without pity or passion for any, but myself. Damned the fate that made him part of mine, deceived for even an instant that I should hope or think there is salvation, a final reclamation of errant souls as mine.

III

Of life, I have never asked much. To live simply to work in my chosen profession, to marry, have children and look back upon a life spent well and decently. Of death, I only wished that it should come surely, and after a time that I might review with some success my accomplishments. Quick, painless, and finalized by the final prayers of those I have loved—perhaps at some ceremonious wake where other spirits too might be raised as my empty body burns brightly upon a bier.

Somewhere—tucked between the opening lines of these confessions, or lost to those days that haunt me still—there was the impulse to create, to recreate, to represent. To give life to the thoughts and dreams of others, to imagine I somehow understood. I was the vehicle, the uniting force, the tool. It was more than an affected lisp or limp, much more than an arching glance or ambling gimp. All for an image, her image, kneeling in prayer.

IV

And know your loving parents—both—calm in the simple knowledge that, despite every other uncertainty, the family was ever that—a family. No separation of distance or death or time would intercede. No fateful summers erase, deny.

It would not be so. Life has never been so simple, fate never so kind. And all that might be desired would lose its substance, yield to every other want and preferred reality.

But I have been rent from all I love. The trusts that I have held sounded hollow. The hopes, dashed. I am at once afloat in a boundless sea, strapped to the mast, yet also stranded upon a pirate shore where no flotilla of my faithful adherents could affect rescue. And there are none such. I am carrion only for all the vultures of the air and beasts of the field that ever found genesis in the brotherhood politic.

The divine thirst for vengeance, held by the heavens and which I thought had already drunk its fill of my life, my career, my love, will be sated with nothing less. As I walk, stumbling and half-asleep, into the deep of winter storm, I can still hear the night echo this single phrase: The villain must die; the villain must die.

That night, as I raised my spirits and my hand to do the deed, having secured again the sanctuary of my act and its accomplishment, rehearsed my part as never before, I yet faltered. His daughters had retired promptly at nine and he was to be working on his codices in the study. But he was not.

Oh, he was there, but not at work, as I had planned. Not at all as I had planned. For though he toiled in his study, it was not over volumes of classical scholarship. It was a simple task that had the attention of the grand commander. Simple and particularly identifiable.

As I approached the outer door from the corridor connecting to the main receiving hall I thought at first to hear echoes of those uncertain chords of celestial judgment and anticipation—but stopped short to listen to the poetic lessons of my youth, eerily familiar, yet not altogether remote. Pike was practicing his violin. No, playing.

Once else only in my life did I cry so spontaneously, so ashamedly. Not even at the death of Hand, whose body froze still for no good reason save that of his own friendship and devotion. Not even at the loss of Ella, nor of the bright, dashed hopes of fatherhood. It was a greater loss to which I was witness. The complete and utter loss of everything I had ever been. Everything I had never been.

I was witness to the world of accomplishment wherein I held no place, but as a fiend. The thousand dreams of youth carelessly deferred for any reason but their own until a single moment smashed them with its steadily increasing if unanticipated weight. I could not kill this man. At least he had done something with his life, however vigorously I might have taken exception. If I were to kill, but once more, my true target was never so uncertain.

VI

How can I not but think of her when it rains? The steady, cooling rhythm that once matched our every loving breath. Promises of cleansing passion and fresh beginnings, the laughing shelter from thunderous outbursts she playfully sought within my arms. The striking shadows flashing her face like some envious photographer's ferrotype, vainly seeking to capture a fragment of her soulful eyes. And this night the spring's own proclamation of her rite could do no less for my memory of her.

What perfect form she from the first displayed. That night we met. Her ruffled hem finding rightful censure about her graceful ankles and tiniest feet. I remember wondering at the impossibility of their size. As if she wore the shoes of some child angel who, having no more use for them upon a winged body, bequeathed them to this earthly child of heaven. And with them too relinquished part of the heavenly spirit. For that was unquestionably hers.

And that spirit is now forever inside the rain I hear. This rain that stills the songs of nightingales and sends the tracking hunger of forest wolves deep within their starving dens; recites the chords of inner melody, stirs a different need within the tireless animal of desiring man, quenches other spirits.

And while the rhythm quickens upon my crudely roofed cabin and streams of heaven's fear and respite form veils outside my only window, these thoughts of her too grow. And as they slake my thirst, I shall keep them dry, safe, warm.

My heart pumps louder with the glowering night. Once more I turn my head to end my day without her. Once more I close the eyes that opened once, on her; asleep, dream that same and only dream. And hold my breath that somewhere she might sense and fret my despair, whispering through the dark, "Breathe, my darling, and know my love."

VII

This is not the first time I have had this thought. Until now I have scarcely known how to express it. Still am not sure.

Could there yet be a time when I could return. Could walk as a free man for a short time. Pass my children on some side street or broad avenue. Would we recognize each other? Would the report of my character confuse your ability to embrace the father, the kinsman in me? Would your mother's features alone be enough to call my memory back from what has been an endless time of forced forgetfulness?

It would be so simple, you will think, if all that has befallen you, demanded you be different, isolated, protected from certain truths, had itself been different. If at any moment—be it morning's ritual revival, or any other—you might wake to find your lives serene, unhurried. What of late has been termed *normal*.

VIII

But tonight the mists have cleared and heaven's supporting clouds hover moonlit on a lingering harpoon of horizon. Her vision, sweet upon my brain, breathes new life, and mine can matter no more, while all the world cares again.

IX

You have cause, and with reason, to hate the name you will never own, the father who could never be. The life of simple ease that should have been yours. But if you feel the fool of some fiendish plot of mine, if you even slightly sense betrayal or deceit, a moment's uncertainty in the tenor of my heart, be calm.

Rest sure in this: What I performed I may not say I did for you, yet it is so. What I have dreamed was certainly with your wellbeing in my mind. What could not be was not the fault of what was never wished.

If I could do again what I have done, what surely held no other feasible outcome, I would not change my course. Could I regret that now you live? For what I risked was never mine but in the power of a larger life. And what we choose when we submit to a greater welfare than our own must be done.

X

I have sinned but not without cause. I have surrendered all but only known that I had not forsaken more. I am without comfort, certainty or the esteem of my fellows, but I would dare to say, I have, though in truth it is impossible for my flesh to know just what.

Then hate me, if that hate will in any way relieve your souls. Curse my name and memory, you could not damn me further than providence has already. Abhor our kinship and rue my ever having lived. Hate me, yes, but know, I love you—always.

Antistrophe

I could not look into those eyes. I could no longer murder.

***

> *Father,*
> > *Mother,*
> > > *Sisters all,*
> *God, and myself, I have lost by my fall.*
> *The veriest wretch that goes shivering by*
> *Will take a wide sweep, lest I wander too nigh;*
> *For all that is on or about me, I know*
> *There is nothing that's pure, but the beautiful snow.*
>
> *How strange it should be that his beautiful snow*
> *Should fall on a sinner with nowhere to go!*
> *How strange it would be, when the night comes again,*

301

If the snow and the ice struck my desperate brain!
      Fainting,
           Freezing,
                 Dying alone,
Too wicked for prayer, too weak for my moan
To be heard in the crash of the crazy town,
Gone mad in its joy at the snow's coming down;
To lie and to die in my terrible woe,
With a bed and a shroud of the beautiful snow!

Epilogue
The Dawn

The bearded tyrant sits grim and still. The makeshift door-brace eases precisely into the knife-cut mortise as a fragile darkness assumes its place with eternal acceptance. No guard is there at the top of my quick, rose-carpeted steps. No guard except the conscience I have long persuaded to watch me past the carved colonnades of the outer balcony. And from my temporary cloister, these twice theatrical wings of daring that can wax or melt in an instant—my heart speeding as if the deed were done, the labyrinth sprung—I once more study my final entrance.

The moment holds its breath as next my fingers move to part, if slightly, the damask curtain that now alone separates our cause from his unbearable will, true victory from an untenable surrender, my haunted night from the all-harkening day.

The tyrant's gnarled knuckles claw into the lupine-scrolled arms of his rocking chair perch and his eyes fix upon the evening's play, while he is yet aware that half the house rather watches him—for a movement, a sign, some memento to take home from the theater. The monograph, perhaps, of a once favorite player. This will my hand supply as never before.

Fine powdered ladies in their veils and bonnets, tall grinless gentlemen with their canes and capes, although forgetful of the solemn night's duty, force appreciation of fatuous comedy while surely urged beyond noting the execution of a well-framed speech. Their ancient spirits cry for them to witness the justice done to nature's two-thousand-year-old ritual, turned westward toward the fractured summit. The fabled robe of old stretches as velvet upon the seats throughout the house, its purple plush full-soaked with scents of perfume or cigars. Again, the dice profane the cause with play.

Their usurping standard presumes its place in folded drapes out front the box wherein their blasphemous master dreams. The rifting stripes and impenitent stars signifying only a shroud to trip his steps from imagined resurrection. And his plump Calpurnia, decked in more finery than her frame or character can support, drunken with her pride and porto, clutches at his side, somehow knowing that next, this eve of ides, this modern feast of sacrifice and expurgation, this Gessler will be mine.

Mrs. Mountchessington exits in a flurry and there, too, a single player stands upon the stage. His cue well-met, his lines well-spoken, I cross and play my business out. Half a stride, then face-to-face, I cheer the motto of my faith and countrymen. The powder flashes, the bullet rings, those steel gray eyes last look on me.

I cannot look them back.

***

In my dreams I often see the bearded tyrant sitting grim and still. But it is not Lincoln; and it is not Pike. It is my own untended face. It is that part of all men that would abuse and forsake their souls.

He will not be quieted by violence or forgotten through ignorance. He must be confronted and brought to justice, to the true light. He will tell you he prefers the shadows, that they are enough. You must not yield. You must insist. But do not await or blame another to urge you to accomplish what your soul already understands.

I imagine my grandchildren laying flowers on the grave of President Lincoln, cursing the man who put him there. And I curse him, too. His stage play seemingly unfinished, his part is yet complete. The house lamps lit, the apron backed and still, the wings and flies of the benefit production silenced at last, that none other should ever know nor fear this man in any future.

Yet, does not the classic form always demand a fifth and final act? Might not beauty make another entrance?

Curtain